ANDREA

love stories

Noah Abner Bowen

Thanks to my Dad and all of my friends.
I'm not lucky, I'm blessed.
Thanks also to the girl who disappeared
whom I will always love, but have to let go.

CONTENTS

PREFACE

These stories represent a turmoil of emotions. Perhaps they're anger or indignation. Agony. Some are contempt, some are pain. Love has an end. That's what this book is about: the death throes of a once-good thing. Make no mistake, these are horror stories. We are all in bondage to our pain.

Noah Abner Bowen
May 2021

BULLDOG

Linda and I were on the rocks.

We argued a lot over semantics.

After a while we stopped talking. We'd sit and drink our beers beside each other in silence on our cellphones. Even our sex life had deteriorated. We serviced each other from time to time, but only with our hands; intercourse wasn't worth the effort anymore. Linda was beautiful but her body had ceased to inspire me. It had become like the drive to work, familiar in a bored sad sort of way. We kissed passionlessly; they were cold quick kisses. We were going through the motions, fulfilling the requirements of our relationship like a ghost might sit down to eat, but what we'd had was gone.

We both knew it.

There were no commonalities between us, only shared memories, and we'd recycled those so many times they were threadbare. Still, we'd bought the house together. We hung on; we languished. For three years I dragged myself out of bed each morning and made the drive into the city.

Linda worked from home.

She had an office filled with law books.

I kept the garage to myself and used it for hobbies.

We were together, eating dinner in front of the TV when the doorbell rang. We were both tired and annoyed; our doorbell never rang. We looked at each other, exasperated, but curiosity drove us to our feet.

We opened the door. There was girl standing on our porch, covered in blood and pointing a gun in our faces.

"Move," she said. "Step back slowly. I'm going to close the door. If either of you panic, I'll shoot."

She was small, supple looking, wearing a long grey sweater over tattered jeans and yellow Converse. Her hair was blond. Her eyes were black. She had a pretty face but the muscles beneath it were ugly.

She was inside. She kicked the door shut behind her, reached back and flipped the deadbolt.

"Now strip," she told us, waving the gun.

Linda opened her mouth in protest and was met with a smack; the girl lurched forward and drew the gun down across her mouth before she could speak. I turned defensively and froze, halted by the barrel thrust between my eyes.

"Back," she said.

We moved slowly into the living room. Linda holding her jaw where she'd been hit, tears streaking her face and spoiling her makeup. "What do you want?" she whimpered.

The girl smiled.

"An orgasm," she replied. "Now sit and keep your hands in front of you."

We did as we were told, sitting down on the loveseat opposite the TV. Our dinner trays were stationed on either end supporting half-eaten meals and we sank into the cushions toward the middle, pressing against each other like we'd never fallen out of love. Linda was shaking.

"That's perfect," the woman said, standing before us. "Now do like I said. Strip."

"Look—" I began.

"It'll be harder with a bullet in you," she glared, sliding a hip onto the edge of a table beside the entry. It was dim in the room. No lamps were on. There were logs stacked in the fireplace but no fire. The television screen lent the air electric blue. We'd been watching Friends. The show was paused on a close-up of Courtney Cox, blurred by motion.

Why had we both come to the door?

I dropped my hands into my lap then took hold of my shirt, pulling it up and over my head. Linda looked at me disgustedly. The drapes were open. I could see outside. The street was dark. It was raining.

"That's a start," the girl grinned. "Now the rest. And you too, wifey." she said, eyeing down the pistol sight with one eye closed; it looked like she was winking. "Quick."

Linda and I both stripped.

I felt ashamed, sitting there, lifting my hips and sliding my Levi's down off my thighs. There were rolls on my stomach that hadn't been there before. I was out of shape. I blamed it on too much beer. I'd always had a good metabolism.

I'd start hitting the gym again.

I'd bounce back.

Linda left her underclothes on, a sexless white bra and panties. Her body looked pale and heavy in the low light. Her breasts were soft and matronly and her stomach was like mine, a paunch; doughy additional flesh hanging over the waistband of her underwear.

"The rest too," the girl told her.

After a pause, Linda complied. She shook her breasts free, then stuck her thumbs in her panties and rolled them down her legs, dumping them onto the floor with the rest.

"Now what?" I asked when she'd finished, noticing that Linda hadn't shaved in a while; surprised by it. Surprised that I hadn't known.

"What's your name?" I asked the girl.

"Bulldog," she replied. "I work for Cupid."

*

When I was a kid I was preyed upon by bullies. They ran the schoolyard. Kids possessed of size and strength, cornfed and authoritative and cruel. In summer, they were in the hills and the gravels pits till dusk; they built plywood forts in the sagebrush behind my house and threw dirt clods and swung branches. We were all white trash but they called me nigger because they didn't like me and there were no blacks around to use the word on.

I was beat up a lot.

I'd always wanted a bulldog. I'd seen them in cartoons. Big, tough. It was suggested that the devil was a bulldog. My parents said they were expensive; and while my father admitted they were handsome, my mother said they were ugly. Both agreed that they had breathing problems.

When I reached high-school I decided if I couldn't have one, I'd become one. I entered the gym one morning and might have never left. My grades plummeted. My arms and legs expanded in size. My chest grew deep. My voice changed.

I became very tall and the suddenness of my growth left stretch marks on my sides and back. I never joined the football team. And I never got a bulldog.

When I left home for college I never looked back.

For Linda it had been different.

She wasn't the popular girl, but she was the popular girl's sidekick, one of three; she was a beautiful blond henchman. She came from money and belonged to it as much as she'd come from and belonged to Texas, even now. Her family was associated with oil and a variety of endangered species. Then when the economy bellied, they were reduced to average. They sold off their estate and moved to Idaho, where her father played the stocks and her mother acquired a taste for gin.

We met in college.

I remember the moment, not the weather.

It all happened very fast.

In the beginning we talked a lot. We'd both voted for Obama and occasionally smoked weed. We agreed that while we didn't believe in religion, we felt that there was something out there, a force perhaps, and we both admitted to having prayed to it before. These were the things we agreed upon. Important things. We called them fundamental opinions, while sex subtly bridged the cold miles of difference between us.

We graduated.

Linda had a close friend who planned weddings, so we got married; it cost us half the going rate. And then we bought the house. And when the dust settled and the sex grew stale, there was nothing left but quiet remorse.

In the privacy of my shop—in our garage, that is— amid old bicycles, their parts and frames, I often thought of that bulldog I'd always wanted. I wish I'd got him.

Other times I just wished I was dead.

*

"Listen, I'm an attorney." Linda said, twisting to shield her privates. "Is this some kind of joke?"

Bulldog smiled. "No sweetie. If it was," she turned her arm and fired a bullet into the television screen, dousing us into a deeper darkness as it crackled and sparked and collapsed onto the floor. "Then this'd be a water pistol, wouldn't it?"

"Now you," she said, motioning Linda with the gun, "Put him in your mouth for me."

"What?" Linda stammered.

"Suck his dick. I want him hard and you're going to be my fluffer," she smiled. "You know what a fluffer is right? In porn, it's the person that gets the actor's dick big before they roll film. Like between cuts. You're basically the warm up, the vacuum. All you need is a strong jaw and some lung power. Now suck."

Linda stared at the floor. She looked confused; there were tears running from her eyes and her jaw had started to swell and bruise. She glanced at me, pleadingly. I had my hands raised. I didn't shrug, but I thought about it. I didn't know what to do either, so I avoided her eyes and frowned.

Finally she conceded, turning toward me and pivoting on her hips. She placed a hand on my thigh and lowered herself, dropping her head between my legs with a sniffle.

Her mouth engulfed me, gently sucking.

I shut my eyes and felt my body respond. The call of blood. I became hard, tensing against her lips as she bobbed her head.

"Okay, that's enough," the girl said. "Get on the floor. It's my turn now and you're going to watch. If you don't, I'm going to put this gun inside you, stick it in your cunt, and see what the bullet drags out."

Linda whimpered and moved to the foot of the couch. A string of saliva clung to her jaw like a plucked thread. The girl stood up from where she'd been leaning on the table, knocking a picture onto the floor as she did. It was of Linda and I on our Honeymoon. I heard the glass crack when it hit. In the picture I was wearing a Hawaiian shirt and Linda was in her bikini. She had her arm around me and we were both smiling.

In truth we'd never shared love, only loneliness; and even then, our happiness had been as cheap as a heart-shaped box.

Bulldog slipped her jeans off, balancing on one foot and then the other; she tossed her shoes haphazardly over her shoulder, all the while keeping the gun leveled and steady. When she was finished, she wore only the long grey sweater and it reached to her thighs.

Linda lay on the floor on her stomach and wept.

"Be sure to watch, sweetie," Bulldog said, stepping over her. She held the gun beneath my jaw, dropped to her knees, and took me in her mouth. After a minute she climbed onto my legs, smiled, brushing her lips with the back of her hand, and pushed me inside her.

It was nuclear.

Involuntarily I responded. My head fell back against the couch cushions and my hands lifted, grazing her hips with my fingertips and gripping her from behind as she rocked against me.

Fucking me.

As my wife lay face down on the carpet beside us and wept, with the taste of me stinging her lips.

I was reaching the edge. I could feel it. The blackout sensation of falling; expulsion. I tried pushing her away but she slapped my hands and pressed the gun against my throat, laughing. I finished then, firing off into the abyss of her womb as my muscle seized and my buttocks clenched beneath me.

Afterward, she lifted the gun and ejected the clip. She shifted her hips and I slipped from her with an audible plop. Then she stood and emptied the bullets, slowly, one at a time, into the fireplace. Linda was motionless on the floor.

She knelt, ignited the gas, then touched a match beneath the logs and watched as the bullets caught in fits, flaring up in sudden bursts of blue and green fire.

A blast or two ricocheted off the mantle.

When it was over, she gathered her shoes and left, disappearing into the rain in her long grey sweater; with her yellow shoes in her hand and her blood covered jeans left on the floor in our living room.

We waited for several minutes, long after the door had closed behind her. The fire raged, spurred on by its thirst, tearing into the logs, and lighted the room.

The TV was destroyed.

We got up; off the couch, off the floor. We avoided each other and slowly dressed. Linda called the police. I poured myself a drink.

We never heard from her again.

DTF IN THE HOUSE OF GOD

They wanted to know why.

Because the house is haunted, I told them.

First it had been the nurses and doctors, now it was the police. They'd dressed me in a hospital gown and were slowly feeding the blood back into my veins through a needle. It was a miracle I'd survived. But nobody here was interested in miracles. They wanted to know about the events of the weekend, how I'd come to be handcuffed, and why the house had burned.

Because, I said, worn down by the repetition of their questioning, *the house is haunted*. The man in the rumpled coat looked at me—a mix of pity, frustration, and concern—and put his notepad down.

"We'll be back when he's stable," he told the nurse. "You have my number. Anything happens, use it."

The nurse nodded, affecting a tight-lipped smile. Her name was Diane. It said so on the identification card dangling from her neck.

"Thanks," the detective grumbled, rising from his chair. He was followed out by his partner and a very self-serious youth in uniform who took up watch outside the door.

The nurse finished her tasks, avoiding eye-contact, and left the room. She'd started to perspire in the interim. I couldn't blame her for being on edge. Nobody wants to be left alone with a crazy person, especially one suspected of homicide.

*

Sometimes, unexpectedly, paragraphs grow, pages unfold into whole chapters, and all of the sudden what started out as a blip evolves into an earthquake. Life is written in portions—I don't mean days or weeks, years, or even decades; it can't be condensed, there isn't a spine in the universe broad enough to contain it all in a single printed volume.

If anything, life is a library. A sprawling labyrinth of spiral notepads. Stack upon stack, papers on the floor. Pages torn, crumpled, and discarded; moments forgotten. There's unlimited space, but not every shelf gets filled. There's a lot of emptiness. There's a lot of dross. We don't all live well. The greater portion of stories are either boring or the writing is bad. We can't all be Hemingway in Africa. Some of us lead lives that read like stove manuals, ventures in doldrum.

Aurelius wrote Meditations; most of us are mediocre.

Fresh out of college I hit the backboard of my early twenties, so to speak. It was the end of an era. I said goodbye to the school dorms, moved into a boarding house, and started looking for work. One day I turned the page and all of my friends were gone. The book closed.

I kicked off a new start and moved to Boise.

The years that followed weren't inconsequential, it just felt like they were happening between volumes. During that time, I thought about the past a lot. The prior narrative was compacted into a glossary of highpoints and run through often; I was sick with nostalgia, living out a prologue unawares.

Not much happened.

I had my own place, no roommates, and a shared jacuzzi that overlooked the industrial quarter and a gravel pit. Numerous exciting novels start off slow, I told myself.

I kept distracted with work but at every turn I faced reality. The mornings were the worst. Nothing amplifies solitude like bare walls in an empty kitchen, illuminated by dawn and the glow of the stove clock, as you pour and chew your cereal; rinsing your dish, then lacing up your shoes at the door, keys clutched in hand, stepping out and meeting the day with nothing to look forward to but doldrum. That's how it was—copy and paste, copy and paste, over and over—my morning melancholy, all caps and italicized; the monotony of adulthood.

I spent a lot of time doing nothing.

I'd get home from work, kick off my shoes, collapse on the couch, and sigh. The TV churned out programming like an influx of junk mail. I went out with my co-workers a few times; knew people, but never made any friends. The apartment filled up with furnishings but never felt less empty. In a nutshell, I was lonely. Boise was erupting with growth and I was utterly lost, a ghost in a maternity ward. It wasn't the way I'd envisioned it. As a newly minted adult, I carried a job and knew how to scramble eggs.

That was it.

Welcome to the real world, Mark.

Then Cupid came along with his rotary canon, kicked open the book, and deftly unraveled the plot like a ball of yarn down a hillside. Love is the greatest author; solipsism is a hack. Salvation arrived—chapter one, verse one—and Laura was her

name. Laura with the beauty mark beside her mouth, dark eyed
and olive skinned, with a Spanish rose tattooed on her shoulder
and forever blood-red lips.

We met in a minor way.

Time passed.

I felt less alone, I fell in love.

We'd been seeing each other for about five weeks when
she invited me over for the first time. It was normal. She lived
with her aunt. We had no idea where it would go. What had
started out as a one-night stand had evolved into something
more. Two nights, three nights. Four nights because the sex
was great. But then she started staying over for breakfast. We
scheduled coffee dates and started holding hands.

After that it was full tilt.

The paragraph had grown; we were cultivating chapters.

The pick-up lines deepened into compliments; and the
compliments were delivered sober, clothed, and unbidden. She
was over most nights and when she wasn't her absence was felt.
The apartment became ours—not on paper, but in our
hearts—it was a shared occupancy. She gave it life, femininity.
There were traces of her in every room. It started with a panty
drawer and a second pillow, some space for shoes in the closet;
she bought an electric kettle for the kitchen, gluten-free snacks
for the pantry; her favorite mug lived on the counter beside the
dishrack when she wasn't there, and artesian soaps cropped up
in the shower stall. One day she exchanged the old battered
blinds for pleated shades and cool green curtains.

That was her favorite color, green, and she wore it all
the time even when it was mine. Picture her naked in my one
suitable shirt, an olive-drab flannel that fit her like a summer
dress, but with sleeves that extended well-beyond her fingertips
and a decade worth of un-ironable wrinkles. She wore it around
the house after sex and on weekends. It's probably still draped
over the bed, even now.

It probably still smells like her.

*

"How about Saturday?" she asked, cracking a celery stalk between her teeth. It was Tuesday evening. We were at home waiting for the oven to heat up. A pot roast sat on the counter in a tray, leaking blood, also waiting. "My aunt has been demanding I serve you up for an inspection. I thought I'd be able to spare you but it's inevitable really. We might as well get it out of the way. She'll probably rate you on a scale of one-to-five then issue a review asserting how positively unsuited we are for each other, but that's Aunt Sarah, ever in touch with the needs of others."

"Sounds charming," I said. "I can't wait to meet her."

"You say that now."

She poured us each a glass of wine—white for herself, red for her man—then settled in beside me on the couch. "Once you get to know her, you'll find that she's about as charming as a piranha."

"Great."

She tilted the glass to her lips and smiled. Laura loved Malbec. "I'm just trying to prepare you," she said. "My aunt can be very…let's just say, challenging. She's very religious."

"I'm guessing she doesn't approve of this then? You staying over, us sharing a bed—taking a dump, as it were, on the holy sanctity of marriage. She probably thinks I'm the antichrist."

"Yeah, and it's for precisely that reason that she doesn't know, okay? She thinks I've got an apartment with a friend from work."

"Shall I wear a wig, introduce myself as whats-her-name, or would you rather I just don't bring it up?"

"You're funny," she said. She set her glass on the coffee table and came closer. "Don't worry, it won't be that bad," she purred. "It'll only be for a few hours. Just play dumb, Charlie Brown. You'll be fine."

"Do we have to?"

"Yeah or I'll never get her off of my back."

"Okay," I said as she pressed her hands against my chest and kissed me. *Okay,* as her tongue slipped between my lips, silencing the matter.

Before I knew it, the week was over. Saturday had arrived and I woke up in a funk, feeling tense. After so many hours in front of a computer screen, scouring video sequences for imperfections, the last thing I wanted to do was engage in social niceties.

The editing bay had scored my eyes and I couldn't stop blinking. I was exhausted. I felt like a faulty extension on the verge of a crash. Being creative for other people will do that, it knocks your batteries out. At this stage conversational glitches were guaranteed; at any moment during the dinner I might hiccup and say fuck too many times in front of the zealot.

"Idiots," I growled, maneuvering traffic as a pickup truck merged onto the freeway at less than half the speed limit. Rush hour for rednecks, they move everywhere at the rate of tractors like nothing exists outside of the farm.

Laura dialed the volume back on our favorite radio station, hushing Halsey's throaty warble to a murmur. We were on our way to her aunt's.

"There's something I haven't told you," she said. "I have a brother…we didn't really grow up together, that's why I never mentioned him to you. He's a lot younger than I am."

Her words were bitten off, like stiches tugged from an old wound. She was looking out the window, breathing through her teeth. It didn't seem like a big deal. Evidently it was.

I glanced at her, smiled to show that I wasn't upset. "Okay," I shrugged. "I didn't know that obviously, but cool. I'm sure he's great. How old is he?"

"He's nine. I never meant to keep it from you. It's just...I don't know."

"Wait, didn't your mom..."

"He's my half-brother."

"Oh."

"It's complicated. Like I told you, I don't talk to my Dad."

"But your aunt raised you right?"

"Yeah, both of us."

"Alright," I nodded.

"You're not mad?"

"No, I'm not mad. Why would I be mad?"

"Good," she took my hand and squeezed it. "I'm glad you're not upset."

"So, what's his name?" I asked.

"His name is Danny, but...don't laugh okay? We've always called him God." I felt her eyes on me as she searched for a reaction.

I kept my attention on the road and waited for the rest of it.

"It's a long story really," she said. "At school they made fun of him...that was before we knew. The children picked up on it first. They started to calling him Danny Down Syndrome. Then the teachers started noticing things in his behavior and... Aunt Sarah ignored everyone of course, even when it was obvious that Danny was different. But then he fell way behind in class and at the end of his first year he was diagnosed."

We were both quiet.

She stared out the window, letting the road sounds pick up the slack. According to the GPS we'd be there in fifteen. When I was sure she'd finished, I broke the silence. "Well, I look forward to meeting him," I said, smiling. "I'm sure Danny...God...is an interesting guy."

"You're the best," she took my arm and hugged it, straining her seatbelt, then pressed her face against my shoulder and kissed me. "I knew you'd understand."

We pulled into the driveway as the last of the sunlight petered out into pink streamers on full-dark. It was a tiny brick house bordered with Juniper shrubs. The windows glowed and a trail of smoke snaked from the chimney, muscular and grey against the night sky.

The porch light snapped on immediately and the front door pulled back on a thin woman in her fifties. She wore her hair in braids beneath a knitted snowcap. "Laura sweetie," she beamed, wiping her hands on her apron and opening her arms for a hug as we mounted the porch steps. "I'm so glad you're here."

I stepped aside as the two embraced.

Laura broke the hold and wrapped her arms around my waist. "Auntie, this is Mark,"

I nodded polity, showing my teeth. "Nice to meet you," I said. I wasn't sure if I should extend my hand or not. She seemed old fashioned and I couldn't tell if she was the kind for hugging strangers.

Her eyes narrowed, studying my face, then she burst into a cackle. "Praise the lord," she grinned. "he looks just like a matinee idol, dear. Come inside now, come inside. I'm pleased to meet you, young man."

"Thanks," I grinned, following them inside. "And thanks for dinner tonight. I've heard you're quite the cook."

"Oh, have you?" She closed the door behind us, threw the deadbolt, then took our jackets and hung them in the closet. "I wonder who told you that. Certainly not Laura. I can't even remember the last time she was over. When was it dear?"

I felt Laura rolling her eyes as we were led into the dining room and handed crystal flutes of sparkling cider. "Aunt Sarah always keeps a bottle of Martinelli on hand," Laura explained, winking at me over the rim of her glass. "She doesn't drink."

"My brother used to drink red wine," the older woman said from the kitchen. "Laura's father. But he knew how to drink responsibly, that's the difference. Most men can't do that. What about you Mark?" she asked, running a knife through a cabbage. It split in half with a crunch and she quartered it, sweeping the wedges into a bowl with a handful of chopped carrots. "Do you drink?"

"Not so much anymore," I nudged Laura's hip, showing her the tightly crossed fingers I held at my back. She took my hand, squeezed it, and smiled. "Only on special occasions."

"That's good," Sarah nodded. She set the cutting board in the sink and doused it with a sponge.

The house was cramped, not cozy; it was crowded and ten degrees too warm. Religious paraphernalia littered the walls and the tops of several china cabinets. The prerequisite Jesus, framed in oak, hung above the kitchen table; and a bookshelf draped with doylies sagged internally under the weight of several giant-size Bible concordances. The wall sconces all held candles that had never been lit and the porcelain knick-knacks were dollar store trinkets. It felt like a church thrift shop. Everything was threadbare and Biblical.

"More cider?" Laura asked. We exchanged a glance and her eyes said: *It'll be over soon enough.*

"Sure, thanks."

"Daniel!" Sarah shouted, removing a tray from the stove with two mismatched oven mitts on her hands. "Stop whatever you're doing and come for dinner!"

He didn't come.

Laura tugged my elbow. "Don't worry, Aunt Sarah," she said. "Mark and I'll get him."

We walked past Jesus, he was glowing, his hands folded and eyes uplifted, then around a corner and into the living room. Our movement came to a halt at the foot of a plush embankment where the floor disappeared beneath a hodgepodge of colors and textures. There were blankets strewn, stretched between chairs, and pillows methodical stacked into walls and turrets, sprawling in every direction, from corner to corner. Quilts pinned to the arms of couches stripped of their cushions and supported by beams and boxes and lean-tos fashioned of bedsheets. It was the most elaborate pillow fort I'd ever seen.

"Impressive," I said.

"Yeah, geez. Better than the school playground."

Laura crouched at what appeared to be the entry, a blanket dangling between two wobbly card-table legs. She lifted the door flap and peered inside.

"Danny?" she called.

"That's not my name."

"I don't care. Dinner is ready, okay? Let's go."

There was a flicker of light in the darkness, like a lantern at the back of a very deep cave. Laura looked at me and rolled her eyes. "C'mon Danny, you're being rude."

"Who's Danny?"

"A rude little boy who's not going to get any dessert tonight."

"I'm not a little boy."

"I like your fort. Are you a builder?"

"I'm not a builder."

"Okay," she sighed, rising up on her knees and then to her feet. She cleared her throat. "God, would you please come out now and join us for dinner?"

There was a rustling from within, hands and knees scuffing the carpet, then a head materialized from the dark at the mouth of the cavern. "I'm not the builder," the little boy said, clambering into the open. "I'm the creator."

"Same difference silly," Laura said.

The boy bounded to his feet and embraced her legs, casting a bashful sidelong glance in my direction before looking away.

"Danny—"

"My name isn't Danny!"

"Whatever. I'm not going to argue semantics with a nine-year-old," she took him by the shoulders and turned him to face me. "Look, say hello to my friend Mark."

He pushed himself back against her legs and assessed me with the shameless intensity of his age.

"Hey buddy," I smiled. "I really like your pillow fort. Did you build it all by yourself?"

We locked eyes. Something shifted in the air, like a storm cloud passing between us. His eyes were as black as dead embers and his hair was imperceptibly blonde, cut so short that it appeared white. His lips seemed to be molded in the wrong direction, concaving in over his teeth.

Danny's condition was evident, but only if you looked. At a glance, he was darkly handsome. The intensity of his continence obscured the irregularity of his features and bored through you.

He broke free from Laura and ran toward the kitchen.

Polite conversation is usually rife with undercurrents. Laura and her aunt squared off and spent dinner tearing each other apart with niceties. Passive aggression punctuated seemingly harmless remarks, hanging in the silences between mouthfuls. They traded blows like fighters while Danny and I stared at our plates, bystanders. He ate his food and ignored me with bashful deliberation; I was a stranger here.

It wasn't until I served him the largest slice of pie for dessert that he warmed up to me. Sarah coolly protested, but her heart wasn't in it.

Danny ignored her, pushing his fork into the piecrust. Within seconds his face became a royal blue smear of blueberries and vanilla ice cream. He beamed at me through the crumbs, kicking his legs beneath the table.

Then came the questions.

Why do you wear red socks? Why do you and Laura hold hands? What's your middle name? Did you know everything in the Bible is true and that Jesus is God's son but they're also the same person? Where do you live? What's your house look like?

Then: *Can I come live with you? Aunt Sarah defies the laws of creation.*

That earned him a smack. Sarah shook her head and apologized, and Danny stopped asking questions. After desert, he was allowed to wonder off. Sarah cleared the table. She poured us coffee and returned to her seat.

"Such an odd thing to say," I chuckled, clasping my fingers at the back of my head. "What do you suppose he meant by it?"

"Yes, well, Danny is prone to saying odd things," she explained, stirring her coffee. "He's a diagnosed autistic. His mind doesn't work like ours."

"Neither did Einstein's. Did you know that he couldn't tie his shoes?"

"Einstein was a savant," she retorted. "Not all retarded children are the Rain Man, as Laura will attest."

"He seems to get along alright."

"Yes. By the Grace of God, Mark. Danny has the spirit of the Lord in him. Which should come as no surprise. My brother was a great man, a Godly man. He—"

"Let's not talk about it okay?" Laura said, pushing her chair back. "Mark has to work tomorrow, so we should probably get going anyways."

"You haven't finished your coffee."

"It's getting late."

The old woman tilted her head. There was a twinkle in her eye as she pinned Laura with her gaze. "It's funny," she said, warming her hands with her coffee cup; she held the power here as assuredly as she brought the cup to her lips and drank, "Very strange actually, Laura, how little you and Danny have in common. The two of you really couldn't be more different."

"Speak of the devil," I said as Danny returned. He waddled up beside me, carrying a large book in his hands. "Look," he said, holding it out for me.

"What's this?" I asked, lifting the tome.

"It's my love letter to the world."

It was leather-bound, thick as a dictionary, and looked about a hundred-years-old. I set it on the table and hauled the pages back, skimming. It was filled with drawings in pencil, crayon; some red ink; symbols and gibberish, rendered by a master hand. This was no doubt the work of an experienced artist; the final-most opus of a brilliant career, corroded by madness and the voices of demons.

In school I'd met people who'd dedicated their lives to art—teachers and students, the talented ten-percent—and not one of them had produced content of such alarming vision. This was nightmare fuel. The work of a twenty-first century Goya. A schizophrenic perhaps, no nine-year-old boy.

I closed the volume and smoothed my hand across the cover. "Who did these drawings Danny?"

"My name isn't Danny."

"I'm sorry. I meant to say God. Is this your book?"

"Yes."

"Who drew those pictures in it?"

"I did," he said, grabbing it off the table and taking it in his arms. "Not Danny. God."

"You did?" I glanced at Laura for support, then at Sarah. "That's not possible buddy. Little kids can't draw…pictures…like the ones in that book."

He studied me for a moment, face slack, expressionless. A shadow of a disappointment passed beneath the dark surface of his eyes and he lowered his head.

"Goo-goo-gah-gah," he muttered, turning dejectedly and walking away with the book held tightly against his chest.

Laura stood up.

"I'll go talk to him," she said. "He's probably just tired."

As soon as she left the room, Sarah's head snapped in my direction like a manned turret. Her mouth creaked open on a loaded smile. She'd been waiting for this.

"Mark, are you a believer?" she asked.

"Uh," I sipped at my coffee and considered lying.

"Do you attend church?" she clarified. "Do you believe in God?"

"Yeah," I nodded. "I believe in a creator. Sometimes I think people are kind of like books or libraries, so—"

"What church do you attend?"

"Oh, I'm not really much of a church goer."

"You've lapsed in your Faith?"

"No," I sipped my coffee, trying to avoid her eyes. "I just choose to pursue it differently. I'm not very religious."

"How well do you think you know Laura?"

"Pretty well I'd say."

"And how well do you know the Bible?"

"I've seen the movie," I smiled, trying for humor.

"So, you're not saved," she asked.

"Saved?"

"Mark, did you know that Jesus—Jehovah, the Son of God Himself, born of a virgin womb—was the product of incest?"

"Um."

"That picture," she nodded at the portrait of Christ above the table. "Hogwash. Idealized and inaccurate. I only hang it there as a symbol of respect for what it represents."

"I don't think that I..."

"Understand? And why not? I'm telling you that Jesus was an incest baby. An autistic, most likely. It's not difficult to comprehend. You see, I've studied the Bible. More than you certainly, but also more than most. My brother, he had the spirit of God in him. He taught me to recognize the truth, to listen and be guided by it. Most interpretations of scripture lack substance, they only reach about as deeply as a fingernail."

Suddenly the eggshells I'd been walking on turned into beartraps. I tried segueing off the topic before one closed around my ankle. "Do you think Laura is finished—"

"You see, we're all God's children," she declared, terminating my question. "It says so in the Bible. Every man, every woman...the virgin Mary even. Do you understand now? God saw fit to impregnate his child, his *own* daughter, Mark. *He saw fit.*"

Then Laura returned.

She came into the room with our coats and we made a fast excuse to leave.

"Come again," Aunt Sarah said at the door.

On the drive home I asked Laura about her father. Her responses were slow, measured. She navigated his story as carefully as a minefield. He was in an institution. Certified insane. Apparently, he heard voices and one day they told him to burn down a building with people inside.

"They sold porn in the back," she explained. "I don't think he knew there were people inside, but he went kind of crazy after my mom died, so who knows. He didn't deny it. I mean, he was always religious but that really pushed him over the edge—I remember him spending hours and hours with a lamp on just poring over the bible. I don't think he slept. He said the preachers had it all wrong. Then after Danny was born, he just disappeared. A few years later his attorney called, asking for bail money. My Aunt just pretends he never resurfaced. MIA. Overseas sharing Christ with the natives, whatever. It's easier for her that way."

"So your mom, what was she like?"

"Normal. Just an Idaho girl. She grew up in Jerome."

"What about Danny's mom?"

"She was there for a while…then she ran away."

"Ran away?"

"Could we talk about this another time?" she reached over, stroking my arm. "I have a headache right now."

The following weeks passed uneventfully. I spent them behind curtains in a dark room, separate from my humanity. Hunched in the chair, with sore eyes and bad posture, working my keyboard down to the wires beneath. Clicking, clipping, cutting.

I had so many clients, I had to write their names down. Spring is always like this. When the flowers bloom, so do the people. They get married then hire someone like me to piece together the memories, immortalized for all-time in high definition video.

I was starting to feel unhealthy.

Physically, my spine felt like soft rubber; my posture was on suicide watch after week one. I had to really work to keep my back straight. It was hard, my head ached. My eyes burned. Stress poured into my subconscious and ravished my dreams with a bloodlust for endorphins.

I felt the need to stretch out in the sunlight somewhere and die, because *saying yes* was becoming a real problem for me.

I said yes one more time and netted a big one, an out of town job chronicling the marriage of an oilman's daughter to the son of a senator. They flew me to three different states with a reoccurring cast of thirty-four, then finally tied the knot in

Sun Valley. The reception was grandiose and expensive; there were three-hundred in attendance. All told, it took ten days to shoot, and then it was over.

I came home.

Laura was waiting for me in a fuchsia nightie when I walked in the door. "Hey sexy," she breathed, leaving lipstick on the rim of her wineglass. She was on the couch. Her eyes were narrowed and bright. She looked high, floaty. Her breasts rose and fell, visible beneath the thin fabric of her top, as her fingers worked in a slow circle between her legs.

I dropped my bag and slipped out of my coat.

"Goddamn I've missed you," I said, pulling my shoes off.

I came to her and pushed her backward onto the couch. She wore a plum colored thong that was already damp, kissing my neck as I ran my hands up the flatness of her stomach and cupped her breasts.

"I was waiting for you," she whispered, sinking her fingers into my back.

"You were?"

"Yeah," she said. "I got horny."

And then her phone rang.

We ignored it. We were kissing like MTV kids, all tongue and teeth, as it vibrated beside us on the coffee table. I hooked a finger in her panties and tugged them aside. She wrapped an arm around my neck and opened the front of my pants.

The phone kept ringing.

"Jesus fucking Christ, okay!" Laura growled, pushing me off her and sitting up. She grabbed the phone and held it to her ear. "Yeah what?"

I closed my eyes, head spinning.

"Okay, I'll be right over." Laura said, ending the call. She looked at me and sighed. "I'm sorry baby, it'll have to wait. That was my Aunt. Something's happened."

"You're the worst," I groaned.

"I know," she said, then stroked my erection and slipped me back into the waistband of my shorts. "I better get dressed."

"Okay," I said. I sat up and rubbed my temples. "But I'm going with you. We'll be sexually frustrated together."

Laura hung our coats in the entry and we removed our shoes. Nobody was home. Sarah had taken Danny to the clinic. *It's a regular thing,* Laura explained on the drive over. *He meets with a therapist. My Aunt just spaced it out and started a roast. She forgot to shut the oven off is all.*

How's that an emergency? I'd asked.

It's an old oven, the thing will literally explode into flames if it overheats.

Jesus, why not replace it?

Because honey, materialism is unbecoming.

I stowed my car keys in the pocket of my coat then followed Laura into the kitchen. The house seemed different now. Empty and without the lights on it felt smaller, oppressive; like the neat artificial environment of a set. Everything was grey but the honeyed glow of the oven light, glaring off the linoleum and into the hallway.

"Okay," Laura smiled, catching me in her arms as I entered the kitchen. "The day is saved. I've checked the oven and everything is fine."

"Great." I took her by the waist and kissed her. "We can go then."

"Uh-uh," she shook her head. "I'll have to watch it."

"Why is that?"

"The roast isn't done yet. Sarah likes it well-done. I'd never hear the end of it if I left her with a bloody roast."

"So what now?"

"I don't know," she whispered. "I guess we'll have to wait."

"And what should we do while we wait?" I asked, shifting my attention to her neck, kissing her throat. "When will your Aunt be home?"

"Not for an hour."

"Perfect."

I snarled my fingers through her hair and tugged her head back. The kiss was vicious, a lashing of tongues. She pressed herself against me like a knifepoint, all nipples and breasts and smooth contours, as we fired off interlocked, bumping the fridge, stumbling, spinning, lost in the throe of passion as we passed from the kitchen into the dining room. We encountered the dinner table. We knocked over a chair. Jesus kept his eyes trained heavenward in portrait, hands pressed together, uttering a prayer for the sinners.

"Hey," Laura breathed. She wrapped her arms around my neck and kissed me once very gently. Her eye sparkled mischievously. "I have an idea," she said.

Shifting her weight, she redirected us toward the living room. We tripped over each other's legs and crashed against the doorframe, sliding down to the floor as the fire blossomed between us. I pulled her over and she climbed on top of me.

"We should do it in there," she said, tossing her eyes in the direction of her brother's pillow-fort. "Under the blankets."

"Sounds kinky."

She pushed away from me and scampered on hands and knees toward the entry. I rolled onto my stomach and watched her go as she paused to remove her shirt. She pulled it over head and threw it at me, grinning wickedly in the low-light. "DTF in the house of God," she said, then disappeared behind the door flap.

I peeled off my shirt, kicked away my jeans.

Then followed her inside.

FIRST DATE

"Do you like dogs?" Her name was Annie and as soon as she asked the question, she met my eyes for the first time since we'd met. All of the sudden our titter-tatter had evolved. It was our first date. We drank in moderation, guardedly sipping our beers to keep our wits sharp. She was twenty-two, slim, blonde. I'm a burly guy.

"Sure," I replied. "I like dogs."

"That's great, because I could never be with somebody who doesn't love dogs."

"You have a dog?"

"Yeah," she nodded, beaming excitedly. "I got her from the shelter. Her name is Annie, just like me."

"That's a funny thing, to have a pet with the same name."

"She's a sweetheart."

"Just like you, I take it?"

"I can be nice."

"Nice like how?"

"Hmm…" Her eyes rolled skyward, searching the cloud I pictured above her head; the thought bubble. "Maybe like this," she said, and darted forward, kissing me on the cheek. She fell back into her seat, her side of the booth, and her face was instantly red all over.

"That was nice," I smiled. "Annie must be a wonderful dog."

"She is. She's the best."

I finished my beer and slid the glass toward the edge of the table. "So, you want to stick around or should we go someplace?"

"I'm not finished yet."

"Oh, I didn't notice."

"No, it's fine. I wasn't going to finish it anyway. I don't really like beer."

"No?"

"Well, not just beer. I don't drink much at all. Like in general, I mean."

"Not even wine, cocktails?"

"Nope."

"And I thought every girl was a sucker for Vodka."

"Not this one."

"How come?"

She shrugged, adjusting her rings; cheapies worn on every other finger with little rhinestones set into the metal in the shape of flowers.

"So, should we go?" I asked.

"Go where?"

"I don't know," I tucked my lips between my teeth and thought about it. "For a drive. Back to my place. Whatever you feel like doing."

She kept her eyes pinned to the table.

"Actually," she said. "Would you mind taking me home? I think I'm getting tired."

I frowned. "Why?"

She said nothing, shivered a little, and it looked like she was trying to disappear. Her whole body seemed to shrink.

"Have I done something wrong?" I asked. It was unfriendly, accusatory. Irritation came through in my voice like something slow and poisonous. "Do you not like me?"

"It's not that," she squeaked.

"Then what is it? What am I supposed to think?"

"I'm just...really tired." Her eyebrows knitted together, furrowing the skin. She wouldn't look at me. She just stared at her hands, working the knuckles, anxiously kneading the flesh like a nervous squirrel.

I exhaled through my nose.

"Okay," I said, sliding out from the booth. "Come on then, let's go."

We walked to the front of the restaurant and I paid the bill.

"How was your meal?" the waitress asked.

"Great." I told her.

She smiled and handed my card back with a receipt. I balled the paper and tossed it into an ashtray on the way out. My truck was parked just outside the front door. Annie climbed inside and I reached across the cab to help her with her seatbelt.

"Sometimes it sticks," I explained, starting the engine. "Personally, I never wear one."

I tossed my arm in back of her seat, twisting at the waist and watching for smaller cars as I backed out. The truck was oversize by design, made even bigger by an additional six-inch lift kit and Gladiator Mud Terrane tires. Parking lots always provided a challenge.

Annie stared out her window as we pulled into the street. She sat as far away from me as she could, shrunk against the door on her side of the cab, hugging her arms like she was cold. She hadn't said a word to me since we'd left the restaurant. Then, out of nowhere, she sat up and asked, "Are you a Christian?"

"No," I said. "I don't believe in that crap."

"I am," she murmured, fingering a small cross on a chain around her neck. I hadn't noticed it before. Her blouse had the neckline of an Amish cape.

I wondered what else she was concealing.

The little crucifix is probably still warm from dangling between her tits, I thought. And then I imagined running my tongue between her breasts, over the necklace, and then licking her nipples. She probably sweats when she's aroused.

"Is that why you don't like me?" I sneered, rolling down my window to spit. "I'm not Christian enough for you?"

The truck lurched as I turned off the street and onto a dirt road. The headlights picked up tire-tracks and clouds of dust, casting shadows off the barbed wire fence posts on either side as we plowed into darkness.

"Where are you taking me?" she asked.

"Home."

"Then why did you pull off the road?"

"Shortcut," I said, watching the road. The truck thumped and the shocks creaked, heaving in and out of ruts, where the ground had been eaten away by rain. Idaho is rural state. Roads like this are everywhere, even near the city. And the fields they cut through stretch for miles all around. That means abandoned barns and cabins and old tractor carcasses, places to go where no one can hear you; places where you won't be bothered.

I know them well.

"My Daddy wasn't a Christian."

"Good for him."

"He never went to church with me and Mamma. Always said it wasn't nothing but crap, same as you believe. I loved him though. He wasn't a very good man and he wasn't my real Daddy, but I loved him."

"A real sweetheart."

"He brought me home when I was seven."

"Where from?" I scoffed. "The free clinic?"

"I was adopted."

I glanced at her. She was still pressed against the door, clutching the little cross. Her eyes reflected the barley fields and the beam of the headlights. I kept my speed at an easy thirty as we climbed a hill. Rocks scattered noisily against the undercarriage and bounced off the wheel wells.

"He used to hurt Annie," she continued. "Used to beat her and treat her real cruel, make her lick up his piss and stuff."

"What are you talking about?"

"My Daddy. He wasn't a very good man."

"Poor you. Hey, make yourself useful and hand me one of those beers," I told her, pointing at a twelve pack I had tucked beneath the seats. "Open it for me too."

She didn't move from her position against the door.

"Hey," I shouted, startling her. "Are you deaf? Hand me a beer."

"Where are you taking me?" she asked.

"We're pretty much there. Any place will do."

"Where are we?"

"A spot I like to take my girlfriends."

"But...I'm not your girlfriend."

"Sure you are, we went out tonight didn't we?"

"I'll scream."

"Go ahead."

I pulled off the road. The ground gave way beneath the tires, scattering rocks as we came to a halt on the shoulder. We'd crested the hill. We were pitched on a tilt, faced by stars and sagebrush. Everything looked grey. I threw the truck in park, rolled my window down and dangled an arm through it. A breeze entered the cab; I killed the motor and pocketed the keys and we listened to the noises drifting in on the currents. A stream gurgling down below in the irrigation ditch and the sounds of insects chirping, scraping their legs together in the tall grass.

I stretched out behind the wheel and took a deep breath.

"You can scream all you want, Annie." I said. "Not much point in it though unless you want to piss me off. I'm not going to hurt you. I just want to make good on time spent, that's all. Me paying for dinner and the beers, I figure I've got something coming, right? You got to pitch in, princess. Even-steven. Do your part."

Her door swung open with a snap of the handle. She got about halfway out before I grabbed her. I coiled her hair in my fist and pulled her back, dragging her in along the seat. She reached overhead, grasping for my wrist to alleviate the stress on her scalp.

"Wouldn't bother running, either. See, I grew up around here. I know these roads like I know the lines in my face. You ever look at yourself Annie? I'm sure you do. And what do you see? Do you see the kind of girl that can run so many miles through crops and uneven farmland all the way back to town? You'd break your ankles."

I let go of her hair and took her by the arm, pushing my thumb against the underside of her wrist. Her pulse was fast, terrified. I twisted the arm and saw the tiny scars etched into her skin like bracelets.

"Well look at that. You a cutter, Annie?"

"Are you going to kill me?" she asked.

"Kill you? Shit, I'm just a regular guy. Like I said, all I want is to make good on my time. And then I'll take you home, just like you asked me to. How's that sound?"

She stared silently at the roof of the car. I felt her relax in my grip, giving in; the muscles in her arms untensed and she closed her eyes. "My Momma, she wasn't much of a looker but she was a good Christian. Always going to church and stuff. But one day she walked in on my Daddy when he was hurting

Annie, she just closed the door and went back to cooking. Had to pretend she didn't hear nothing too, cuz Daddy was always loud. And so was Annie, whimpering and crying out like she did."

With my free hand I undid my belt buckle, yanking it from the loops. I wound it around her wrists and then through the steering wheel and pulled it tight.

"But then Annie got real mad," she said. "Started snarling all the sudden, showing her teeth and stuff."

"Jesus Christ," I complained. "Would you shut up already? I don't care about your Daddy or your damn stupid dog either. Just shut up."

"Arthur?"

I glanced at her face and saw that she'd opened her eyes. She was looking at me for the first time since we'd been at the restaurant.

"You lied to me when you said you liked dogs, didn't you?"

"I don't care about them none, either way," I said, grabbing the front of her shirt and tearing it. I tugged her upright and stuck my tongue in her mouth. Her bra was clinical in its plainness, like something from a hospital. I saw the cross hanging between her breasts, gleaming against her skin.

"We'll do away with that one too," I said, taking it in my fist, breaking the chain and tossing out the window.

"Arthur?"

"What?"

"You shouldn't have lied to me about liking dogs," she said.

"Oh yeah?" I grinned. "Why, because lying is a sin?"

"Not because of that, but because...I'm not like Momma. I won't just close the door and go away while you hurt Annie."

I started to speak but she bit my bottom lip. Blood welled up through her milky teeth and flooded my mouth as she tore it from the bone, separating the flesh from my jaw with an audible oily squelch.

I lifted my hand and brought it to my mouth, saw the blood on my fingertips, tasted it, touched it; the slender rows of teeth slick beneath my fingertips. Then the pain came, firing through my ears to the front of my skull.

I screamed.

I set the horn off, flopping against the steering wheel and door, kicking the peddles. One arm fell through the window, clutching for the handle. I needed to get out. My teeth were exposed. My mouth felt cold, like an open window in a snow storm. All my energy was draining down the front of my shirt.

Annie freed her wrists from the steering wheel. I watched her chew and swallow what had once been a piece of my face, then stretch her legs out. She wrapped the belt around her neck and did the buckle. It hung from her throat like a leash. I was fading, losing consciousness. The last thing I saw was her hand slipping down the front of her pants as she arched her back.

"Good girl," she whimpered, hips bucking. "Good girl, Annie," panting, tugging her clit in the moonlit cab as the blood slid down the back of my throat.

BURZUM

I.

Johnny liked the way his skin fell apart when it opened, the tendons and blood vessels breaking and unfurling like weathered cloth as he drew the scissors across his left wrist. It looked cool. Threadbare. Like he was some tangled mess of humanity worn deep and down to the bone, bleeding.

Fuck yeah, he thought, watching the blood well. *Mariana's Trench, motherfuckers. In my fucking arm.* The blood came slow, like an underwater emission seeping up from the riff.

Split wrists.

Wrists unseaming, wrists unraveled.

But Johnny didn't want to die.

"Yo anyone who says I wanna die is fucking dumb, man. I don't fucking wanna to die. I wanna *fuck* Lady Death, you know? Like in the ass, man. I wanna fuck Lady Death in her fucking ass," he sneered. "Could you imagine?"

He'd had the phone pressed to his ear for over an hour, sitting on the roof above his father's garage. The night sky was clear above him. *Studded*, he thought. *Like God's a bitch with pierced nipples.* He was framed in radiance, cloaked in the stars and their void and the luminous wet-looking moon; it didn't cast light so much as the light seemed to just leak from around the edges, slickening the rooftops.

Johnny carved another wedge out of his arm then put the scissors down and lit a cigarette.

"Trust me, dude," he said into the phone, holding it with his shoulder while he cupped the little butane lighter, protecting the flame from the wind. "You ain't seen shit till you've seen Death in a magenta thong."

He looked down at the street, at the row of houses, driveways, and garages, their glowing windows, curtains, and honeyed blinds. You don't have to grow up in a place for it to be familiar. All neighborhoods look the same. The homes go dark and parked cars sleep in runny moonlight.

This night was damp.

Tumescent shadows crawled through the luminous drip and huddled beneath the warmth of the windows, in the porch-ways, and in the shrubs and bushes that surrounded the latticework beneath them; tilting away from the street lamps and moonlight, revolted by suburbia.

Johnny pulled a storm into his lungs, then released it back through his teeth. *SOS I'm bleeding.* Smoke signals carried away on the wind.

"All that skeleton grim reaper shit?" he said. "It's bullshit, man. Fucking bullshit. The creepy hood and all that— it's just for kids. They make that shit up for kids, you know? I'm telling you, man. Let me fucking tell you. Death is hot. She's a bitch and she's fucking hot."

He stood up, coughing on the tobacco.

He was excited, worked up by the wounds and the rush of adrenaline that accompanied them, and he started to pace.

"Yeah, yeah, yeah," he said into the phone, the gum texture of the roof, still-warm rubber shingles and smooshed cigarette butts, springy beneath his boots.

He shielded his eyes as a car appeared on the street, rolling up and over a speed bump, sweeping its high beams into space then back down again, bouncing light off the asphalt. The darkness broke. Shadows scurried and thinned; they went flat like when rats collapse their heads to get under doors, shrinking beneath the roofs and window ledges.

It looked like an Audi. *An R8, maybe?* Driven drunkenly by some corporate-looking jerk in a fancy jacket. The vehicle swerved, mulching a patch of gravel in the margin as it passed.

Sounds like teeth. Johnny thought. He felt lightheaded, vaguely stoned yet determinedly sober. The pain was running up his arm now, waking his brain.

Imagine that. Car tires with fucking jaws and teeth and tongues and shit, chewing up eternity by way of an asphalt genocide. I like that, he mused, twisting on his heel to face the backyard. *It sounds fucking hardcore.*

The highway holocaust.

Death to trees and people.

That's all this is anyways, a death cult of dollars and cents. Big cars and money, right? We're raping Mother Earth with our cocks, our industry, oil rigs like twisting steel penises. With our AIDS and cellphones and factories and shit. Studded tires drudging up old ugly blood to turn a profit, kicking up dust and scaring the poor bitch's back deep with heavy-duty treads and tractor blades. Then all the stress from our shitty fucking jobs, of course, polluting the air.

He reached for the bloody scissors, thought better of it, then kicked them down into the lawn.

You can smell the fear-stink of desperation in any city. It comes up from the ground. And here I am above it all, on Dad's garage with holes in my skin like ripped denim. Like I'm my own pair of goddamn lucky jeans.

"Whatever," he said, returning his attention to the call, his voice shrill and sounding like a raven. "Fuck all that anyway. It's not important. You'll see tonight. I swear to fucking god I'm going to do it."

He continued to smoke, watching the cigarette paper shrinking away from the ash.

"Yo, what did you say?" he wheezed. "*Am I going to use a condom? Is that what you said? Like a prophylactic?*"

He flicked the cigarette off the roof.

"Yeah right man, if that's what you said. Yeah right. I never use that shit. Not with anybody. Fuck that. And besides, if I put it in her ass who cares? She'll be shitting my seed tomorrow morning and isn't that fucking philosophic?"

A moment lapsed.

"Yo Ramon?" he pulled the phone away from his ear and glanced at the display. It was dark and dead, in need of a charge.

"Piece of shit," he muttered, slipping it into his pants pocket. *Phones die nice though, don't they? No kicking and screaming. No pain. Like Jesus Christ, they die and rise again.*

By the time Johnny got off the roof and walked into the kitchen he'd lost a lot of blood. He filled a glass with water from the sink, drank half, then hurled it against the wall where it shattered into a million pieces.

Fuck diamonds.
Everything is a sham.
I see nothing but broken glass.

His father ran several red lights on the way to the hospital. His knuckles turned white, gripping the wheel, with Johnny flopped down in the backseat, wrapped in a towel. They burst into the ER just as Diane came on shift, looking prim in spotless scrubs.

She took one look at Johnny, pale, staggering, bleeding down his father's shirt with an arm around his shoulder, and groaned. She didn't roll her eyes but she thought about it. This was nothing new for her. He always timed his emergency visits for when she was working. Date night opposite an IV drip. They met a year ago at the Neurolux. Lots of cigarettes and beer and overly-grim shitty bands. Johnny was in a group called Hormones—stylized *WhOre MoANs* on the drumkit. He played bass and he played it ugly, throttling the frets like he was running his fingertips down a face then gouging the eyes out. They played their full catalog of three songs and afterward Diane French-kissed him beneath the stage lights.

She had the longest hair he'd ever seen, gold-flecked green eyes, and what Johnny called a *dick-suck smile.* She was pretty too. Especially in a crop-top with her bubble butt packed so tightly into her booty shorts the seams threatened to burst or disappear altogether.

You're an easy target for a heat-seeking missile, he'd told her at about 5 a.m. while bathed in her sweat. That was their first time together. It was a corny line but she liked it and she added him on Instagram as soon as her phone was charged. They were in a relationship now but they didn't call it that. They didn't give it a title or talk about it; they just fucked and held hands sometimes when his friends weren't around.

"Johnny what the heck?" she said, taking his arm as she and another nurse helped him off his father's neck and onto a gurney. "This is the third time this month."

"Fuck you," he murmured as they pulled an oxygen mask over his face.

The doctor walked up, smoothing the lapels of his hospital coat. He reached for Johnny's father's hand, and forced a smile. "Sir, we meet again," he said. "I'm sure you remember our last conversation…"

Johnny remembered.

His father standing in the doorway to his bedroom, a frail broken man, relaying the information. The doctor advised counseling, group therapy.

Fuck that, he'd said, shoving the pamphlets off his bed. *Fuck that shit Dad,* he snarled. *Father. It's not like that. I'm not fucking suicidal, okay?*

I don't want to
Fucking
Die.

Diane squeezed his hand as they pushed him through a set of doors and down the hall. It hurt like hell but he didn't ask her to stop.

They parked him in a private room.

Diane took his blood pressure and the doctor came and made a swift examination of his wrists before sewing them shut again. They wrapped the wounds in sterile cotton and gauze then plugged him into an IV for the blood loss.

After a little while his vision came back into focus and his head stopped spinning. He blinked his eyes and looked around the room. The walls were blank except for a laminated nervous system chart and a little blue clock. There was a pitcher of water on a tray beside his bed and the ravished ends of a balloon-tie tethered to the stainless-steel frame, a trace distinction amid the antiseptic sameness.

Johnny insisted on staying overnight. Nobody argues with a suicide, he'd learned. The doctor conceded, of course. Johnny got his way and his father drove home more annoyed than sympathetic, tiredness descending upon him like a vulture in the aftermath of the alarm.

"This is getting ridiculous John," he'd said. "What would your mother think of you doing this, cutting yourself? I don't know. I just don't know. If there's a heaven above, I sure hope they've got plenty of wine."

Right.
Like I give a flying fuck.

He closed his eyes and rested.

When he opened them again, the hospital had sunken into a calm. Johnny, propped up on pillows, smiled as the painkillers took hold. The lights and the air trembled electric. He heard the machines, their fans whispering, and the slow off-gassing of life beneath them. Gasping, wheezing.
Suction cups, fed by wires, in search of a pulse. Bones fusing inaudibly beneath swollen purple flesh and plaster, and all the eyeballs like scalped grapes roving restlessly beneath stark sunken lids.

Welcome to the earth-purgatory, he thought. *Our gleaming transitory barge between life and death. The medical system. The monolith.*

Johnny would have painted the walls black. Down a pint of blood and milk-white, his skin almost disappeared in folds of his bedsheet, in the sterile white interior. Without his dark jeans and jacket on, he felt washed out. Otherwise, he fit in fine. His personal aesthetic catered to the dead. He was always this pale; he always looked like a corpse. His hair was dyed black, bunched against his pillow-case, then there were the little black stars tattooed on his shoulder, and his eye makeup standing out stark against his face.

Diane joined him on her break.

She sat beside him, sipping a coke.

"Why do you keep showing up here like this?" she asked, affixing her lips to the straw, slurping the coke. "I mean, what are you doing to yourself? Do you want to die? I don't get it."

He sat up, wincing, and reached for his jacket.

The buckles made a ruckus, slapping the steel bedframe as he dragged it onto his lap and removed a package of cigarettes from the pocket.

He put one in his mouth.

"Hey!" she hissed. "You know you can't smoke in here."

"Yeah, I know I *can't fucking smoke in here*," he sneered. "No shit. I just feel better with one in my mouth, okay? Is that alright with you?" He got the lighter out just to spite her, summoning the flame with his thumb and then holding it up, watching it dance between his eyes. "You know what they say about playing with fire. Maybe I'll burn this place down tonight."

"Maybe so," she frowned. "I don't get why you're so obsessed with dying anyway. You say you want to live but—"

"*I'm not*," Johnny growled, extinguishing the flame. He dropped the lighter in his lap and thrust his arms out with the bandages face-up. "Did you see these cuts? Did you even fucking look? They're the wrong way, man! I did that shit with fucking scissors. I'm not obsessed with dying, you bitch. I'm obsessed with *Death*, a concept clearly beyond you."

"Oh wow, you're so original. What does that even *mean?*"

"I don't expect you to understand."

"Well good. I don't."

He looked away, settling his eyes on the glowing caduceus through the window. The hospital faced a McDonald's, opposite the highway, and the golden arches stood taller and brighter than the caduceus. Boise twinkled in the backdrop, all-smiles.

"Okay fine," she blurted out. "You win, okay? You're obsessed with death, not dying. I don't get it, but whatever."

"That's right," Johnny said. "You don't. Whatever." He shifted his legs and his jacket slid off the bed, crashing against the floor tiles.

"What did you even do today?"

"Shit."

"What?"

"I did *shit*," he turned and glared at her. "And then after that I was talking to Ramon for a while."

"Cool. Did he get his tattoo?"

"I don't fucking know."

"But you were talking to him."

"Yeah, *on the phone*. No shit. Jesus Christ. you're stupid sometimes."

"You don't have to be with me, you know." She lifted her phone, disappearing into the palm-size glow of the screen. They sat in silence while she scrolled through her Instagram and liked photos. Johnny examined the bandages on his arms. He chewed a hangnail, then moved his eyes around the room. He wanted a cigarette.

"Hey come on," he finally said. "Sure, you're a little dumb sometimes but you're great at sucking dick."

"Oh?" She raised her eyebrows without looking up, then lowered her phone and held it in her lap, waiting for more. "Is that all?"

"You've got pretty hair."

"Everyone tells me that. What else?"

"You've got a nice ass," he grinned. He reached out and tapped her waist with his finger. "I can tell even in that stupid uniform."

He moved his hand down her leg and squeezed her knee. She stifled a smile and pushed him away, careful of his injuries.

"Okay, you're forgiven alright?"

"Do I get a kiss?"

"Yes, but just for that last part about my ass in these ugly scrubs. Even though we both know you're full of shit it's still kind of nice to hear sometimes."

She stood up and leaned over the bedrail. Their tongues met in each other's mouths like warring serpents, darting back and forth. He wrapped his arms around her neck gingerly, careful of the stitches in his wrists, and they stayed like that for the better part of a minute.

When it was over, she pulled away and adjusted her top. "That was a porno kiss," she said, licking the corner of her mouth. "I'll have to redo my lipstick now."

"Why bother?" he grinned. "You'll just have to do it again later when you come back for round two."

"If I can Johnny. I *am* here to work you know. There's stuff I need to do."

"Don't worry bitch, I won't get lonely or nothing."

"You're a real prick Johnny," she smiled, wiping her mouth with a tissue. "You don't deserve a girl like me."

"See you in an hour."

"What are you going to do if I don't come back, kill yourself?"

She blew him a kiss at the door then moved through it and down the hall. In the distance he could still hear the squeak of her shoe. She wore yellow Doc Martens; they were her trademark. She called them her duck boots and by magic got away with wearing them in the hospital. He could always identify her by the sound of those boots.

It's perfect, she'd explained, kissing his neck. *This way you'll always know when it's me, even in the dark.*

Johnny waited until around 2:00 am to unplug the IV and crawl out of bed. His blood was replenished and the dizziness he'd felt before was gone, replaced by the dull ache of the stiches holding his wrists together.

He carefully pulled his leather jacket on, pushing his bandaged arms down through the sleeves, then dressed in the torn jeans and army boots they'd stowed beneath his bed. With tangled hair and his eyeliner smeared, he looked like a rock star. Shirtless beneath the jacket, malnutrition made his abs pop and he felt very cool.

He pulled the door open, swiping the hair out of his face as he inched forward and checked the hall. Not a person in sight. He was free to move, stepping out, clutching his coat buckles to keep the noise down, and crossed the hall to the opposite room.

The door opened with a soft click. The lights were off but the room glowed, jittering grey-blue with playback. The beam of an iPad bounced off the wall, projecting voices. The occupant was propped up in her bed, breathing through a tissue she held to her face.

Johnny closed the door and tried the next room. This time the lights were on but the patient was sunken down in his bed, buried to the neck in quilts, and fast asleep. Johnny slipped through the door and found the man's phone plugged in beside the bed. He took the charger cable and coiled it, stuck it in his coat pocket, and dropped the phone into the trash bin on his way out. From there he continued down the hall and entered into an empty room. He locked the door behind him, plugged the charger into a wall socket and connected his phone.

Then he waited.

It didn't take long. The phone booted-up, white with resurrection, and he entered his passcode. The first thing he did was text Ramon: *Yo I'm here.* Then he texted Diane: *No round two? Who's dying tonight?*

Diane responded immediately: *Me maybe. I'm stuck on file duty upstairs. I might have to miss round two. I'll try and make it for round three tho. Why aren't you sleeping?*

I'm not tired, he typed.

But you need to sleep!

Why? For real tho is somebody going to die tonight? Tell me.

Idk. Some of the girls were talking about a patient that might not last till morning. How come?

Curious George.

Really why do you want to know?

What room number?

Idk he's on the third floor I think. Why??

He put the phone down. His battery was at 5%. It needed to charge. He tucked the laces back into his boots then checked the room out, riffling through the cupboards for a scalpel, or maybe some syringes or a stray bottle of morphine—anything interesting—but no, nothing but dull paraphernalia. Band-Aids and Q-tips, some popsicle sticks, and a thermometer. A jar of cotton balls and a broken wrist watch. All of it worthless.

He checked his phone again. It was 23% now. *Enough to get by.* He unplugged it, jammed it into his back pants pocket, and headed for the third floor.

II.

By night the hospital reminded him of winter. It was too warm and too bright, like going snow blind, trapped in coat layers and over-hot. Darkness pressed against the windows like black bloodied snow. He felt confined, suffocated. The air tasted like something sucked from an artificial lung then breathed back through plastic. The smell of unwashed bodies, mop-water, and bleach.

He vacated the stairwell onto the third floor.

If he was seen he could always lie. *Or maybe not.* He'd been witnessed, rushed through the ER with his wrists slit open, bleeding down his father's shirt, and his father shouting. It was only hours ago. They'd remember that and recognize him from all the times before. Johnny, suicide king, was a dangerous boy and they very well couldn't have someone like him roaming the hospital.

It wasn't safe.

He had to be careful, cautious. If he were apprehended, it was over. The new surplus of scars will have been acquired for nothing, running up his arms like ladder rungs; the wasted blood and his chance to ball Death gone up in smoke.

He'd have to slit his wrists again.

And maybe even again after that—a dozen times more, slicing his arms apart, aching for Death and that she would be there, scooping out yet another soul as he sneaked up behind and had his way with her. But it was a gamble and each time the risk increased. He was now down to the wire. He'd played too often and lost. He knew it wouldn't be long before the doctor persuaded dear old dad into having him committed.

It has to be tonight, he told himself.

It's fate, the stars have aligned.

He closed his eyes and concentrated. He wasn't sure how he would find the dying man but listening seemed the most viable option.

You can't see through doors or smell through doors, or touch or taste through doors, but sometimes shit can be heard through them. Like sex or loud music, there's a ruckus to passing. The fabled dying breath. Death makes noise too if you squint your ears and really listen.

He was reminded of his childhood, blaring *Darkthrone* and *Mayhem* in his bedroom to the continuous ire of his parents. Then later with Diane, whenever she stayed the night, tangled in passion. Noise through doors, sounds of welcoming or warning. When his mother died the little boy next-door said that he'd heard the cancer gripping her ovaries, and that it gave him nightmares. They say that dogs sense it too; dogs smell cancer. *Death wears a licorice perfume and her gill-green eye shadow probably smells like sour apples.* He imagined the odors beneath, the tantalizing body-stink of exertion as she went about her business, gathering souls escaped from their bodies like loosened balloons. He imagined finding her, dropping onto his knees and winding her thong in his fist, suffocating himself on the scent of her arousal; the slender divide of pink-purple lace, drenching his fingers.

But Johnny wasn't a dog, his olfactory senses were limited and he wasn't hearing shit through any of the doors either. He opened his eyes and continued down the hall.

Keeping quiet wasn't easy, by default his passage was a noisy one and he was forced into constantly clutching his jacket buckles to deaden their jangle. His boots made noise too and he had to walk slow, letting the soles down easy. They weren't subtle footwear. He called them his fag busters; they were the kind of boots made for stepping on heads.

He reached the end of the hall and saw the reception area, the sizable oasis of computers and counters, crisp in the focused glow of lamps and overhead lights. It faced the lobby like a desert island, Formica countertops sheening opposite the pastel patterned chairs.

The night woman chewed bubble-gum. She was middle aged and fat, dressed in purple scrubs with her died-red hair tied up in a bun. Johnny watched her blow a bubble. It snapped between her teeth and the phone rang. She threw a chubby arm at the handset and brought it to her ear. "This is Janus, how may I help you?"

"Oh," she frowned. She scratched the tip of her nose and checked the fingernail, listening. "Well that's that, then. Better call the doc." She dropped the phone back into place and stood up, coming around the counter and lumbering in his direction.

Johnny turned and rushed for the stairwell. He hurled his boots forward, leaping on his toes—*like a fucking pixie,* hoping the momentum would carry the noise. His stomach knotted when he saw the distance. To reach the exit without being seen would be impossible. The door was too far and the nurse too near. And to really run in the kill boots would be pointless, as futile as attempts to chop firewood with a bayonet, and far too noisy.

He threw himself at the nearest door, seized the handle, and shoved through just as the nurse turned the corner. He slid his fingers in the blinds and watched her from the little window as she marched past, straight for the first room beside the stairwell, and entered.

Moments later, a whole troop arrived with a doctor in tow and they wheeled the dead man out on his bed, arms splayed and dangling over the sides, covered by a sheet. The responding nurse stood in the doorway and crossed her arms, blank-faced and chewing her bubble gum.

So much for hearing death through doors, Johnny thought. To his chagrin, he'd walked right pass the dying man on his way down the hall. Disgustedly, he clenched his fists till the wounds ached. He chewed his bottom lip till it bled black trails down imagined corpse-paint, then looked away.

In that exact moment, dropping his eyes, he saw her. Death. Just the flutter of her hair as she left the room and vanished. A cataract, blinked away—or was it? A glass splinter in your palm, unseen but felt. Death, full-breasted and proud.

He'd missed her by seconds.

"Nice jacket."

Johnny spun, startled, turning to face the voice. A man in a hospital cot smiled at him from across the room. "I used to wear a similar one," he said.

"Good for you." Johnny sneered, returning his attention to the window.

"You in a band?"

"I'm in a fucking *hospital*, man."

"I can see that."

"You're not blind, congratulations." He drew away from the window as the nurses wheeled the dead man past the door toward the elevator. The doctor paused, lifting the pages on a clipboard and shaking his head.

"What's going on out there?"

"Why don't you shut up and go to sleep or something, old man," Johnny said. He stepped away from the door and took in the room. There wasn't much to see. It was a carbon copy of his own but with a different view out the window.

"That's all I do around here," the man said. "Fucking sleep. What's your band called?" He had a round face with short spiked hair, receded above his temples, and a thorny grey goatee. He wore eye shadow and his fingernails were painted black, contrasting with the hospital gown and bed sheets.

"The fuck is wrong with you? Does it sound like I want to be your fucking friend? Do I seem Beaver Cleavers to you, like I give a fuck?"

The smile vanished; the man's face was wet-dry cement, hardening into an impassive grey slab. "Listen to me you fucking *baby*," he snarled, dotting his gown with spittle. "You think wearing your fucking hair like that makes you something? Makes you hardcore? Well it doesn't. News flash retard—*you're a cunt*. You hear me, cunt? You're a fucking *boy scout*. You wouldn't know hardcore if it fucked you up the ass. It's pathetic little wannabes like you that think cutting themselves makes them tough, makes them cool. Try burning a church sometime, baby boy. Try strangling an infant—"

"Yo what the fuck man?" Johnny shouted, halting the onslaught. "What the fuck is this shit, going off on me? I'll fucking hurt you man! I'm dangerous. You better watch how you fucking talk to me."

"Just stop," he said. "Shut your faggot mouth while you're still ahead. I can't stand kids like you, shit-talkers. You're about as dangerous as dirty diaper."

"You fucking stop…man."

"Right," he nodded impatiently. "I'm the asshole. Listen, you come into *my room*, kid—*my* fucking room, parading around in your tight little jeans and leather coat like you're some kind of hot shit. You wake me up. You insult me. How the fuck do you expect me to react?"

Johnny rolled his eyes. "Just chill the fuck out, okay? I'll be out of here in a few minutes." He turned back to the door and peered through the blinds. The doctor was still there. The nurse from reception had joined him and they were both taking turns looking concerned, commenting on the charts.

"What are you doing there?" the man asked.

"Looking."

"At *what?*"

"None of your fucking—" he thought better of it and said, "It's this fucking doctor, taking his damn time. He's just standing there."

"What's the matter, kid? Don't want him to stick his finger up your ass? You playing hard to get?"

"Fuck you."

Johnny removed his fingers from the blinds. He stepped away from the door, stuck a cigarette in his mouth, and paced. He glanced at the ceiling. "Where's the fire alarm?"

"Over there in the corner."

"Bingo." He took a chair and dragged it in place beneath the alarm, then stepped up and detached the device from the ceiling. "And don't give me any shit, old man. Don't tell me not to smoke in here."

"I won't," he said, raising his hands innocently.

Johnny pointed at him. "I mean, you better not fucking say *anything*. I've had a rough day of it and don't need any more shit, especially from you."

"I got nothing to say. What do I look like to you, some kind of poser? If I'd wanted you gone, I would have rung the nurses by now, right? I'm solid, kid. True blue. I said I liked your jacket, didn't I?"

"Yeah well I don't like *you*, old man, so just keep your mouth shut and be quiet."

"Give me one. Buy my silence with a cigarette. I haven't smoked since I got here. They've got me on a diet like liquid dog shit."

Johnny stepped down from the chair. He pried the batteries out of the smoke detector and tossed everything into the sink. "Sure. Why not? If it'll shut you up." He ran the tap, just in case, then walked over to the bed and handed the man a cigarette. He fired up his own and tossed him the lighter. "Do it yourself, old man."

"Thanks."

"Don't thank me."

The man shrugged and lit his cigarette, pulling the warmth into his lungs, and sighed. "Hey, you know who you remind me of?"

"Don't fucking care."

"Ever heard of Euronymus?"

"Fuck you," Johnny said, turning away and shaking his head. "Do I know Euronymus? Fuck you, man." He crossed over to the window and looked down at the parking lot. It was late, there was nothing to see. Parked cars and hedges. He could feel the man's eyes boring into him from behind.

"Yo, what about Euronymus?" he turned suddenly and asked. "What would someone like *you* know about Euronymus?"

"A lot more than you, that's for damn sure. And a lot more than you can find out about on Wikipedia. That's the problem with your generation," he said. "You think you know everything these days because of the Internet."

Johnny pointed thumb and forefinger at the man, then lifted his middle finger.

"You know Varg?" the man asked.

"Yeah I fucking know Varg."

"You don't know *shit*," the man said, drawing on the cigarette. He released the smoke back through his teeth and held up Johnny's lighter. "You ever burn down a house?"

"I'd like to burn this hospital down with you in it, old man. Give me back my fucking lighter."

It arched through space and into his palm. Johnny pocketed it and the man laughed. He was enjoying the cigarette, pushing the smoke out through his nostrils like a fire breathing dragon.

"Yeah, you remind me of him a little I guess," he said, crossing an arm in back of his head relaxedly. "The way you look. And he was all bark and no bite also, a real fucking poser just like you, boy scout."

Johnny closed the distance between them in an instant. He grabbed the front of the man's gown and started to pull, easing off then as the pain came, snaking up through his wrist. He kept a loose hold and pointed his cigarette at the guy's face. "Don't you fucking talk, old man. Don't you *fucking talk*. I'll burn your fucking eyes out like they were ashtrays."

"Say fuck one more time," the man laughed, coughing a little. "Now Varg," he said, clearing his throat. "Varg was *real*. He didn't just talk about doing shit. He actually did it. Whatever needed to be done, he left no stone unturned."

Johnny moved the tip of the cigarette closer to the man's eye, he could see the ash reflected in the pupil, staining the iris red. It looked like jelly, like it had come out of a can or a cellar jar, fruit preserve, or something that had once lived in a seashell and had crawled into a face. He could feel the cigarette burning down between his fingers.

"Go on, kid," the man said. "I dare you."

Johnny dropped him back on the pillows. "What do you fucking know old man?" He put the cigarette in his mouth and inhaled. His wrist was pounding beneath the bandages. *Probably popped a few of the stiches,* he thought.

"I know a lot about those days," the man said, smoothing the front of his gown against his chest and adjusting his pillows.

"So you can read. So what?"

"I was there, idiot."

"I think you're full of crap, old man." Johnny said, dragging a chair into place beside the bed. "Talk all day, but I'm not buying it. Fuck you." He turned the chair backward and sat down, clicking his toes against the linoleum floor. "You really expect me to believe that shit? You think I'm fucking stupid?"

"I don't give a fuck if you believe me or not."

"You're telling me that you knew Euronymous and Varg?"

"Sure," he shrugged. "I knew Varg Vikernes when he was parading around under the alias Count Grishnackh. That was before Mayhem was anything more than a live act with a few tapes. I used to hang out around the record shop, Helvete. Necrobutcher, Blackthorn, Tormentor, I knew them all. Fuck, I knew Dead when he was still *alive*."

"Fuck..." Johnny winced, flinching as the cigarette scorched his fingers. He dropped the butt and ground it out beneath his boot. "That's straight-up, if it's true. I mean that's fucking insane, man. Un-fucking-for-real. Most people have never even heard of those guys."

"Look at where you live. You're from Boise Idaho, kid. What do you think, that the whole wide world lives in the same culture starved dairy farm?"

"Fuck Boise." He fixed the man with a stare. "And fuck you too. What you're saying is crazy. Like maybe not even fucking possible."

"Why shouldn't it be?" he snorted. "A lot of people where there. I just happen to be one of them." He dropped his own cigarette butt into a glass of water beside the bed and smiled. "Thanks for the smoke. I'll bet that doctor is gone by now."

"Did you play?"

"What, an instrument? Not really. I dabbled a bit, played guitar some, but I was never any good at it. I wasn't there for that. It was more about the lifestyle."

"I can fucking imagine. All this shit now, the way the world is—man, it makes me sick! Like I want to fucking throw up. People these days. Even in music, you know? Everyone is so fucking weak. Back then it was different. Those guys stood for something, man. Nobody is like that anymore. No fucking way. It's just a bunch of fucking peons now."

"That's right," the man smiled

They locked eyes and he winked. Johnny wasn't accustomed to empathy, his opinions usually incited conflict, and he found the mutuality unnerving. His narrowed his eyes at the stranger, then looked away. For Johnny, the world was always *over there*, something apart from himself. He didn't like thinking otherwise. *Commonality is such a bore.*

"Fuck it," he said. "So were you like, a part of the black circle and shit?"

"Sure. I wasn't super involved, few people were, but I went to my share of the parties."

Johnny nodded. He removed the cigarettes from his coat, put one in his mouth, then extended the package to the man, who waved them away. "So why are you here?" he asked, patting his pockets for the lighter. "In this country I mean. But also like...in this *place*. I mean are you sick or something?"

"Kid," he scowled, taking hold of the sheet. "I'm the worst kind of fucked up."

With a swift tug he threw the covers aside, uncovering his lower half. Johnny felt the wind hit the back of his throat. The man's legs were gone. What was left of them looked like ballpark franks. Spindly quadriceps sutured and bruised purple, tapered into stumps, and poking from beneath his gown like thumbs.

"They took my legs, kid—my *fucking legs*," he wheezed. "Can you even imagine what that feels like? I guess they got tired of me breaking the damn things off up their asses, that's what I think. Cops and politicians, they hate that. This what they do to shut us up. Anyone who sees through their shit. First, they stick us in prison. Try to break our spirit. Then when that doesn't work, they start taking limbs off. Put us in places like this. *Public* hospitals," he tried to spit but didn't make it far, a thread of saliva clung to his chin. "But you know what, kid?

They'll never stop us. Not ever. And even this, kid—the fools don't know, but it beats the hell out of prison."

"Fuck, man," Johnny cringed, averting his eyes. The cigarette had fallen from his mouth and he hadn't bothered to pick it up. He watched it burning a stain in linoleum and wished the man would cover himself. "It's fucking overwhelming," he said. "I mean, how does that even work? Like, who did this to you, the government?"

"More or less."

"And just because you spoke out about all their shit?"

"That's right. I exposed them."

"Fuck that's heavy."

"Martyrdom always is."

"So wait, you were in prison?"

"Yeah," he held up two fingers. "Twice."

"So what'd you do to make then so mad? Two times—man, that's insane! Its fucking crazy. It must have been some serious shit. Like, you don't go down twice and get your legs cut off for nothing I mean." He shook his head, uncrossing his leg, and picked up the cigarette and put it out on the underside of the chair. "Let me guess—you burned down a church or something. Fucking Christianity, right?"

"Nah, kid. They never caught me with the matches."

"Okay, so maybe you fucked some rich piece-of-shit's good girl little Christian daughter?"

"Son," he smiled.

Johnny furrowed his brow. "What?"

"It was his son. I fucked—raped, that is—forcibly screwed, violated, whatever—some rich bastard's teenage *son*. And let me tell you, kid," the bed squeaked as he leaned forward. "That time, they caught me dead to rights with the matches."

He was viper quick. His hand shot out and seized Johnny's hair, snarling it through his fingers. His eyeballs glowered, red rimmed with hate like they'd been with the ash.

He twisted his fist, yanking Johnny forward, and laughed. "He was just like you, actually. A fucking poser with a smart fucking mouth."

Johnny couldn't think, it'd happened too fast. He didn't scream, he didn't shout. The antibiotics had dulled his senses into rubber. He felt his hair being pulled and his wrists throbbing, the adrenalized race of his pulse pounding at the stitches and his head being dragged down, spinning because of the meds. Then it hit him all at once, the horror of the situation, as the man drew the gown up over the remnant of his legs and exposed himself—the purplish cock, engorged and lapsed heavily across his thigh, sprung from a dark thatch of hair.

Johnny reeled.

Stomach acid splashed the back of his throat, a combination of terror and rage, as he fought the urge to vomit, curled his fingers about the buckle at the end of his sleeve and threw his elbow into the cripple's stomach. He imagined it was a shovel—*aim for the motherfucker's spine through his stomach and gut the bastard*—pushing in till he struck bone through all the layers of meat. He rolled out of the man's grip, feeling his scalp tear as he twisted away, latched onto the bed rail, and pulled. The cot tipped up onto its wheels, teetered, then went over and down, smashing against the floor. The legless man hurriedly rolled onto his back and started to scream.

It was louder than a fire alarm.

Not good.

Johnny staggered over and stepped on his throat. He didn't know what else to do. He felt righteous though, poised with his foot up. Victorious, even. *Like Captain Fucking Morgan.* Watching the man's eyes bulge and plead, their fires doused, as his cries were reduced to a gurgle. He pushed at Johnny's boot and his hands slipped helplessly up the leather. His face turned purple. *Like crushing grapes,* Johnny thought, lifting his boot.

Squelch.

Blood splashed the tiles.

Like a trampoline, the flesh gave then resisted. He dropped the boot again. The man juddered, soft beneath his heel. And again, and again. Stomping the neck flat, splashing his bootlaces. There was nothing left in the world but the boot and the throat; the springy tissue losing its bounce and the milk-white tips of smashed vertebrae poking out from the tears.

When it was over, he fell back panting. He slipped in the blood, braced himself against the window sill, and decided not to laugh. He wasn't happy, it wasn't funny. He was scared. And once hysteria took hold, he knew he was sunk.

He couldn't allow that.

A sharp intake of breath alerted him to the door. It was open. He saw the nurse backing away, jamming her thumb against her pager. The resulting alarm welled up from the depths of her lungs as she dropped her clipboard, shrieking, and ran back into the hall.

He looked at the cripple. The eyes were open still and there was blood in them staining the cornea red. More of it came from his nose and mouth and out from his ears. He had the look of a dirty hot spring. His throat was smooshed inward, ragged as a torn balloon and with the consistency of a mud puddle.

Johnny idly wondered if CSI could pull a footprint out of the carnage and make a mold. Sweat ran down his face and neck and alongside his ribs, dampening the waist of his jeans. He was exhausted. His stitches had broken and the bandages were soaking through. He could feel the blood dripping down his hands and fingers and onto the floor.

"Fuck," he said, and wobbled for the door.

III.

Night, *like the inside of a stomach*, dripping wet. The rain came without warning. It fell from a yellow cloud and left the city slick and acidic. Nothing was cleaned or swept into the gutters. It wasn't a purging rain, just a sprinkle. Enough water to dampen the asphalt and vitalize the filth.

Downpours in the country are different; afterward, the air smells like flowers. A fresh, life-giving scent. But in the city the earth is buried beneath layers of gravel and concrete. Wet newspaper takes the place of the earth-smells and petrichor becomes the sharp tang of water-logged cardboard and sour milk.

Johnny could smell the blood dripping down his fingers. It ran between his knuckles, looking like black lace, like he was on his way to a funeral, gripping a veil, and his hands were pale as his bones beneath. He was sopping. His clothes and hair were plastered to his skin and mascara bled down his cheeks from his eyes.

He was several blocks from the hospital now, crossing the street. He hurried through a parking lot. Rainbows danced in the oil stains. Down alleyways, grease-smears on dumpster iron reflected thunderbolts and droplets rolled off the garbage bags in trickles. Silent night, deadly night.

Street lights in the haze.

No sign of police.

He found himself an alcove in back of a restaurant and threw himself against the brick, catching his breath. He looked at his cellphone. 7% battery. *The cold sucks the juice out like an anxious whore.* He zipped his jacket, pulled the throat buckle tight, then dialed Ramon. His thumbs left blood on the touch screen. "Answer, you fucking prick." he breathed. "Answer your fucking phone."

He slouched and groaned. The dial tone throttled his eardrum, causing his head to ache. He felt cold. Dangerously cold. And he pressed his face against the bricks in the alley wall, clenching his jaw tight against the shivers.

"Christ," Ramon answered. "You know what fucking time it is Johnny? Jesus. What the fuck are you doing calling me so late…early I mean…whatever. It's like three in the fucking morning, man."

"Just shut up and listen."

"Yo where the fuck are you? The hospital still?"

"No, I had to leave. Look," he licked his lips. "I'm fucked up bad, okay? I think I've lost a lot of blood. I need a place to stay. To get warm while I wait for Diane to get off…she'll know how to fix me up."

"Yeah? What the hell happened to you, man?"

"I don't have time for…to answer a bunch of questions, alright? I'm about to die, like my phone…the battery is almost dead. But listen, I can't call Diane…they might be expecting that, so I need you to call her and tell her to come get me as soon as she's off, and to bring some medical sup—"

"Fuck, Johnny. I can't just let you come over here. It's the middle of the fucking night. My parents…"

"Fuck your parents."

"Yo, my Dad's a cop, Johnny! If you're in some kind of shit I could really get fucked, man. My Dad wouldn't hesitate to put me out on the street. Besides what makes you think you'd be good here? You think I could just like…what? Hide you under my bed or something? *From my Dad?* He's not even asleep. He's right fucking downstairs right fucking now, man, watching TV. And my Mom's an insomniac so she could be up any time. If they saw you…"

"I'm going to *fucking die* you coward," Johnny hissed, scowling as a jolt of pain ran up from his wounds and into his teeth. "You want that on your conscious Ramon? Fucking buddy? Pal. You want to have to live with that? Letting your best fucking friend bleed out in some dirty fucking alleyway? I'm not asking you for your last stick of bubblegum, Ramon. Jesus Christ. I'm asking for *your help*."

"Look, Johnny…I'm not trying to bail on you, man. It's like I said, my Dad's a cop and…ah, fuck. You know what, where you at? I can come. I can call an ambulance. Whatever you did, Johnny…if you're going to die, it's not worth running, man. It's—"

"Just shut up Ramon, you fucking pussy. Fucking bailer. I'll take care of this on my own. I'll save my own fucking life. But after this don't you ever expect *shit* from me, you fucking poser."

His phone made a noise—the indicator, the death gurgle that sounds like a wind-chime.

Low Battery.

"My phone's about done. Look, just call Diane, alright? It's the least you can fucking do for me. Tell her to meet me at Bartholomew's. He won't let her inside, but… Yeah, just tell her I'll meet her downstairs, okay? Tell her to ring the buzzer and I'll come down."

"Bartholomew…"

"Don't say *shit* Ramon," Johnny growled. "You don't fucking speak. Better pack your bags, chickenshit. I don't think Bartholomew is going to like—"

The phone snapped off and powered down.

Johnny felt it go cold against his ear. He put it away and looked down at his hands. His fingers curled toward his palms involuntarily, tugged along by swollen tendons—the aching tightness in his forearms—and the bandages had come loose and rolled down around his wrists like rows of bloody bangles.

He staggered toward the street.

He thought twice about the phone, turned back, and hurled it down the alleyway. It struck iron and landed in a puddle. *Trace that you sons-of-bitches.*

Bartholomew lived on the top level of an abandoned carpet factory. Inner darkness dragged the sky toward boarded windows and the property was surrounded by a frail chain-link fence. Inside, the floors would be strewn with broken bottles and litter. Spent condoms, hypos, and spray cans; all the paraphernalia dragged in by the destitute, from teenagers to hobos to gang bangers and junkies.

Weeds grew out of the scorched foundation, shooting up amid hunks of blasted concrete and shotgun shells. Sooner or later they'd crush the whole thing flat and build apartments; it was inevitable, the city was growing and needed housing-space for all the Californians.

Johnny picked his way through the rubble toward the entry. He crawled through an opening in the fence and tore his jacket. Gravel chips stuck in his boot treads, clicking against the pavement, as he came to the door. The meds had worn off and his wrists felt like sacks of broken glass. He couldn't move without pain and he'd lost a lot of blood.

Staggering. *Blood loss feels like outer space,* he thought. *Like all the gravity is leaving your body, thundering out through the wound. A deluge of gore and physics. Gravity dripping down from your sleeves. And the droplets like sledgehammers on concrete or against the tips of atomic bombs.* As if the pain were sticks of dynamite ripped open by a charge then rewound and exploded again—that, on repeat. Each and every movement, each and every throb a brutal detonation, jarring his nerves.

He leaned in the doorway and pushed the buzzer. Coming was a risky move. *But why pray? God hates devil worshipers.* He could only hope Bartholomew was in good spirits.

The intercom blinked: "What?"

"It's me, man…Johnny…I need your help. I'm hurt…bleeding."

"Cops?"

"No man…just…it's just me. No trouble. I just need some help, a place for a few hours…then I'm gone, okay? Swear to fucking god."

"Don't. He's not here."

A buzzer set the locks whirring and the mechanism clicked. The door popped back—there was no handle, just a bric-a-brac of boards and caution tape—and Johnny pushed, stumbling against the façade as it swung inward. He waited for his eyes to adjust then moved slowly toward the stairs as the door clicked shut behind him.

There were three floors to the top.

Six flights of stairs.

Each step he took felt weighted.

He put his shoulder to the wall, displacing his weight, and dragged himself up the first set of stairs. He would have used the railing but his hands didn't work. And the thought of squeezing the rail, clutching it and pulling his weight forward, made his stomach turn. He imagined his forearms cleaving open to his elbows and his palms bursting; funny bones split down the center, ringing, as the gore welled up through tangles of little blue veins and muscle.

He reached the second floor and thought of sitting down.

Just for a moment.

But.

Dragging his boot heels, enveloped in darkness. He felt terribly alone. Losing his mind in the din of the stairwell. Shuffles sounding like bats, spinning. Divebombing down. He held his hands in a shaft of moonlight. The blood had dried and turned black. Lifting them, touching his face, a lively trickle flowed down his sleeves and pooled in the elbows of his coat. He kept on.

Time passed, plodding up the endless stair.

Mostly, he thought about water—he was intensely thirsty. He'd missed Death twice now, and by a fraction each time. The second instance, a sort of summoning even, when he'd stomped the cripple. He imagined her tilting her head, descending in her panties and high-heels and casting the dead man's soul sideway to hell. *But the nurse...* She arrived first, so he had no other choice. He was forced to run, missing his chance.

And now what?

He reached the landing and paused, leaning against the rail, to catch his breath. *If I don't bleed to death first, they'll get me for murder. I'll have to lay low and recover, then find a way out of the country. Dodge the law and live on, blacklisted for life.*

So fucking what?

He crossed his arms against his chest, cradling his wrists, and continued to the next level. It was worth it to kill the guy. He was obviously a fag. Killing him would win points with Bartholomew and that was good. Points went a long way with guys like him. Points were how you gained respect.

He stopped, measuring the distance.

Three steps to the landing and the dark steel door. He felt anxious. He'd started to sweat and couldn't tell the difference with all the blood running down his arms. His hair stuck to his forehead and he felt feverish. *The man behind the door, is he a Nazi, a Satanist for real? Is he even human? Like with a conscious.* He climbed the remaining steps, barely keeping his feet. The door felt cool against his face. He raised his arms and feebly knocked.

The intercom clicked.

"Took you a long time, Johnny." Bartholomew growled through the speaker. "A long fucking time."

"I'm sorry..." Johnny said. He was reeling, pushing his head against the door to keep from falling over. "I'm...not doing too good..."

The door swung inward, catching him by surprise, and he staggered through it. He tripped and fell, twisting just in time to save his wrists as he went down and his shoulder impacted the floor. A moment passed. Bartholomew watched disgustedly as Johnny scrambled onto his knees and gained his feet. He stood up, wobbling. One of the bandages sheaved from his arm and slapped the concrete, so dark and blood-soaking-wet it looked like a placenta.

"That's fucking disgusting," Bartholomew said.

He was shirtless, wearing American flag 'stars-and-stripes' suspenders and army fatigues tucked into polished brown leather boots. His hair was buzzed into a tidy mohawk and his eyes were like musket-balls embedded in his flesh. He looked like the bad guy in an action movie—too tall for conventional doors, all muscle and bone and stern-faced villainy.

Eight-eight was emblazed on his chest on a cross that stretched from his navel to his neck and the eagle tattooed on his throat carried a swastika in its talons.

"What the fuck did you come here for?" he scowled, crossing his arms over his chest. "I should waste you just for bleeding on my fucking floor."

"I didn't have anywhere else, man. I'm dying…I had to run…" he pleaded, searching for sympathy where there was none. "The fucking police, man," he said. "They—"

Bartholomew dropped his arms and came toward him. His hands slammed into Johnny's chest, grabbing his jacket. "You fucking punk," he growled, yanking him forward. "The police? What about the *fucking police* Johnny?"

He dragged him into the bathroom, kicked the shower curtain aside, and shoved him into the tub, then removed a revolver from the waistband of his fatigues and pointed it at his face. "You bring the police *here?* To my *fucking home?*"

"No, man! No," Johnny shouted. "I swear to god I didn't. It's not like that, man. I swear to fucking god." He held his wrists up between himself and the firearm. "I cut myself, that's all."

"You did that to yourself?" he asked, titling his head. "Why?"

"Because I..."

"Because *what*, Johnny? *Because fucking what?*" he grabbed Johnny's hair and jerked him forward. "What did you do? Tell me what you fucking did or I'm going to waste your stupid ass right here in the shower."

"I did... Bartholomew, listen man...I did us one good, okay? For the cause, man. I killed this fucking faggot in the hospital...but then...then my...the stitches, man...they broke and shit, so I had to run. I didn't get the chance to...you know, like...enjoy it or anything. Diane is going to come here and fix me though, man. And...and then I'm leaving town, okay?"

"Diane? You mean the *cunt*? That fucking cunt *Diane?* That one? Is that the Diane you're talking about?"

"Yeah man...that one. Look, she won't come up or nothing. She's just picking me up once she gets off work..."

He let go of Johnny's hair and lowered the gun.

"Fine," he said, straightening his back. "You've got one hour."

He turned and left the bathroom. *Spawn of Satan* was carved across his back in arching letters surrounded by skulls and serpents. "You want a beer?" he asked from the other room.

Johnny struggled, using his elbows against the sides of the tub to get out. "Yeah, thanks," he whimpered, banging his wrist against the faucet. "You have any old towels for the blood? I don't want to like...bleed all over the place, you know?"

"Under the sink. When you're finished primping your candy-ass, your beer is on the kitchen counter. I'll be in the other room. I want to hear about this fag you supposedly smoked."

IV.

They were sitting across from each other on matching couches. Johnny on a sheet, shielding the upholstery from his bloody clothes. His hands were wrapped in a faded grey towel. Their conversation was a game of tag. Johnny was never 'it.' Every time their eyes met, he diverted his gaze to the floor.

"So tell me about the fag," Bartholomew said, lifting the beer can from his lap. He tilted it to his lips, drinking deeply, and the beer flowed from the corners of his mouth.

Johnny felt dizzy, worse than before, the beer having gone straight to his brain after the first three swigs. "It's like this," he said, speaking slowly, spacing his words as the pain blossomed between breaths. "I was in the hospital tonight...like, just a few hours ago...for this shit about my wrists. And..."

"You said you did that to yourself, *right?*"

"That's right, but not to like...to die."

"Oh, okay," Bartholomew nodded. "So you did it to live. I get it now. Yeah, that makes total fucking sense." He leaned forward and his smile became a threat. He looked like a shark. His jaw was broad and square and blasted with acne scars. "But tell me *really*, what was it—you take a long hard look in the mirror and see something not worth living?"

"I did it because...to try...I mean, to get into the hospital." His mouth was dry and the words hurt his teeth. He sipped the beer and the alcohol stung his throat. "A few weeks back I also did it...my wrists, like...I mean...but that time...was for different reasons...like, just to scare people, you know? I was fucking pissed off and...

Dad took me to the hospital.

For some fucking reason the place was packed, like everyone was dying all at once. So they stuck me in this room with an older guy. Old but not like, ancient, you know? Just like forty or some shit. Anyways, he was in rough condition, man. This fucking guy, he'd gone over his handlebars. Like on a motorbike, man. Crack! head first in the center of the fucking road. He'd hit a rock or something, like his tire did. So you can image how his face looked. I mean it was all bandaged up, so.

But you could tell.

He was on a breathing machine and shit and they had him in all these different casts. Fucking guy looked like an Egyptian, you know? Like a mummy. All wrapped up in bandages and plaster. And quiet, man. He was real fucking quiet too. Just lying there with his arms and legs all up in the harnesses and shit. Like in a fucking cartoon. Like Wile-E-Coyote, you know? You remember that shit? The roadrunner and all that. He looked just like that. Like somebody had dropped a fucking piano on his head.

So I'm lying there with my hands all taped together, right—duct tape—and I'm on enough drugs to fuck my own mom, when all of the sudden this guy kicks. He fucking dies right fucking there in front of me. I know because I hear the machine going off, beeping hell, and then the heart thing—whatsit called? that little line on the monitor they have—it goes flat as shit. Anyways, yeah. He dies.

I'm like, well fuck.

But you know what man? It looked kind of nice. Peaceful like. I mean he was just gone and all that was left was the plaster and the shell, his skin and his bones and blood and shit. I thought—you know, this guy—this motherfucker, he's got it sort of good. And most people would never think that, man. Most people would never even think that. But I did.

Then holy shit, it's like fuck—before the nurses get there something crazy happens. I mean, someone else comes in first, like on cue. Like they'd been waiting outside the fucking door for this. And yo. Yo and behold, man, it's this hot fucking bitch, okay? And at first, I'm like what? I think it's his wife, right? Kind of obvious. Like she came to visit, say goodbye or whatever. But here's what's wrong with that man, here's what's fucking crazy as shit. She's practically fucking naked. I mean, like, she's got these big fucking titties and they're hanging out and bouncing when she walks and shit. And it's not like she's just shirtless, either. She's

*got nothing on, man. Just this little bitty pink-thong and high-heels.
Stilettoes, I think.*

Whatever.

The kind stripers wear.

*And yo, my dick goes hard almost instantly. I'm telling, this
bitch is stacked. The crème-de-la-crème. Built to fuck and all that. And
you know what else? I can smell her too. Like massage-oil, man. Licorice
massage oil. But not just that. I can smell something else too...like below.
There's another smell there beneath the sweetness. Like, a pussy smell for
sure but also a death smell.*

*Anyways, I'm lying there, spotting my fucking sheet, right? Hard
as a fucking rock while this goddess walks up the dead guy's bed—and
then you know what she does? You won't believe it, man. She looks down
at him and starts to play with her nipples. Next thing I know she's tongue
kissing him. The dead guy, man. She's kissing the fucking dead guy. I'm
starting to think she's going to climb into bed with him and fuck him,
when all the sudden she rips his fucking soul out! She stops kissing him
and takes it out through his...*

"...through his fucking mouth, man. Pulls it out with,
like...her fist. I mean, she shoves her whole arm down his
throat...like, all the way...and out comes this...this...soul, I
guess. It's like, *writhing*...in her hand...sort of like a jellyfish."

Bartholomew stared at Johnny. He was wordless at
first, then his mouth twitched and he burst into laughter.
"You're a cunt Johnny," he said, crushing his beer can. "A
fucking cunt. So let me get this right, you're telling me that you
saw Death incarnate claiming some guy's soul. And that she's
got great tits. Right? That's your story? You witness her tongue-
fuck and gutting some paraplegic and it turns you on. So then a
few weeks later you open your wrists again with the hopes that
she'll come suck *your* soul this time, preferably out the head of
your cock."

Johnny knew better than to contradict Bartholomew.
He couldn't remember why he'd even told the story. This

wasn't about Death, it was about biding time, earning his keep till Diane got off work and picked him up.

"Yeah, like that. You're not far off, man" he wheezed, feeling the ice in his veins. "I did it again to go back…and again even, actually. This was my third visit…tonight."

"Okay, Johnny," Bartholomew said, his smile deteriorating into a frown. "I laughed. We're done. You're a suicidal little bitch—a cunt, and you tried to kill yourself. Great. Do the world a real favor and try harder next time. Now what about this fag you say you killed? Or was that just another one of your *jokes?*"

"No joke, I swear. It happened tonight just like I said. In the hospital. I was hanging out. Like, prowling around for pills…morphine and shit, when I had to duck into this guy's room…and lay low while the nurses…" he coughed and it was wet against his teeth. *Wrists, bleeding down the back of my throat.* "…while the nurses were in the hall…and wait for them to leave…" He closed his eyes and felt the weight of his head dragging him forward.

No.

Get 'em open.

Don't go toward the darkness.

"So this guy starts talking to me," he blinked. "And then out of nowhere he shows me his cock and…he's a fag, so I drag him out of his bed…and…he didn't have any legs, man…he didn't have fucking legs but I stomped him…I mean, I kicked the bastard in throat until it looked like cherry pie, man. You know…? But then, the nurses came…and I had to go…but fucking Ramon, chickenshit bastard…he bailed on me. I didn't have anywhere else to go, man."

Bartholomew opened another beer.

"You know what's pretty fucking annoying, Johnny?" he asked, taking a long swing. "Listening to you talk. Those cuts aren't that bad. Why don't you sit the fuck up straight and finish your beer instead of acting like a little bitch?"

Johnny, in a fog, lifted his beer. He drank deeply despite how bad it made him feel. Maybe with a buzz he could make it back down the stairs.

"That's better," Bartholomew said. "Relax. That's good work what you did to that faggot—*if it happened*, I mean. We'll see what's in the papers tomorrow." He stood up and paced to one of the large grey windows, hands clasped behind him, clutching his beer against the small of his back. "We'll see if I regret having put you up or not."

"You won't, I swear it's…I'm not lying to you."

"Except that shit about the bitch. Death incarnate."

"Yeah," Johnny nodded reluctantly. "That was…a joke, just a bad joke…"

He'd started his decent through the couch cushions toward hell, sinking between them and into the fold of darkness, his consciousness slipping out through his wrists and into the towel, a dwindling flood.

The Red Sea, the seepage.

All those broken stitches, caught in a riptide, awash in the ebb and flow of his sluggish pulse and pink froth clinging to the ragged shore of his skin and bone. The wounds were raised at the edges and raw, puckering furrows of bleach-white flesh. They looked like fish gills. *Fish gills in my fucking wrists*, he thought, dozing. *Bitch, I can do underwater handstands like…forever.*

"I'm like Niche, you know that?" Bartholomew spoke. His was staring out the window at the fading stars, low-slung in the void and his silhouette was sheathed in hammered aluminum. "People were distraught when he pronounced the death of God. It made them angry. God is dead, three small words. Well you know what I say? Bullshit. He was exactly wrong. God could never die. He has regenerative powers. And that's the problem, that God *isn't* dead. It's the Devil that's passed away. Satan. He's dead and his throne is empty. Hell today is in shambles. What's happening down there is the same *goddamn shit* that happened to the Reich after the fall of the empire. The Führer is gone, Johnny. We're just waiting for a new Satan to take the throne."

Johnny startled at the sound of the buzzer. He opened his eyes and commanded: *think*. But the pain-fog was thick. It took him a moment to remember where he was at.

"Sounds like your bitch is here." Bartholomew said.

Johnny inched forward on the couch, He hunched over and wobbled and the beer slipped from his fingers and spilled on the floor.

"I should make you clean that up."

"Please…"

"But I won't. I'll clean up your fucking mess, Johnny. This time. Next time I'll cut your fucking balls off for coming here. Now get the fuck out of my home. I never want to see you here again unless you've got something to sell."

Johnny got to his feet and headed for the door.

"Hey," Bartholomew called after him.

He stopped. *Don't look back. This is part where he puts a bullet in your head.* He shut his eyes then half-turned, holding his breath, and waited.

"My towel. Leave the fucking towel. I'll use it clean up your mess."

Johnny unwrapped his arms and set the bloodied towel on a table beside the entryway. "Thanks," he mumbled. He opened the steel door and leaned in the entry.

He looked back.

"Ramon's dad is a cop, by the way."

He gave himself over to gravity, barreling down the stairs, tripping on his boots then catching himself at the last possible moment on a shaky leg. *I could do this blindfolded. I could do it with broken ankles if I had to.* He was numb. He felt nothing. What little blood he had left lubricated his palms and prevented them from sticking to the rails.

Clatter, clatter, clatter.

The basketball sounds of steps in a stairwell. Despite himself, he occasionally yelped. He couldn't help it. He was almost there—home free.

He reached the bottom and collapsed on the final stair.

His ankles buckled in his goddamn boots and his knees gave out, spilling him backward against the steps. He slumped into an artless heap. The door stood open, a short distance away, and the outside glowed, beaming within.

Just a few more steps.

But he remained.

He patted his coat pockets. Found and retrieved the pack of cigarettes. There was one left. *My lucky day.* He had a difficult time getting the lighter to spark; each roll of his thumb against the ignition was sheer agony, but at last he brought the fire.

Smoke this cig just like I smoked that fag, he thought. *Everybody smokes or gets smoked in this life.*

Yeah.

Just this, a little break…one quick cigarette then I'm out of here. Stand up again, keep going. Diane will be outside waiting. She'll fix me up. By tomorrow I'll be good enough for quick fuck.

He tossed the package into the dark.

Something scurried.

He shifted his feet. He brought the cigarette to his mouth and the tip glowed orange in the dark. The smoke was grey and ghost-like. It ran from his nostrils in slow curling circuits as the tobacco cracked and turned to ash.

He narrowed his eyes against the dawn. It came through the door and reached all the way to his boots. *To have a minstrel cycle like dawn, is to bleed through the door every day.* The light felt like daggers stabbed through his eyes and scraping the bone. Through the pain he saw her silhouette. She came to the entry etched in fire. Thigh-gap and hips.

Diane.

Sweet Diane who he would marry after this; and who he would flee the country with and burn churches with and maybe even get to fuck Death with. The two of them together—a threesome with fuzzy cuffs in a funeral bed— Johnny tugging aside the magenta thong, getting off, while Death entered Diane, his love, with a delicate forked tongue.

She stepped inside and the door closed shut.

Johnny blinked.

Nothing glowed in the dark but the cigarette smoke, detaching from his tongue like river-rapids on air. He couldn't see her, but he could hear her feet. He listened to the steps, slow, steady, approaching through the dark, and he tried to smile.

He dropped the cigarette because he couldn't hold it anymore, the weight was too much. It bounced, scattering ash, then disappeared off the edge of a step. He was fading, listening to the click of her heels against the concrete. She was at his side then, cradling his shoulders.

She lifted his hands and his fingers brushed her nipples. She kissed his wounds, sucking the flesh. Her lips felt cold and so did her tongue. And Johnny's consciousness slid out through his nose and eyes like steam off of hot coals—winding, twisting, dissipating—working itself out of existence and into the *burzum*.

Diane, was his final thought. *Her shoe.*

It hadn't squeaked.

HAUNTED

Dear _____,

I've written this letter and placed it in a bottle, hoping that you will find it one day. I've lost you in the long halls of my haunted house and I'm quite unsure of how to proceed. I occasionally hear the creak of a floorboard, but when I turn, you're never there.

Some people's minds are mansions, colosseums, or ballrooms. I was once swallowed by a castle and was lost there for two years. But it wasn't unpleasant. Her esthetic was grandiose; mine has always been Grand Guignol. There are certainly more pleasant places to be lost than in my mind and heart.

While you are here, avoid closed doors. There are many and there are skeletons secreted there. The bones drip and they never dry and the wire hangers have grown rusty. The skeletons, they hate you for your fingernails and freedom.

Ignore the cobwebs, my dear. There are no spiders, only metaphor. My house has grown dark and the memories reside in vague networks. Though frightful, they are harmless.

The basement has flooded since we danced there and the attic has lost its glass—the shutters bang and the shingles flap. The roof leaks.

Yet I stand there sometimes before the shattered lens, watching the overgrown path, wondering where you are...

FIRE POPPIES

The last time we had sex? I don't even remember it. I remember the flight home. I listened to the new *dvsn* album and slept. We didn't talk for days after that. And when we finally did, coming around to each other through text, it was just to complain. We had nothing in common.

Air fares dropped that summer but the visits were costing more than they were worth. We ate out needlessly, chewing our food in silence. We browsed the mall and shopped for clothing with passionless disregard; neither of us cared what the other wore. Not anymore.

Mostly, we argued.

The urgency was gone, convenience had outdone desire. We still held hands but stopped as soon as our palms began to sweat. Contact wasn't worth the price of discomfort. We rarely kissed. A few months later it was over. She told me I was her soul mate; it didn't compute. I told her she was lonely and dropped her like a bag of hammers.

Now she's dead.

They found her upper half stuffed into a garbage bin.

I'm sitting at the airport, waiting for a cab. In Boise, cab traffic is about as dense as the skyscrapers; the city has thirteen tall buildings, none of which make the cut. Visible taxis can be counted on the fingers of one hand. Mine pulled up to the curb and I climbed inside.

"Super 8." I told the driver.

It was the only hotel I knew. Maddie and I had used it before, back when being together meant certain sleepless hell for her roommates. After months apart, our reunions were dependably seismic. Out of respect, we started booking the room and spent our first nights in private. Immediacy drove us to the Super 8. It was the nearest available bed, located just opposite the airport, across the freeway. Within minutes of my arrival we'd be pressed together and stripped of our clothes.

But that was then.

Now it was just a dive, a big yellow sign glowing in the night. Without the promise of company, it was drained of its charm. A week ago, I couldn't have imagined seeing it again. A police officer called and in a span of fifteen seconds I was informed of her passing. The way she died I found out later, online. She'd been severed, cut in half. The police were still looking for her legs. They weren't interested in me. I'd been dismissed as a suspect. I was in another state when it had happened. A regular guy with no priors. It was a courtesy call, nothing more.

Oh, another thing, the cop said before hanging up. Her voice will be burned into my head forever. It sounded callous, police hardened—not solidly, but in the same way as an innertube, something made hard by force. I pictured at the other end of the line, holding the phone. The self-conscious type of gal who wears a long ponytail and more than anything wants to be made to feel pretty and soft but spends too much time with the boys. I imagined her in her uniform. The hat, the badge, the belt and boxy black shoes. *She was four months pregnant. Did you know that?*

My mind did the math, running its calculations. Four months ago, I'd been in Maddie's bed. And at some point, we'd made love. When you think you know everything about somebody—you don't. In truth you know very little. I felt lightheaded as the police woman said goodbye. The phone slid from my hand and struck the floor.

I didn't know she was pregnant. How could I? She didn't tell me. I couldn't even remember the last time we'd had sex, or if I'd used a rubber or not. I might have cum on her stomach. All the forgettable couplings bled together. Her bottom sheet was too big for the mattress and kept slipping off at the corners.

Sex was a dirge by then. We each expelled the minimum effort and our orgasms were forceless and weak. We didn't *have sex*, we just did it to each other like strangers bumping knuckles. It was fond perhaps, but passionless. We hadn't been in love for a year. We'd been coasting on fumes and the fumes were running thin.

I checked into my room, threw down my backpack, and fell face first onto the bed. The duvet smelled like spray arousal and cigarette smoke. It was midnight, mountain time.

No one knows I'm in Boise. I don't know why I came to begin with. I threw a bag together and drove to the airport without a second thought. When my plane touched ground, I thought I knew. But Maddie wasn't waiting for me at the gate; she was dead.

Now I'm standing outside her door.

It's nine am. I ring the bell and wait. There's a wasp trapped behind the exterior door, banging its head against the wire mesh. It escapes into the house as the door opens behind it. Emily smiles at me. "Come inside," she says, pushing the screen back. If she's surprised, I can't tell.

We hug and we're both aware that it lasts longer than it should. "You want a coffee?" she asks.

"Yeah, that'd be great."

She's wearing a faded pink sweatshirt and jeans, with her hair pulled back and piled on top of her head in a messy bun.

"Place hasn't changed much," I observe, following her into the kitchen. "Same girls?"

"It's always changing. We swapped a Jenny for a Racheal last semester, so now we've got two Racheals. And then Laura moved out, so…"

The kitchen is small and cluttered. The counter needs a wipe-down and dirty dishes are piled into a warzone beside the sink. If its edible, it's been tagged. Labels declare ownership, revealing a backlog of spite. I see a death threat pinned to an avocado: *Don't eat this Amber.* The cabinets are plastered with post-it notes and reminders and everything is segregated into piles. A magnetized white board on the refrigerator door tells me that it's Jenny's turn to do dishes.

"Sorry it's such a mess."

"No worries."

Emily gets the coffee pot, sets it in the sink, and starts the tap running. She leans on the counter and looks at me. "Nick, I'm just going to say it. I'm really sorry. What happened to Maddie… It's unimaginable. I mean, everybody is devastated, but you must be—"

"Em, don't." I catch her eye and force a smile. "I'm okay, really. Thanks."

She nods her head, then looks away. She turns, loading a filter into the little coffee maker, and pours the water inside. "All I've got is Starbucks," she explains, holds up a silver bag of coffee beans. "You can thank my parents, they're oblivious."

"Coffee is coffee. I'm not picky."

"You still take it without cream?"

"Yeah, black as Monday morning."

"Okay, now you get to choose your mug."

"My mug?"

She opened one of the cabinets and pointed to an array of pottery. There's a post-it-note taped to the shelf: *Emily's Collection, Don't Break Please.* I pick a green one shaped like a gourd.

"Good choice. That's my latest masterpiece."

"You made these?"

"I sure did," she beamed. "I needed a few extra credits this semester, so I took up ceramics."

"Pretty cool. You must be about finished, right?"

"Yep, this is it," she says, pouring the coffee. "One more semester and I'm done for good." She smiles and hands me the mug. "Let me know if it's okay. I made it strong."

Emily's the type of girl you don't always recognize when you're young. She's beautiful, inside and out, and with a strong sense of self. From the moment we met, we clicked. Our chemistry was on-point and undeniable, and I looked forward to seeing her near as much as Maddie whenever I visited. We'd exchange music suggestions and talk about the books we'd read. When things got rough, she was my rock. Maddie didn't care. She wasn't the jealous type and Emily and I weren't the kind to cheat. Toward the end, the arguments got bad. Some nights, I took to the couch and Em kept my company. She'd make coffee and we'd talk, and the talking always helped.

I sipped my coffee now, remembering.

"Em," I said. "I need to see her room."

"Okay."

"The coffee is perfect."

"Black as Monday morning," she smiled.

I set my mug on the countertop. "I'll be back for this," I said, then walked up the steps to Maddie's room. The door was the same, decorated with a glitter-swept sign that said: UNF*CK YOUR BRAIN.

I turned the handle and stepped inside.

It smelled like her. *Victoria's Secret* body spray and cotton candy, her essence. And there she was, the imprint of her body on the bedlinens, the pillow. The quilt was crumpled and kicked down to where her feet would have been and the under sheet was pulled back on itself, exposing the left corner of the mattress.

I felt like crying, but the tears wouldn't come.

In a matter of months, Maddie had become a million miles removed from me. My heart ached—standing in her room, knowing that she was dead—but it didn't break. Maybe I'm sick, unemotional, or sociopathic. No matter how badly I wanted to feel remorse, I just felt dizzy; and the guilt of that burned hot in the pit of my stomach.

Four months isn't a long time, but emotionally, it's forever. We'd been drifting apart for a year. We were never close to begin with, I'd decided; ours was a relationship built on sex and loneliness and not a lot else.

I looked around the little white room and the effect was like stepping back in time. Here were the fairy lights, strung along the wall beside her bed; the dreamcatcher, the succulents crowding the window sill; her makeup and hairdryer, still plugged in, protruding from an open drawer; pajamas on the dresser, closet door pulled back on a row of dresses and jackets. The police had taken her notebooks and computer, leaving her work space uncharacteristically blank. It was the only thing in the room I didn't recognize: the surface of her desk.

I closed the door and returned to the kitchen.

"You okay?" Emily asked.

"I don't know to be honest," I took my coffee in hand and we walked into the living room. "I don't even know why I came."

"The funeral doesn't have a date yet."

"I know."

"Hey," she said, curling a leg beneath herself as she dropped onto the couch. "If you need a place to stay while you're here..."

"Thanks, Em," I smiled. Her eyes were profoundly beautiful and blue. "I've got a place."

"How's California treating you?"

"Same as always. I hate it."

"Are you working?"

"Yeah."

"Same job?"

I didn't answer. I joined her on the couch instead and took her hand, the free one, absent coffee mug and resting on the cushions. The contact came as a surprise for us both. Her fingers responded. She squeezed my hand and narrowed her eyes, searching my face for answers.

Instead she got a question.

"Em," I asked, self-conscious, hearing the vulnerability in my voice and knowing that she heard it to. "I know this is a shitty thing to ask, but...was Maddie seeing anybody else? While we were together, I mean? Those last months, they weren't the best and I wouldn't blame her."

Call it a byproduct of any long-distance relationship, too much time apart leads to suspicion. Months between visits are plagued by doubt and insecurity. I'd considered it before, of course. Maddie had always had a lot of guy friends. She was the proactive type, too. Always trying to get ahead, pragmatic about everything. Maybe she foresaw the end of one relationship and helped herself to an early start on the next.

And why not?

Could I blame her?

Companionship and company are supposed to go together. When they don't, something ceases to operate. The problem is, a lot of long-distance relationships don't have roots enough to sustain them. When the weather gets bad, they've got no anchor, no food source. Before they get the chance to grow, they're pushed away and swept apart. The roots never form and the love-blossoms die. They're fire poppies, they come up quick and fade just as fast, there and gone again before gaining any real timber. The curse of a beauty brought to life by a bush fire, born of fleeting flame, and doomed to parish.

A few collective weeks together won't cut it. Memories don't go far when you're lonely, and sometimes availability is the most attractive asset. Your eyes open and you start seeing it in the people around you. Bound by nothing more than attraction, it doesn't take long. The relationship crumples. You drift apart. You stop talking and resort to text. Nicknames are dropped and compliments go by the waste side.

It doesn't take much to lose interest. The difficulty comes when somebody gets hurt. They either get cheated on or abandoned, left for dead to the rise of crippling self-doubt and the wide range of insecurities that come with being dumped. And they never see it coming, either. People settle for less all the time, just to not be alone. We sink our bets, blinded by desire, and more often than not, it's selfish. Relationships can be so one-sided.

With the way things were between Maddie and I, it made sense. We'd left the soft sensual surf and gone barefoot on the rocks. Gone were the days of romance and passionate kissing. Without substance and respect, it was inevitable. We'd met at the very bottom; what we'd shared at the time were low-points in both of our lives. Then time passed and we didn't even have that. We had nothing in common and the sex was too far and few between, never enough to build upon.

Maddie and I had run our course and we both knew it. The end was as tangible as the turn of a page. In the end, maybe she met somebody she liked and didn't want to miss her chance for it. She made an investment, a down payment. Somebody knocked her up and she didn't know it. Maybe she got cold feet, broke it off, and changed her mind. *I've decided that you're my soulmate*, she'd said, effecting a complete 180 at the precipice of our separation. It didn't compute.

Maybe she was seeing someone else, did it matter?

Did I really care?

"You want to know if the kid was yours," Emily said, dropping her eyes before I could see the disappointment in them. She pulled her hand away and joined it with the one holding the mug. "Right?"

"Yeah. I need to know." I pressed my fist against the couch cushions and gained my feet. "I don't know why, Em, but I need to know."

She avoided looking at me. Her eyes were fixed at a spot on the carpet. She sipped her coffee then shook her head. "I'm sorry," she said. "But I don't know."

"She never said anything to you about it?"

"We didn't see each other a lot. Our schedules were complete opposites this semester and Maddie got a job, so she was never here. I didn't even know she was pregnant until a month ago. It wasn't super visible and I don't think she was sure if she was going to keep it right away, so she wasn't telling anyone."

"The father…?"

"I never asked," she shrugged. "I guess I didn't really want to know. There was this girl…Ezmer, I think her name was. She might know something. They worked together and carpooled a lot."

"You have her number?"

"No, but there's an address on the fridge. See the little gift card? Maddie put it there and nobody has bothered to take it down. Employee party I think."

"Thanks, Em. It's something."

I got the address from the kitchen and then we finished our coffees on the couch. We didn't talk about Maddie again. We reverted to the old ways, communing over the interests we share. It was nice. It felt normal, natural, and once again I was taken by her and by the chemistry between us. The attractive tilt of her jaw, halfcocked, whenever she prepared her response, pausing before speaking.

"If there's anything else I can do," she offered at the door.

I stepped down onto the sidewalk and looked back at her. "I might come for another cup of coffee."

"I'll have something better than Starbucks next time."

Elizabeth Short, they cut her in half too. Split her open at the waist, spread her legs, and carved a smile across her face from ear-to-ear. She was drained of her blood and posed atop her organs in a vacant lot in LA. She was 22 years old. They never found her killer and her murder remains unsolved, the subject of countless books and documentaries.

Maddie never wanted to be famous.

I took a bus downtown and from there walked to the address I'd taken from the card. It wasn't residential. It was an anonymous beige building filled with desks and dividers. They refer to these as call centers, but they always look more like prisons. This is where Maddie had spent the last months of her life, answering phones and dealing in policies. Working overtime maybe so that she could save up money for the kid she'd decided to keep.

I walked inside and was met at the front desk by a small Asian woman wearing a padded blazer and too much lipstick. I smiled. She didn't smile back.

"Can I help you?" she asked.

"Yeah, actually. I'm from out of town. I was hoping I could speak with Ezmer if she's available?"

"Define available," she said. "This is a call center, she's working."

"It won't take long, just a few minutes," I worked my mouth into a cautious smile. "It's important."

She returned her eyes to her desk and frowned. It was natural to her face. Her mouth was the downturned shape of a horseshoe, indented into her jaw, and her heavy lipstick stuck to the fronts of her teeth. Her eyes were lifeless and dark, but I could see that she was thinking.

She lifted a phone and asked Ezmer to report to the cafeteria. "She has a guest," she said, dropping the phone back into its cradle. Then to me, "Down the hall on the right. She has five minutes."

"That should be plenty of time. Thanks again."

"Mm-hm."

The cafeteria was well suited to the work environment, one of depressive small-scale corporate greed. It was a sterile room with unpleasant lights—florescent bulbs run along the ceiling in plastic sheaths—and linoleum flooring. The standard rubberized tables and folding chairs were the only furnishings. I sat down and waited. A few minutes later the door opened behind me and she entered the room.

"Ezmer?"

"Yeah. Who are you?"

She looked a lot like Maddie, but Hispanic. A dwarf Kardashian with pronounced lips and breasts and very long fingernails, immaculately manicured, painted, and inset with twinkling rhinestones. She wore a chili patterned camisole crop-top and jeggings and her eyes were the kind that bled fire when provoked. She sat down across from me, swooping her hair back, and crossed her arms.

"So?" she said haughtily.

"Sorry, my name is Nick." I extended my hand, a friendly gesture that was received with annoyance. Her hand felt like crushed velvet in my grip and her bracelets rattled when I shook it. "I dated Maddie."

"Yeah, I know about you. Heard all about it right after you broke my girl's heart. Listen," she said leaning forward. "I know your favorite drink, I know your favorite meal, sex position, and the size of your little *pito*. Maddie told me everything, *cabron*. What do you want?"

"I want to know if she was seeing anyone else."

"*Puta madre*," she rolled her eyes. "Typical man. Only thinks about himself."

"You were good friends," I entreated her. "I need to know if the child she was carrying was mine. She was four months, that puts it around the time we last saw each other."

"*Por qué esto importa?* Why does this matter? You abandoned her, *cabron*."

"We broke up."

"She was your girlfriend. You left her."

"We were in a relationship, it ended."

"Then don't you know? *Muy pendejo*. Or do you just *derrama tu meca* without thinking? Maddie was right about you," she huffed. "If you think it was your kid, you should know. You were the one. *Vamos a coger*, no protection maybe? I wasn't there, *cabron*. Only you were."

"Maddie wasn't seeing anybody else then?"

"I don't know, was she? If you had been my boyfriend I would have. But Maddie *no vio, el novio verdadero*. Then it was too late."

"Didn't she—"

"Maddie hated you. You broke her heart. That's all I have to say." She stood up. "I'm done talking to you."

I expected to be slapped. Her eyes had turned into balls of fire. But instead, she turned her head and spat.

"If you think of anything," I said, holding out a card with my phone number on it. "Let me know."

"*Chinga du madre, pinche gringo*," she snarled, leaving the room. "*Estás pero si bien pendejo*." As she walked away the spikes of her high-heels kicked up fire, her bracelets rattled, and her hair swung angrily against her back. The door closed behind her and I was alone.

Maybe she wasn't as ruthless as she seemed. She'd snatched the card out of my hand on her way out.

The Boise police station is as anonymous as its surroundings. It looks like a strip mall actually, but with a larger parking lot and some flagpoles. It's located near the shopping mall; near a complex network of one-ways and crowded intersections; a spot where traffic violations would be plentiful and quotas readily met.

I opened the door and walked inside. For a half-second I was the center of attention. Everyone turned their heads and assessed the entry, looking over the partitions that separated their desks, over clipboards and computers and up from their phones. Satisfied, they went back about their business. Guns weren't drawn. A skinny cop approached me. He stared me down then passed by, moving through the door and out into the daylight.

"Can I help you?"

The voice was female.

I turned and recognized her immediately—the ponytail and boxy black shoes, uniform as well fit as a one-size-fits-all Halloween costume. It was the cop I'd spoken with on the phone, the woman who'd called and told me about the murder.

"Yeah," I responded. "Well, actually I'm not sure who can help who here. My name is Nick Sothern. I was called last week about... I think it was you I might have spoken with. You called me about the girl they found."

"Oh," she frowned. "The ex-boyfriend. From California. Yeah. I remember. What are you doing here?"

"I thought I should come."

"That's nice of you. At least you're not here to buy up our real estate. That's what most Californians seem to be doing.

These days local people can't hardly afford to live here anymore, because of all you driving the market up."

Her phone chimed, she read a text, and typed a response. "They haven't scheduled the funeral for your friend yet," she said.

"Yeah, I know."

"You have information about the murder?"

"No. I mean, not that I know of anyway. I just wanted to check in. Any developments with the case?"

"Can't say, mister. It's an ongoing investigation. Soon as we've got something to share, you'll see it in the papers."

"Sure," I nodded. "But about... You said she was pregnant?"

"That's right."

"Do they know who the father was?"

"Jesus H. Christ," she sighed, rolling her eyes. "It's like I said, what we know might be significant to the investigation, so details like that will not be available to the public until further notice. All I can tell you is that she was about four months. If you're curious about if it was yours or not, just do the math."

"Thanks."

"Have a nice day," she said.

I walked back through the door and into the sun. My phone vibrated as I passed the flags. It was a text message.

I remembered something, it read.

I typed back: *Ezmer?*

Yah.

Hey thanks what is it?

Meet me later?

Sure. Where?

I don't get off work till six. I'll send you the address.

Sounds good. Thanks

I received the text around seven. *Be there at eight*, it said. The address took me to a ramshackle little building on a dead-end street. The windows were grey with dust and impenetrable. Whatever it was, it had been closed for years. The surroundings were bleak and industrial. Cottonwood roots burrowed beneath the sidewalks, buckling the concrete panels, and weeds straggled up from the gravel-scattered cracks.

It was a dead zone.

The *Lyft* driver waited while I double checked the address. "Yeah, this is it," I told him. "Thanks."

I shut the door and he drove off. The car turned and disappeared back down the street. It was 8:04. The area was deserted. "Great," I said aloud. "She's fucking with me."

But she wasn't.

She arrived and she wasn't alone. At first, I didn't get it. They came wildly, kicking up dust. Four separate trucks, bumping up over the curbs and revving engines. In movies, the hicks all pile into the back of a single pick-up. That couldn't be further from the truth. Each vitriolic slob needs his own representative vehicle.

The doors opened and they climbed out.

There were nine of them. Guys and gals, coupled-up, and a burly dude with bandages on his face. When he opened his mouth, the bandages pulled back revealing a narrow row of sooty, crooked, yellow teeth. He leaned against the front of his truck and scratched himself.

Ezmer stood beside a blond-bearded giant in a sleeveless flannel. Her head barely reached his armpits. He had muscles in his chest big enough to crush beer cans with, and they flexed uncontrollably.

"This is Bobby," Ezmer said, flashing a wicked little smile. "He's a *real man* and he would never abandon me like you abandoned my poor girl." She removed her arm from his waist and Bobby stepped forward. He was wearing a baseball cap with a peaked bill, blue-jeans, and imitation leather Vans. "My man is going to beat you within an inch of your fucking life, *cabron*."

This kind of shit still goes on in the twenty-first century. I keep forgetting that I'm in Idaho. In California, we have drive-by shootings and street gangs. But here, even the teenagers vote republican; punishment is dealt out with fists in vacant lots and with a crowd cheering on the axe-man.

"Bring on the beers," someone screamed, dragging a cooler from the back of a truck.

Bobby's fist impacted my stomach and the effect was like de-corking a Champaign bottle; a surge of bubbly spilled down my chin. I puked while staggering backward and the ground wobbled beneath my feet. I doubled over, gasping for air, and he kicked me. His heel collided with the side of my head and I crumpled.

The guy with the bandages walked over and kicked me in the ribs. I saw lights, flashlight beams and fireflies sparking against the backs of my eyelids. There are many forms of pain. This one was entirely new for me.

The others joined in too, one at a time, and the girls were the worst. They giggled, compensating for lack of power with sheer nastiness and blow placement. Afterward, someone spilled warm beer on my face.

The last thing I remember as they climbed into their trucks was her voice in my ear, "You're not a man, *puto*. I should have let them kill you."

People move here for privacy and they get it. When I came to, I wasn't in the hospital. It was morning. The sun was up and I was still laid out in the gravel. Idaho is a private place, a rural state, even the city is full of dead zones and farm silence. It's the perfect place to beat someone up, the perfect place to cut a girl in half.

I dragged myself into a sitting position and spit the rocks out of my mouth. All that came forth was blood. It was dried all over my face, down my mouth and chin, and into a hard-black shell between my collar bones. My shirt was ruined. So was my smile, I could imagine. My cheeks were swollen against my teeth and ragged on the inside. My lips were split and my nose felt off center.

My phone was dead, of course. The screen was smashed into a fatale cobweb where it had been kicked.

It took me a while to get up. I sat there dozing, familiarizing myself with the pain, before finally wobbling onto my feet. I'd never been roughed up before. Learning to walk again was a steady challenge. I headed for civilization with limp.

Traffic was nonexistent, not a cab in sight.

I reached a thoroughfare and followed it to a restaurant, where I asked to borrow their phone. The manager called the police and the police called me an ambulance. I tried not to think of the bill.

I was out of the hospital by mid-afternoon with a thirty-three stitches and a bandage compressing my ribs. I told the police nothing. As a curtesy the front desk called me a cab. I got my things from the hotel and asked to go straight to the airport. But no. As we left the parking lot, the driver cursed, spilling his coffee in his lap, and I changed my mind.

Maddie was dead. It wasn't my fault. Whoever killed her would be caught and sent to prison. He'd die and I'd celebrate. Maybe I'll never know about the kid and that's alright. I don't have to. There's closure enough when your ex gets cut in half.

I leaned my head against the seat and watched the city pass through the tinted window. Maddie was gone but she left an echo. It's like that with relationships, the chambers of our hearts remember the soft words and longing. Traces of occupancy, scorch marks and splinters.

Maddie is etched into a tree somewhere.

I mourned for her and the child she was carrying, the boy or girl that might have been ours, but I couldn't make myself love her, not even in death. The driver pulled up to the curb and let me out in front of her house.

Emily was at the door before I reached the steps. I heard the sharp intake of breath. Her eyes went wide and she covered her mouth. She came running then, barefoot in the grass. I dropped my bag on the curb.

"Got any coffee?" I asked as she flew into my arms.

SATYR PLAY

I.

She'd had a cleft lip when she was younger, and because of that she looked a bit like a snapping turtle. Her mouth was sculpted flat, smoothed over by the surgeon's scalpel, and her teeth showed on either side when she half-smiled. Oddly enough it only enhanced her beauty. She was ravishing. Her eyes were wide-set and hazelnut, and her hair was combed-caramel lapping at the straps of her fuchsia bikini top. She wore a light beige skirt and sandals and her belly button was pierced through with a silver hoop.

Her name was Adelaide.

She could have been nineteen or thirty. An ageless angel type, the MTV type. You could imagine her in faded denim studded with rhinestones and a lace-back crop-top, holding a microphone or with a headset plugged in to one ear, singing her heart out on a glossy stage.

I met her inside that flashing blue dungeon, Space Bar, located a block away from the capital building. It was seven o'clock. She'd just come off the river and was leaned against the Iron Maiden pinball machine, smelling of sunscreen and licorice, drinking craft beer out of the can.

"You play?" I asked, nodding at the machine.

"Sometimes," she replied. "I'm not very good though. Actually I was just hoping a table would open up."

"Yeah it's packed tonight."

"Where are you sitting?"

"Over there with some friends."

"You mean the group by the Nintendo?"

"Yeah."

"My feet are killing me. You mind if I join you guys?"

"Not at all," I smiled. "But only because your feet hurt."

Her eyes sparkled, she winked and the effect was like the sway of a gold watch. I felt myself falling under her spell. "Thanks cowboy," she replied, and as we walked to the table the rhythm of her hips was a further hypnosis.

"Guys this is Adelaide," I announced, scooting through the menagerie of chairs toward the group. "She's going to join us. We're getting married on Sunday."

"Addie," she said, "It's a lot cuter that way. And we're not getting married until Tuesday."

The joke was lost on most. Kevin laughed. The Deathlord smiled. Michele rolled her eyes, fixing her lips over her soda straw. They introduced themselves one-by-one, all six of them, while I made room for an extra chair and scooted it in beside my own.

"Hey, you want another beer?" I asked, touching her elbow. She was shaking hands with Elizabeth and glanced back over her shoulder, eyes flashing between the strands of her hair.

"Sure," she smiled. "But only if you're having one too and I buy the first round."

"Okay," I shrugged.

"I always buy the first round," she explained to Elizabeth. "My taste in beer gets more expensive as the night wears on."

They both laughed. Elizabeth glanced at Kevin, covering her mouth. Women bond over laughing. It's a fact, just watch *Sex and the City*.

Addie threw her arms around my neck. "We'll be right back," she told the table, pressing her chest against my ribcage. She tugged me toward the bar and said, "I've been in the sun all day. I need some serious good vibes and double serious beerdration."

"*Beerdration?*"

"Yeah, aren't I clever?"

She took my wrist and we weaved through the arcade arm-in-arm. It felt more like the beginning to a rom-com than a one-night stand. I almost couldn't believe it was happening.

Space Bar is not a place to hook-up.

We skewered the crowd surrounding *Street Fighter II* and she threw herself at the bar, leaning in on her elbows with her smile on full-tilt as the bartender walked over. He bypassed the others in line—a bunch of guys in t-shirts, anxious for their next drink—but nobody complained. It was the natural order of things, everybody knows: hot girls first.

"Hi," Addie beamed. "Remember me?"

His eyes lit up right away. "How could I forget? PB Stout, right?"

"That's right!"

He had a beard and wore his cap backward. Cheap fitted vest, narrow shoulders. He rattled the silver watch on his wrist and grinned, checking her out, while I stood behind her, the invisible man.

"What was the name of the brewery again?" she asked, crossing her arms beneath her breasts, pushing herself forward on the bar top. "You told me before."

"Belching Beaver."

"Oh yeah," she giggled. "Belching Beaver. We'll take two of those."

His eyes darted over her shoulder at the word "we". I smiled and waved and the friendliness leaked out of his expression like air through a broken tire valve.

"Sure, coming right up," he grunted as his smile continued to deflate.

He gave her the beers. She paid him then showed him her back, passing me one of the arty red and brown cans.

"Cheers," she said, pulling the tab.

"Cheers."

We knocked our drinks together and titled them to our lips as *Rock the Casbah* battled through the speakers over the sound of the arcade, 8-bit missiles and turbines, repetitive phrases and countless winking defeats.

"What do you think?" she asked. "Pretty good, right?"

"Yeah. It's sweet, but not too sweet," I said, tasting it on my lips. "It's very…peanut butter. Like a Reese's, but beer."

"Exactly, that's the point."

"It's good."

We paused briefly at the *Mortal Kombat* machine before working our way back to the tables. Four impassioned nerds were trading insults, taking turns. A big guy with pimples seemed to be winning. His tee-shirt said GAYMER, spelled out in rainbows across his back.

"It's actually pretty cool," Addie said, tilting her head back. "Some people get so into it."

"Yeah, for sure."

"Which one do you like best?"

"I don't know." I answered, sipping my beer. "I don't really play. Centipede maybe?"

"You don't?"

"Not really. What about you?"

"Oh I'm terrible, I just like to watch. But I'm surprised that *you* don't play. You seem…"

"Don't say it." I groaned.

"Don't say what?" she asked, smiling amusedly. She held the beer can against her lips, nipping the rim with her teeth. "That you seem like the type?"

I nodded. "Yeah, that."

"Well, that isn't what I was going to say." She stood on her tiptoes—which really wasn't necessary—and kissed the corner of my mouth. "I was just going to say that you looked cool. Like someone who does a lot of different things and is also into retro gaming."

"So like a hip nerd?"

"Just shut up," she smiled, taking my hand. "You're dumb."

Back at the table they'd blundered into politics. You could tell from the way Kevin stared at his phone. He was scrolling idly, checking his calendar. Beside him, Elizabeth was nodding her head. She was blinking her eyes as The Deathlord explained recent upheavals in the Super Smash Brothers community and how they mirrored state elections.

None of us are gamers. The Deathlord even; he's just called that because it's cool. I don't know why we came here in the first place.

Addie and I sat down and Wesley studied us from across the table with ghostly indifference. He started to wave, then Michele spilled his Kombucha. He calmly looked down, watching the liquid spread, then flinched as it rushed off the table and spilled into his lap. Daniel Kerr witlessly handed him a single napkin then returned his attention to the conversation; he'd memorized the Bible verse of the day on his cellphone and was patiently waiting for the right context to interject it.

It was an odd group. Everyone was a different age and on a different page. Kevin and I do that sometimes, social engineering. We arrange these stilted gatherings for our own amusement, assembling groups of obvious polar-opposites then watching them twitch and struggle to find commonality.

Wesley stood up and excused himself to the restroom. His chinos were soaked through, stained purple with Kombucha. Addie laughed at something Michele said and the two of them engaged in a gleefully mocking conversation, deriding some poor girl's haircut. Kevin looked up from his phone, caught my eye, and sighed.

We both nodded.

Sometimes we forget how exhausting it can be.

"Hey," Addie said, leaning into me, sliding her hand across my thigh. "What are you doing tomorrow night?"

"I don't know. I don't have any plans. How come?"

"Well, this is really embarrassing, but…"

"I knew it," I slapped my hand onto my forehead in mock dismay. "I should have known it was too good to be true. You have a boyfriend, right? And it's date night tomorrow and you need someone to babysit your kids?"

"Hey buddy! Do I *look* like I've had kids?"

I froze, dropping the hand.

"I didn't say that."

She tried holding a straight-face, narrowing her eyes against a smile, but lost it. We both laughed. I could feel the curve of her hip pressing against my thigh as she leaned toward me. Her hand alighted on my chest, fidgeting with a button. She looked into my eyes, lips parting ever-so slightly, and brought them within an inch of my own.

"Fine," she said, pulling herself straight and away. "I won't tell you then."

"C'mon. No more jokes I swear." I drew a finger across my chest and grinned. "Cross my heart."

She lifted her beer, hiding a smile behind the can. I could see the raised corners of her mouth and the mischievous sparkle in her eyes. "Okay, fine!" she said, showing a flash of teeth. "So there's this party tomorrow night a friend of mine is having. It's like a campfire party. And...well, I need a date, so."

"Yes."

"Yes what?"

"Yes, you can ask one of my friends," I said. "Except for Kevin, he's married."

She slammed her fist into my arm.

I grabbed the back of her head and pulled her to me and our mouths came together like the jumper cables on the wrong post. When it ended, she was smiling and soft. Her eyes had changed. They'd been reupholstered, vinyl to velvet. Confidence poured into my bloodstream.

"Your friends seem really nice," she murmured. "But to be honest, I was kinda hoping that you would be my date."

"What time should I pick you up?"

*

She pulled into my driveway at half-past six, looking small and cute behind the wheel of a battered red pickup. I watched her park. She let the engine idle, staring into her lap, and a moment later I received her text.

Here.

Coming, I replied.

I paused at the door and contemplated bringing a coat. I'd dressed in a flannel and jeans. How far were we going? Boise is warm but further North the climate changes. Once you hit the mountains the temperatures drop and the forests are quick to cool. I decided against the coat, shoved a beanie in my back pocket, just in case, and left the house.

She waved at me through the windshield then stretched across the seats to throw open the passenger side door.

"Sweet truck," I said, climbing inside. "Reminds me of home."

"Thanks," she smiled, twisting at the waist, watching for traffic, as she backed down the drive. She was wearing a cherry-red and white plaid button-up beneath a caramel colored cardigan, grey yoga pants, and UGG boots. Her makeup was subtle—eyeshadow and lips gloss—and her hair was tied back in a ponytail.

"So where's home?" she asked.

"Carey."

"Nice. I grew up in Burley."

"That explains the beerdration joke."

"That's Burley for you. Why would I ever move, right?"

"Sarcasm?"

"Mostly," she shrugged. "You ever been?"

"Once or twice."

"Then you know what it's like. It's a shit hole. The only things I ever miss about it are living at home for free and my dentist."

"Your dentist?"

"Yeah. Actually he was an orthodontist. I had the biggest crush on him in high school. I even wrote his name on my Vans."

"Sharpie?"

"Yeah, a silver one."

"And I thought nobody liked their dentist."

"He looked like Ashton Kutcher," she beamed, piloting the old pickup into traffic. She downshifted at a stoplight then threw it back into gear and roared past a Subaru on the left.

"So you came here for school?" I asked.

"No, after. I came here for a social life."

"Burley wasn't big enough?"

"I got tired of all the redneck jokes."

"I know what you mean, Carey's the same. More tractors than people."

"Exactly," she said. "What about you? Go to BSU?"

"CSI," I said. "In Hailey of all places."

"I had a cousin that worked up there for a few years. My dad always used to joke that that's not really Idaho."

"He was right. Sun Valley, Ketchum, all that—they might as well be California. It gets worse every year."

"I almost went to Michigan State," she shrugged. "Ended up at U-of-I. I guess I wasn't ready to leave either, who knows."

"Home is home."

"Yeah."

We passed the Rhodes skate park beneath the on-ramp to the freeway. A group of homeless loitered in the usual spot, ghost-faced or scowling. Their sleeping bag rolls and backpacks were piled against the underpass wall while they stood at the street corner, holding their signs. Most of them looked healthy. I wondered who paid for their tattoos and piercings.

"Hey, you want to hand me a cigarette?" Addie asked. "They're in the glove box."

I opened the compartment and reached inside. "Don't you know that smoking is bad for you? In the twenty first century, it's practically medieval."

"Yeah well, oral sex is illegal in thirteen states, you think I care?" A row of traffic cones guided us past a roughed-up patch of asphalt. We slowed, merging lanes, and were waved on by a construction worker in a neon vest and hardhat.

"Really, is that true?"

"Yeah," she took the box of cigarettes from me, held it to her mouth and pulled one out with her teeth. "In Idaho too, it's one of the thirteen."

"That's crazy."

"Yeah, whoever passed that law must have had a real puritan for a wife, he obviously had no clue what he was missing out on."

"Either that or he was ahead of the times."

"How so?"

"I don't know. Maybe he was a feminist. Seems like something a feminist might do, outlawing blowjobs."

"Not the ones that I know," she said. "And besides, the law isn't limited to just *male* oral sex, it cuts both ways…" she looked at me and smiled. "You know that, right? All the feminists I know love it when their man goes down."

"I think we're talking about two different kinds of feminists."

"For sure. The kind you're talking about aren't even feminists, they're just a bunch of prudes who don't like sex anyways."

"Sounds about right," I nodded. She handed me the pack of cigarettes and I returned it to the glove box. "So what kind are you?"

Her lips raised at the corners.

"Hand me the lighter," she said throatily. "It should be somewhere in there." I found it beneath her registration papers, a little pink butane, and passed it over.

"Cute," I said. "So where are we going anyways?"

She lit the cigarette then rolled down her window, releasing a trail of smoke between her teeth. "Out toward Lowman."

"To a campsite?"

"No this is out in the woods for real. You'll see."

"Cool."

"If the smoke bothers you…" she started to say.

"It doesn't."

"Either way…I'll make it up to you."

"You're that kind of feminist, huh?"

She smiled. "I'm not a feminist at all."

It was dark by the time she pulled off the road and said *we're here*. It looked like nowhere. The roadside gave way to grass and a towering wall of forest. She inched the truck off the road, into the gravel and weeds, and killed the motor. "First things first," she said. She reached across my legs, opened the glove box, and place her phone inside. "No phones tonight."

"Really?"

"Yep, that's the rules."

"What if there's an emergency?"

"There won't be."

I shrugged, powered it down, and tossed it inside. She closed the hatch and kissed me. "We have to walk from here," she said, throwing her door open. "20 minutes or so."

"You're sure this is the spot?" I asked, glancing both ways at the empty stretch of road. "It all looks the same."

"Stop being such a worry wart. Look," she pointed at a florescent mile-marker beside the truck. "We're right where we need to be."

"And we're the first to arrive too from the look of it."

"I doubt it. There're other ways in, this is just sort of my spot. And don't tell anyone either, Peter would be pissed if everybody started parking along the road. The last thing we need is the forest service getting on our case. They see one truck, they don't care, they keep driving you know? Figure it's some dumb farmer. But if there were a bunch..."

"I get it."

"Especially with all the fire warnings."

"My lips are sealed."

"Not for everything, I hope." she winked, igniting a small flashlight.

The forests in Southern Idaho aren't particularly dense, but they're heavy with undergrowth. Sagebrush in the foothills gives way to pines and the woodland floor is choked with their gnarled remnants, sudden outcroppings of rock, boulders, and fallen branches, and the earth is visible in patches, hard-baked and beige beneath carpets of dark needles, twigs, and pinecones. Lichen grows on the rocks in bright orange plumbs, or on the trees, clinging in furry tufts to their riddled bark; and patches of green stand out, here and there, in the dark like Martian flares. Everything is dusty with pollen and the smell is robust and organic.

"This is an old deer trail," Addie explained, illuminating a vague pathway through the forest with the murky beam of her flashlight. "There are tons of them out here but this one leads right to where we're going."

"That's convenient."

"Yeah, but it's also creepy if you think about it."

"How so?"

"It leads right to the highway."

"And that's creepy?"

"I mean, not really, just that it's probably served as a death march for a lot of animals. This stretch is famous for deer crossings. In the spring especially, the roadside is littered with carcasses."

"Like *Frogger,* but deer and no replays."

"People die too though. The deer cause a lot of really bad accidents."

She stepped over a fallen tree. The evenly spaced branches projected skyward like the scorched ribs of a dead whale. In silhouette, even the dead take on a certain spectral elegance, moonscapes carved out by shadow.

We carried on like that, swatting aside branches and picking our way through underbrush until we saw firelight flickering ahead of us through the trees.

Addie paused. "This is it," she said, glancing over her shoulder.

I could make out the tents and camp chairs as we got closer, and a dozen or so people surrounding the fire. Their voices carried, feeling out of place this deep in nature, like loud music in a study hall.

We breeched the tree line and were bathed in firelight. Dream-catchers tinkled above us in the branches and the open sky showed clear with stars.

"There's Dan," Addie said, tugging my arm. He was seated on a stump at the edge of the camp, whittling a branch with a pocketknife. "Adelaide!" he chuckled, standing up. "It's been way too long, missy."

He sunk the knife into the ground and they embraced. "I'm glad you made it, dear," he said, drawing back just enough to look at her face. Her clapped her arms fondly. "You're looking great as always."

"Thanks, and when have you ever known me to miss a party?" She reached for my arm and pulled me forward. "I want you to meet my guest."

"Hi. Lucas."

He took my hand and we shook.

"Dan," he said, grinning through broad polished teeth. He was a lanky man with skin like old leather, freckled shoulders, and a large handlebar mustache. His face was long and brought to a point by a patchy blonde beard. He wore a beaded vest and faded jeans, and his hair was pulled back into a ponytail.

"Welcome to the party," he said.

"Thanks."

"Come on and say hi, join the fire." he said, turning toward camp. "Can I get you two something to drink?"

"I'll take a beer if you've got one,"

"Make it two," Addie said, hugging my arm.

I leaned into her. "Were we supposed to bring something?"

"We're fine, they've got plenty of drinks." She slowed our pace just long enough to kiss me, then hurried forward. "Besides, you brought more than enough already."

"My sense of humor?"

"I meant your body, stupid," she winked, taking my hand.

II.

We sat on logs surrounding the camp fire, everyone there was a type. Within an hour the circle of attendees doubled, then tripled. Stragglers breached the dark, wandering in from the trees. Beers were cracked. There were jokes and laughter. Some of them passed a joint.

It was a unique crowd. There wasn't unity here in any common sense, it was plain togetherness. Looking around, no one seemed to match. There were rednecks as well as hipsters, the well-to-do kids, the hippies. All ageless and glowing. The woods will do that. Nature has a strange power over us, the effect of dwarfing the individual and amplifying our humanity. All of the sudden we're more or less the same: hungry, thirsty, vulnerable, alive. Hicks pause before speaking and laugh off disagreements; they're not so one-sided. Jocks mingle with nerds and both trade war stories. Debutants and bohemians coexist in the firelight.

Katie and Rebecca are from the UK, here on tourist visas. They'd been commandeered for the party by a guy named Rick who'd passed out drunk in one of the tents. They both have sparrows tattooed on their wrists. We talk for a while. They argue over the merits of globalization and birth control.

Time slows to a crawl.

The stars are out above us and the size of first love. Addie keeps dipping her hand into my lap, testing the burning logs with a branch as she leans forward, sliding her grip along my thigh. We all watch the fire, the coals twinkling beneath the flame, cinders of blackened pine shrinking, dissolving to ash. Its hypnotic, relaxing. The steady crackle and bursting of sap.

It speaks to our souls.

As the night wears on people shift spots, they go for toilet breaks and return to different openings in the circle.

Companions change and the conversations evolve with added perspective, gaining fresh new dimensions.

I return from the forest, having emptied a few beers worth into the ground. I'm wobbling with a nice buzz, buckling my belt. Addie sits cross-legged in the dirt. She's wearing a yellow headlamp, carefully sketching henna on a slim girl's hand. Dan sits on a tree stump beside her, wringing his wrists, turning his bracelets in slow steady revolutions. He smiles at me and waves, bleary eyed and stoned.

I find a place to sit and topple down beside a guy with a nose piercing, wearing a fedora.

"Nah, it's the Californians," he says, addressing a half-circle of flunkies, perched on logs, listening. His name is Marshal. He wears dessert boots, skinny jeans, and a faded rib-knit cardigan. "What happens," he continues. "Is they come to Boise and start some lame business. Maybe they buy out your grandparent's place or whatever. Then they renovate it a little, right? Just enough so it feels cool and modern. And then what they do is jack up the prices. And people here go for it because they're scared of being considered too country if they don't. Like they're ashamed of being from a rural state or something, you know?"

Everyone nods their heads.

"Right?" he smirks, pleased with himself. "So what happens then? The owner makes a fucking killing of course, because they're getting *California* prices without having to pay California wages. And then the city wants in. Duh. Same old story, right? So they jump taxes and the rent goes up, and now everybody has to charge California prices just to keep in business. And what does the state do to set thing right? Does Idaho raise its minimum wage? Fuck no. I pay thirteen hundred bucks a month for rent, man. For an apartment. And minimum wage is *still* 7.25. Can you believe that shit?

"But in California," he pauses, reading his audience masterfully as he tilts a beer to his lips and drains it.

"In *fucking* California," he says. "It's 15.00 bucks an hour. That's why they come here. Low minimum wage. And that's a major fucking problem in my opinion."

A few of them clap, everyone agrees. From there the conversation mutates into an exploration of wealth, classism, and the horror movie *The Purge*. I haven't seen it. They spoil the ending for me. I get up and go for another piss.

It's getting late. So many hours on the beer-clock and all of the sudden standing support is a requirement for getting your fly down. I leaned against a tree and relieved myself with a groan. In a blur, I return to camp.

I'm sitting on the ground, staring up past the trees, following flakes of ash as they drift into the sky and join the stars. Moments later they wink from existence and I'm left feeling sad. Everybody wants to be a star, don't they? The plight of the ashes reminds me of a video game I used to play, one I always lost. It's like that—three or four beers in and it all comes together, every little thread of existence. You start to appreciate the small things, the details. Memories gain epic proportion and feel profound. Then several more beers on top of that and you might as well be on drugs.

I'd stopped counting awhile back.

My head was swaying, drawing stick figures in the dirt with my finger. I'm sitting across from a business grad now. He's been going on about real estate for what feels like eternity. I drop in and out of consciousness and imagine the skin sloughing off my face, tugged away from the bone by meaty wrinkles and decay. I imagine that I'm dead and that he's still right there talking, unawares, immune to the stink as my corpse begins to congeal and rot. I know deep inside that one day I will become a fossil. And that he will be there, sitting on the log beside me, debating the housing market as the planet slips over the edge and into oblivion.

Someone passes me a beer and I take it.

The business grad yelps. I'm vaguely aware as a soccer ball smashes through a pile of empty cans and ricochets off his forehead. The guy who kicked it throws his arms up and roars. He's wearing spotless *Air Jordon's*, ripped jeans, and a leather blazer with suede lapels. He looks like a member of Def Leopard. Beneath the blazer his t-shirt is dalmatian print and he's wearing a red UFC baseball cap over long curly hair.

"Sorry," he says, extracting the ball from the undergrowth.

"You're playing soccer?" the business grad blinks, rubbing his eye. "Out here?"

"Nah. It's not even my ball. I just found it and saw the cans."

"Beercan bowling," I interject, grateful for the intrusion. "It's a real art."

"Yeah," he grinned. "Who are you?"

"My name is Lucas," I extended my hand and he ignored it, smiling.

"Cool, well I'm Dillon," he said, crossing his arms over the soccer ball. "My sister is here too. Her name is Racheal. When the shit goes down later on you better not fuck her or I'll cut your balls off, okay?"

"Noted," I said. My head feels like it's wrapped in neoprene. The business grad stands up, brushing his pants, and wonders off. I look at Dillon and smile. "You don't have to worry," I assure him, slurring. "I came with a girl."

"So?" he sneers. "You really think that matters? It's like I said—put your dick near my sister and you're dead okay?"

I blinked my eyes and wondered if this sudden hostility was Oedipal. "What makes you think I—"

"You're the type. *Her type.* I can tell."

"Okay. I'll keep away from Racheal"

"I'm not joking, buddy. You better."

He walked away with his soccer ball and I lowered my eyes, staring at a wet patch of dirt where some beer had been spilled. Moments later, two girls with big hair rescue me from my confusion. They plop down beside me on logs. Short, curvy brunettes with manicured nails bordering on masterworks of art. Their names are Maddie and Ezmer.

"Don't let Dillon bother you," Ezmer says. "He's *un pendejo.*"

"Yeah," the other girl agrees. "Trust her, she's right. He's my roommate's brother so I have to put up with him all the time. He's super protective."

"Thanks," I grin. "You girls want a beer?"

"I'm not drinking," Maddie frowns. "But thanks."

"And I've had too much already. My boyfriend would kill me if he knew I was drinking this stuff." Ezmer lifts the can of Coors, squints at it, then drains it and burps.

"My boyfriend's a Bud guy," she explains. "Like hardcore. Bud Light Bobby, that's what his friends call him cuz like…he won't drink nothing else, not even whiskey."

"That's cool," I nod.

I feel like I'm smiling at them through a tight sheet of visqueen. Opening my mouth to speak, but then I can't think of anything to say, so I just stare at the fire. After a few minutes they give up on me and leave. With a reassuring arm around Maddie's shoulder, Ezmer says: "He's just wasted, don't worry girl it's totally not you."

"Yeah."

"Besides…let's get the fuck out of here, anyway. Bobby doesn't know I'm here and he would be pissed. Let's go back to your place and watch something."

After that, I switch to water for a while. There are several two-gallon jugs of Crystal Geiser lined up on stump at the edge of camp. Beside them, a tray of empty mason jars. Gradually my head starts to clear. It's like that for me, the buzz never lasts long. I sober-up quick.

I wonder what time it is. It's getting chilly but my beanie has disappeared and I don't want to button my shirt.

Addie joins me beside the fire.

She leans against my arm and kisses me. Her fingers curl, tracing my stomach, as she guides them to the small of my back and pulls us closer. Our jaws clash, tongues lashing, gliding between our teeth, and our mouths open wide, working in perfect tandem. It goes on till our lungs give out and we back our mouths away, panting. The scar on her lip is accented by the firelight, a subtle seam in the fabric of her skin. In that moment she looks like the love emoji, with hearts in place of her eyes, smiling dreamily, and I'm very much in the mood to advance. It's sudden, like I've just been awakened to the possibility. Heat pours through my blood and I'm horny. I go to kiss her again but we're disrupted by someone shouting.

"Welcome friends!"

Across from us, seen through the flame, a man stands and raises a guitar over his head, drawing everyone's attention. He's wearing a loose-fitting sweater with the sleeves pushed up to his elbows, designer jeans, sandals, and an ankle bracelet. His hair has thinned above the temples and is pulled into a long grey ponytail.

"That's Peter," Addie whispers. "He's in charge."

The chatter drops off and the campsite settles into silence as our host moves his eyes slowly over the crowd. Firelight catches in his jewelry, silver bracelets and turquoise rings worn on every finger; it flickers in the blacks of his eyes, on his fingernails and against his skin.

Everyone is quiet, watching.

There are about thirty of us left. I don't see the business grad anymore and the two girls, Maddie and Ezmer, must have also gone. Katie and Rebecca are still here. They both look drunk, pressed on either side of heavyset dude in a tank-top. Marshal's there, cleaning his glasses. Dillon, of course, arms crossed and glowering. As I glance at all the faces, I find myself wondering which one of the girls is Racheal.

Peter lowers the guitar. His eyes don't leave us for an instant as he brings it into place, cradled against his stomach, and gently strums the cords. He starts to play, summoning a familiar tune. His fingers flutter against the strings, shifting at the frets. He smiles and nods and the music floats on the air, soft at first, intermingling with night sounds, and then gets louder. We all start to sway, shoulder-to-shoulder, beside each other on the logs.

I can't place the melody, but everyone knows it.

Dan stands and, with a solid clap of his hands, begins to sing. It's euphoric. Addie squeezes my hand, holding it in her lap. We're chanting *Kumbaya*, smiling, rocking together reverently in the glow of the campfire.

It's magical.

I feel twelve again, at summer camp with a sunburned nose and grass stains on my knees. The smell of hotdogs cooking, too much ketchup on paper plates, and pitchers of lemonade. Dixie cups blown over by the wind. Then I'm fourteen, smuggling video tapes down into my mother's basement with my two best friends, watching Jason Voorhees butcher clueless camp counselors in analog high-definition. I'm eighteen, working for the forest service and paying for my own gas, driving to Prom.

Now I'm twenty-eight.

It's the present and everyone is super chill.

That's what we always say when we're drunk or high. Super Chill. They're our words, they belong to us—to our generation—ages twenty-five to thirty-five. He's super chill, she's super chill, the party was super chill. *How's the weed bro?* Super chill. *Are you guys dating?* Yeah man, it's super chill.

Call us what you will. Millennials, whatever. We're Generation Nintendo. Generation Go-Green. Diet Planning Rights Ranting Misguided Depressives. Generation Prone-to-Suicide. Generation Wrist Slitters, Hope-Shot-Down. Skinny Jeans and Track Shoes.

We're Generation Sad About Greed but Compliant. Lil Wayne: *I Feel Like Dying.* Generation Stress. Generation Steve Jobs. Go-To-College, Get-A-Job, Buy A House.

We're truly cynical, we believe in nothing.

Generation Godless.

And that's what shapes us. We won't survive when the power goes out. When we lose our phones and our parents die, we'll be lost. We're contrarians because we're scared to have opinions. We argue because we're insecure. When we become offended, it makes us feel important. Hurt lends weight to our feelings, counterbalancing our deepest fear of insignificance. We've established ourselves as a generation of victims. We're empowered by it. Weakness has taken the place of bravery. And now asshole men with money are a girl's best friend and abuser, and little boys don't dream of slaying dragon anymore. We wave banners and join clubs and take up activism to fill-in for the parts of ourselves both God and our parents left out.

We're the generation that grew between the cracks.

Generation *Why Bother?*

We didn't have the courage or self-esteem to be punk, so we pierced our eyebrows and dyed our hair. We were emos, goths, bulimics, and gamers. We treated our acne with meds that worsened our depression then wore our bracelets cut into our flesh; today we cover the scars with long sleeve shirts and wrist watches, Livestrong bands, and low self-esteem.

We're generation Bummed Out.

Cool Backpack, MacBooks, and *Eight Mile.* Eminem: *Lose Yourself.* Generation Sober but Aimless. We're narcissistic, *nonpareil.* Overnight Bisexuals. We redefine ourselves because we want attention. Generation Look-At-Me. Respond-To-My-Texts. The World Revolves Around My Jokes, Insecurities, and Small Talk.

We're the flavonoids.

No substance.

Generation Love, but only on the surface. We don't get married, we sign papers; we don't wear rings anymore, we run them through our noses and say: *Yah*. We're young, we're free. We're all on drugs. We're opened minded because it's easy to be open when you're empty.

Generation Lost.

Generation Not-Our-Fault.

We're the product of soft-touch childcare and absent parents. Too much reassurance and not enough initiative. We're spoiled, selfish. Somewhere Enya screams and 2Pac isn't really dead, he stuck around long enough to take a shot at politics then died when Hip-Hop genocided with mumble rap and was reborn in rainbows. Generation XXXTentacion: *Sad!* Full of contradictions. The young rapper brutalized his girlfriend, pimp-style, with a wire coat hanger, then died, celebrated, months later at twenty. They called him the "Voice of a Generation" in subsequent write-ups. You see his picture on religious themed shrines against chain-link fences, blown-by by newspapers with headlines lambasting other older abusers of the same ilk.

R. Kelly.

See? By our standards, every coward has a good excuse if he's young enough. Being bullied turns fledgling narcissists into martyrs and every villain is a misunderstood human. When mediocrity is applauded, everybody is a winner.

Generation *Thank You, Next*.

Generation Twenty-Hit-Singles but Nickelback Sucks. Percocets, Codeine, and Molly. We drop in and out of addictions like breathing, from designer drugs to Instagram.

We believe in nothing deeply.

We assume popular opinions and call ourselves alternative. We grew up Nickelodeon, then graduated from Rocketpower to Adult Swim and Pornhub in the span of a school year. The same year we lost our virginity and supplemented Gatorade for Monster.

Now we're Generation YouTube. Internet Clairvoyants and Accidental Entrepreneurs. Generation On-My-Phone. We're the ones that turn our reads off to feel in control of each other, twisting the knife to gratify our egos while the hopeful carry on. We play the game because we're empty and bored.

The Ghosted Generation: we're hollowed out.

The first of us have passed well into adulthood and the rest of us are on our way. It's irreparable. We're approaching middle age and it feels like cancer. We've hardly lived. We don't know who we are. Generation Identify-as, and reaching.

But right now, sitting around the campfire, it feels different. Something changes. These are the moments, the *super chill* moments, that make us feel whole. We'll be okay. We'll overcome time and stress and money and we'll do it together. We're unified now. Look at us: rocking together in the glow of mankind's first vital discovery. We've come home. We'll be young forever and everything is going to be okay.

But that's just me, what I think. That's the type of shit that comes into my head whenever the buzz wears off. Right now, singing *Kumba-fucking-ya.*

I feel enlightened.

"First, I want to thank you all for coming tonight," Peter says. He flattens his hand against the strings and lowers the guitar. "When we join together God smiles. I know this because he told me so. He who has ears, let him hear. In Matthew 18:20, the lord sayith: *Where two or more are gathered together in my name, there am I in the midst of them.*"

His eyes brush over us. The fire pops, launching an ember, and he passes the guitar to Dan.

"Friends," he proclaims, raising his arms. "Brothers and sisters, tonight we are as one flesh! *Now ye are the body of Christ,* wrote the apostle Paul in his letters to the Corinthians, *and each a part of it!* Children, tonight we bond in sacred union, for it is ours to take joy in this! Eat, drink. Take pleasure. For *I cometh quickly sayith the lord!*"

There is a roar of applause.

Everyone claps. They cheer and grin and go around slapping each other's backs. I couldn't imagine any one of them Christian, or religious at all, they were just varying degrees of drunk or high. But hey: they were having fun, moved by the moment. Generation YOLO. It wasn't about the words; it was about spectacle and emotion. The power of being there, being seen, and sharing it.

Peter looms over all, somehow taller—a head above the rest, and visible from every viewpoint. He might be the only person I've ever encountered that actually *looms*.

His presence is elevated, glowing, like you might believe there was some special force within him drawing the campfire up out of the logs. The set of his jaw, firm, fixed, and confident, and those fire-eyes that look out upon us with such strange knowing. His countenance inspires awe; both down-trodden and divine, he comes off as a prophet at peace amid the destitute.

I look at Addie and she kisses me. Taking me by the hand, she pulls me to my feet, and leads me toward the tents. "I'm going to make you eat my pussy," she says, glancing over her shoulder. "Then we're going to fuck all night like animals."

Generation DTF. I'm very okay with it.

We come to a halt. She throws back the zipper on a midsize purple tent, then crouches and draws me in through the flap. The uneven ground forms lumps beneath the nylon, jabbing our knees and palms as we crawl to the center, tearing at each other's clothes, and kiss. She yanks the shirt over my head then does the same for herself, exposing breasts which are small, perfect, and round. I follow her down, kissing them as she wiggles onto her back. She kicks her shoes off, lifts her waist, and rolls her leggings down. The tent is filled with her smell, like fresh bread, an intoxicating sourdough aroma.

She thrashes her legs, getting her panties off. "Eat me," she says. We tongue-kiss then she pushes me down. The heat from her sex draws the blood to my cheeks. It happens fast. I'm blushed, incensed, and overwhelmed as she clamps her thighs over my head. She tilts her hips, thrusts them upward. Her fingers twist and pull.

It's like eating honey from a jar—no spoon, all probing tongue and drowning as she arches her back and whimpers softly. Her taste is like spring greens, earthy with an underlying sweetness and the tart of her juices. Forcing herself against my mouth, straining, turning her head, and twisting beneath me. Her leg muscles clench, tensing with the ebb and flow of her lust. I think: *this is the purest high.* Spinning then, losing myself in her excitement as she pulls my hair. Her body shudders, stiffening. She cries out, and then it's finished.

I'm kissing her shoulders, stroking her hair. My neck aches. Its dark in the tent, but the whole of her glows. Gooseflesh beneath my palms as she rouses herself, slides on top, and guides me between her legs.

She grips me, then lifts on her knees and drops. There's nothing subtle about it. With a grunt, I'm plunged inside of her and destroyed. I take her waist in my hands, she's weightless, lifting her, pressing my thumbs into the softness of her flesh. She throws her head back and tosses her hair, firing herself at me, jackhammering her pelvis with a hand on her clit.

It's louder than it has to be.

We work it like that for a while, her on top, me lunging below, and then fumble apart and wildly advance. She climbs onto her hands and knees, reaches behind, and looks back me while spreading her thighs. I shuffle forward, knocking the tent poles. Had we not been drunk, we might have used protection. As it was, we were stupid.

I gripped her shoulder and pulled her onto me; she pushed back with a growl. She drops her head, flexing her spine, and grinds her backside against my hips the way you rub out a stain. I coil a fist through her hair and yank it. She falls forward and reaches between her legs. This is good sex:

passionate, forceful. I'm getting close, losing dexterity. My eyelids raise and my head starts to spin. Focusing on the vigorous bounce, the thrust. Harder, faster. A second pair of hands climbs my waist. Fingers trace my stomach and throat and lips press the nap of my neck.

Awareness strikes me like a thunderbolt, but it's too late. I flood her womb, registering panic as an unfamiliar hand reaches between my legs and fondles my testicles. Spasming, firing into her but scarcely feeling it. Addie squirms, arching her back. She rocks against me and groans, driven over the edge, as I fumble away from her and turn.

"What the fuck!" I shouted.

The girl drew herself back, partially silhouetted against the open tent flap. She licked her lips and smiled. "What's wrong?" she asked.

I glared at her. "Are you kidding?"

Addie was still out of it, face down on the floor of the tent and writhing, gyrating her hips against the nylon as the aftershocks surged through her body. The stranger was crouched, animal-like. Her face was covered with freckles, but not a trace of blush showed on her skin.

"What's wrong?" she asked again, knitting her eyebrows together. She seemed genuinely confused. "Tonight we're one flesh." she said.

Her eyes sparkled, she reached out and touched my face and I pulled away. When her hand came back there was a droplet of jism on her fingertip, which she smilingly devoured. "Backsplash." she whispered, sucking her finger.

"What the fuck are you doing in here?"

"Joining you."

"No. You're not. Get out."

"Uh…okay…?"

"You weren't invited."

Addie drew herself from the floor. She pressed her face into her t-shirt, moping the sweat, then crawled past me. She took the girl by the hand and kissed her. "Of course she's invited," she said. "We're all the same tonight."

I felt dizzy. Seeing them kiss made my stomach turn. This is where I differentiate from other guys: girl-on-girl action has never turned me on, threesomes make me sick. The two least appealing things I could think of confronted me. I felt angry, overwhelmed. Most guys would feel different about it. For them, it would be a dream come true. Nine out of ten men jack-off to this kind of thing, it's been trending for decades. But not me, I'm the one percent. Intimacy isn't meant to be passed around. I don't view sex as a communal act and I think lesbians are for lesbians.

Pop aberration don't appeal to me.

Sex should be a love act between two people.

That isn't to say I'm vanilla. Like anything, it's taste. Everybody has a preference; I have mine. Some people fuck horses and that's sex too, bestiality, but the thought of drilling a house-pet turns my stomach. Like cellphones and plastic, some things just aren't natural.

"Get out," I told the girl.

"Why?" Addie hissed. "What's wrong with you? She doesn't have to go anywhere."

I looked at her. I could see we weren't on the same page. I was too zonked to articulate. Maybe I was in shock. After sex I felt drained enough and the thought of arguing drained me further. To explain wasn't worth it. Words fall on deaf ears when there's a barrier as deep as preference and abhorrence. Right or wrong, it doesn't matter. When people feel judged, their empathy vanishes.

"Okay," I said. "Then I'm out."

"What the fuck is wrong with you?"

"I'm not into this."

"What kind of man are you? This is every guy's dream. A threesome with two hotties. Are you fucking kidding me right now?"

"No." I said, gathering my clothes. "I'm leaving."

I tugged my shirt out from under her knee and pulled it over my head.

"I thought you were cool," Addie groaned. "I didn't realize you were such a…"

"Such a what?" I growled. "I don't have a say in what I like and don't like without being considered less of a man? Aren't I entitled to a preference? Or are preferences reserved for whores and perverts these days?"

"Who are you calling a pervert?"

"Nobody." I got my pants on and started tying my shoes.

"I think you're scared," she said.

"Think whatever you want. I'm not worried about it."

"I think I need to find a beer and another tent maybe," the other girl said, backing out through the flap. I found my flannel in the corner of the tent, ran my arms through the sleeves, and followed her through.

"Sorry to spoil the party," I said, buttoning my shirt.

She crossed her arms and shrugged, "Didn't you know?"

"Know what?"

"Oh boy." She rolled her eyes and walked away.

Through the tent flap Addie called for a guy named Max. "Max," she shouted. "Come and fuck me. I'm in the purple tent and my pussy is wet!"

I gathered my bearings and moved through the tents toward the fire. There was a breeze, it tickled the dreamcatchers, ringing their chimes, but I could barely hear them over the whisk of flailing nylon as bodies jounced against the tent poles. Cries of pleasure ripped through the night. Their heavy breathing. The grunt, the slap. The slow shrill whine of a female pile-driven to completion.

I felt sick.

All around me, the tents shook.

I glanced down an aisle and saw a dozen or so campers in the open. They were mounded in a half-circle around the fire, interlocked. Bodies chained together like orgiastic paper dolls. They looked like the exposed roots of a tulip—pale, bound, and ensnared—trailing from the discarded bulb. This is the weird flower: entropy in bloom, humid and ripe. A writhing mass of flesh, straining in the firelight like so many maggots in a rot blossom. They were conjoined vaginally, anally, orally. Every orifice skewered. Fluids spilling from the steaming folds in opulent trails as their bodies collided and were penetrated. The ones that took it up the ass grimaced, their pained expressions turning toward the firelight.

I locked eyes with a short-haired girl bent backward over a log. A man knelt between her thighs while another dropped onto his knees at her front, thrusting into her mouth.

I looked away.

Felt the ground tilt.

There was a smell, it overpowered the wood-smoke and pines and made the air seem thick. The sex scent of cock, tongue, and fingers breeching the moist hollows *en masse*. Real or imagined, my stomach clenched. I doubled over, spewing a pint of hot beer onto my shoes.

Generation Rome, the corporeal playground.

I wiped my mouth on my sleeve and started for the tree line. Outside one of the tents I found a can of Budweiser. There was a little left and I washed my mouth out with it, spitting a stream into the grass. It must have been around four in the morning.

The woods were an open door that looked shut, impossibly dark on all sides of the camp. To a man without a cellphone or a flashlight, nature poses a solemn threat. I wished for a lantern and a hatchet, then stepped in amid the pines. It was worth it, swallowing back the fear. Anything to get out of camp. The chances of encountering a bear were slim, I told myself. To the cougars and wolves, I had no rifle. I came in peace. My brief intrusion would hardly justify an impromptu mauling. They'd stalk and follow perhaps, peering through branches, but they'd leave me alone. I posed no threat. Besides that, what was a morsel compared to the smorgasbord I was leaving behind. If the animals were hungry, they had access to a buffet.

I ducked a branch weighed down with dreamcatchers, gently bumping the chimes, and glimpsed Dan a few yards away. He was standing between a man and a woman. It looked like an argument of some sort. The beam his flashlight bounced off the trees and tents as he held them apart. "Hold on!" he said, keeping the girl back as she lunged forward. "Just calm down now."

"I'm going to fucking kill him!" the girl snarled.

"Jesus H. Christ, lady. Hold on."

"You know what he did to my sister?"

The man in question raised his hands. "I don't want any trouble," he said, backing away. He was a big guy with a disfigured face. Dirty stitches ran along his jaw where the wounds were still raw and clotted. Exposed teeth glinted in the absence of a bottom lip, reflecting the beam of Dan's flashlight.

"You know he's got fucking AIDS?"

"You need to calm down, lady." Dan said, tightening his hold on her arms. "Yelling won't get you anywhere."

The guy with the stitches smiled grotesquely. "Yeah," he said, carefully scratching his jaw. "Calm down." The girl went ballistic. She threw herself at him, but Dan held her back. Her hair fell across her face and she showed her teeth like a wolf pup, panting.

"Look—if you can just calm down, we'll listen to you, okay?"

"That fucking bastard," she shouted. "He gave my little sister AIDS at the last one of these things. She didn't want to do it either. He made her do it, he raped her!"

"That's a lie." Stitchface said.

"No it isn't, you son-of-a-bitch!"

"Whoa there!" Dan shouted. "Calm your horses."

"Whoa there?" the girl raged. "Are you fucking kidding me? Really? Did you not just hear what—"

"I remember your sister." Stitchface said. He stepped forward confidently and smiled. "She was very horny."

"Arthur."

"You gave her AIDS you—you rapist bastard! I'm going to—"

"Lady, stop." Dan said, giving her a shake. He looked tired, bored with it. "You're being crazy here. This is a peace gathering. Whatever happened to your sister, didn't happen here, okay? I can assure you of that. And Arthur, he didn't have nothing to do with it either. Did you Arthur? If your sister caught something, that's not on us or anybody else here. Okay? Even if she did, weren't nobody made her come out and take her clothes off either way. That would have been her choice."

"You know what?" the girl laughed. "That's fine. Get AIDS. I hope he gives it to you all. But especially *you*, fuckface. I hope he blows his AIDS infected load right into your fucking eyes!"

She tore herself away from Dan and stepped back, rubbing her arms. "Fuck you all," she said, then turned away and marched into the forest.

Stitchface tried to spit, an action made difficult without both lips. Failing, it clung to his chin and he had to wipe it away.

"I don't know what she was talking about, Dan," he said. "I got pretty drunk last time and I don't remember much, but you know me, you know I would never lay a hand on a girl unless she wanted me to.'

"That's okay, Arthur. The girl clearly has some problems. As you know, there's no helping who gets in. Sometimes we get a loony, is all."

Dan clapped him on the shoulder and they walked together toward camp. "So forget it," he said. "Be the better man. Tonight is about unity and peace."

"Crazy bitch," Stitchface said. "I'm really sorry about that Dan, but I know you're right."

"Nothing to apologize for."

They disappeared, wandering back through the tents, and I made a decision. I turned into the woods and ran after the girl.

III.

"Hey, wait up!"

I bounded through the brush and caught up to her, huffing. She turned on me, brandishing a rock. "Back off asshole!" she hissed. "I won't hesitate to beat your fucking head in if I have to."

"Oddly enough," I panted. "You're not the first person to threaten me tonight. The first was some guy named Dillon, worried about his sister."

"What do you want?"

"Nothing," I shrugged. "A ride home, maybe."

She narrowed her eyes. A solitary beam a moonlight breached the foliage, skewering the air between us. She shifted her stance and crossed her arms.

"Why?" she asked.

"What they're doing back at camp…I'm not into that."

"You were there, weren't you? Or did you just happen upon it, lah-dee-fucking-dah, walking through the woods?"

"I was there, yeah. I thought it was just a party. I didn't know anything more, until I did. Then I decided I'd rather walk than stay. I saw you leaving so I thought I'd ask. It's a long way back to Boise. I doubt I could hitch-hike."

"You don't have a car?"

"I came with a friend."

"And?"

"She's staying," I explained.

The girl stared at me, chewing her bottom lip. The rock was still in her hand. Either the moonlight did wonders for her, or she was beautiful. She had nut-brown hair so long it reached her waist, fierce eyes and eyebrows, and a smattering of freckles across the bridge of her nose. She was wearing blue floral-patterned leggings and a pair of Doc Martins; the boots were fashionably battered, the laces scalped and the eyelets threaded through with colorful ribbons. On top, she wore a loose blouse and a jean jacket about three sizes too big with the sleeves rolled back on an exposé of bracelets. Looped around her neck, a silver chain and a razorblade with a name on it. *Johnny*, engraved in the steel, glittering against her chest.

"Okay," she said. "I'll bite. But don't think I'm a cunt. You walk in front. And just keep in mind what I said before. I've got this rock, one wrong move and I'll lobotomize the back of your fucking head, buddy. The only reason I'm trusting you at all is I'm fuck-all afraid of getting lost."

"Fine by me." I stepped past her. We started through the woods and she followed at a careful distance, watching my back. "I'm Lucas by the way."

"Diane."

"Well, here we go Diane. Where did you park?"

"Alongside the road."

"What direction?"

"I don't fucking know, straight."

"I just don't want to lead us off a cliff or something."

"Fine. And I don't want to hit you either, so just watch yourself. If there's a cliff, you're going over it first."

We were quiet after that. I turned my attention to the ground and kept a steady pace. The trail was indistinct. Neither of us had a flashlight so we had to watch our feet, being careful of rocks and branches. We moved slowly, navigating tight copses of brush and fallen trees, kicking up carpets of pine-needles and sheaves of discarded bark as we clambered over them, working our way through the darkness. Moonlight breeched the canopy on occasion, tracing our path in and around the trees. Tufts of grass and mossy boulders were bathed in radiance before plunging back into shadow.

I was far away, locked in my head.

It's always like that. Whenever I walk at length, the wheels start to turn. My mind fires up, attempting to sort through all the crap and de-stress. Usually it works. Tonight I was overloaded. Bummed out about Addie and feeling the early ache of a hangover blossoming in my temples.

I wasn't paying attention when the man appeared. I was staring at my feet. Diane gasped. I looked behind me at her and walked straight into his chest, startled, grabbing for support as I tripped over a root and fell backward. Diane pushed me away out of her way and hurled the rock at the figure. It bounced off a tree somewhere and hit the ground near our feet.

"I'm not going to harm you," the man said, lifting his hands. The sleeves of his sweater were loose, bagged-out, and hung open against the whiteness of his wrists.

"Don't think it goes both ways cocksucker," Diane said, leveraging a branch from a blackened stump. It broke off into a jagged point and she thrust it at him. "Now back the fuck up!"

"Do you ever not swear?" I asked, climbing to my feet and brushing the dirt off of my clothes. I recognized the man immediately. "It's fine, he's the—"

"I know who he is,"

"Okay then, chill. I doubt he's out here to steal our kidneys."

"Honestly, you startled me as much as I seem to have startled you," Peter said, lowering his hands. "I didn't expect anyone else would be out here."

"Fuck that, what are *you* doing out here, buddy? Diddling kids?"

Peter pursed his lips. He bowed his head, absorbing the insult, then calmly replied. "Meditating, actually."

"Right. And I've got two cunts. You expect me to think that you came out here just to meditate? And miss out on all the fun they're having back there. Listen asshole, women get to vote these days. Do you think I'm stupid?"

"I never participate," he replied. "I am the head. As such, it is not my place. There is a clearing in the forest and a small stream that overlooks the lower valley. Very peaceful. I was just returning from there."

"Sounds glorious," she sneered. "How very yogi of you. But while you're out frolicking in the woods my sister is back home trying to work up the courage to tell our parents that she's got AIDS. How do you think that's going to go over? Especially when she tells them that she got raped at an orgy. I was there too. A guy forced himself on her. One of your buddies. You know who I'm talking about," she drew a finger across her chin. "His face is all fucked up now."

"Understand," Peter said. "The individual does not exist within the mind of our community. We gather for worship, to be as one, and all are invited." He looked at me. "I know very few of the attendees on a personal level. As with all flocks, they come and go."

"If the police knew about these little parties of yours, I think they'd be pretty fucking repelled, maybe even inclined to take a hard look at whatever shit you're trying to pull with this crap. Orgies are one thing, but knowingly spreading a disease, that's a fucking felony."

"I don't understand."

"Read my lips, asshole. You could go to jail. Back to whatever madhouse you came from. That guy with the face? He spreads his disease around and you're fucked for enabling him. The bastard gave it to my sister and who knows how many others. Do something about it."

Peter frowned. He sighed and touched the tips of his fingers to his brow. "Obviously I knew nothing of this," he said, looking up at her. "I will see to it upon my return."

"You better," she said. "Because I've got your fucking name. Peter. You were in with Laura's dad. I've also got your Facebook account. That'll be enough to go on. I'll see to it you're fucked on either end by a judge and a lawyer for accommodating criminal transmission of a disease."

"This information makes me no happier than it does you. We're a peaceful community. If this individual you speak of poses a threat, then he must be expelled. Certainly. Christ has no tolerance for such men in his sacred temple."

"That's right, asshole. Now you're getting it."

"I am in your debt for this. I will pray for your sister's recovery."

"There is no recovery."

"All things are possible through Christ who streng—

"Fuck off asshole."

She shifted the spearpoint and motioned him to leave. He smiled weakly. As he walked past, I glimpsed his face. The enlightened glow was diminished. I could see the varnish beginning to crack. Beneath the polish, he was scared, masking his concern with a look of humble indifference. He disappeared into the forest and was swallowed by the dark. We could hear the slap of his sandals against his feet as he receded, making his way back toward camp.

Diane nudged my arm. "Come on," she said. She hurled the tree branch into the woods and we started walking. I buttoned my shirt and stuck my hands in my pockets.

"That was weird." I said.

"And you're surprised? Let's just get out of here."

"Hey, you didn't swear. You must be warming up to me, huh?"

"Shut up. *Shit-for-brains.*"

"That didn't last long. Oh well. We'll probably be at the highway soon. But hey, I've got to ask. If everything you say is true, why didn't you just take that guy to court like you said and be done with it?"

"It's not as easy as you think."

"Rape? Seems pretty straight forward. Then there's that thing about transmitting a disease you mentioned. I'm sure others would back you on it."

"You wouldn't understand. It's complicated."

"Complicated how?"

"Don't push it."

"Do you think he knew? The guy with the face."

"I don't fucking know! Jesus Christ. It doesn't matter anyways. Whether he knew or not, the whole thing is fucked up. What kind of people do this kind of thing anyways? Orgies, really? To look at them, you'd think they're all normal. I'm mean they're our age. It's the twenty-first-fucking-century."

I shrugged. "They like it, I guess."

"Yeah and everybody has a preference too, right? Some guys just like to rape drunk girls. They can't help it. It's an urge they were born with, same as pedophiles. God, I'm so sick of that shit."

"Hey, I'm with you," I said. "That's why I left. I don't even know how I'm going to get my phone back. The friend I mentioned? The one I came with? Well, my phone is locked in her truck."

"Too bad."

"Yeah. I just bought the thing too. Didn't get insurance for it either. I could probably get ahold of her somehow and get it back."

"You don't have her contact?"

"Christ no. I hardly know her at all. We met a few days ago in an arcade and she invited me to this thing. She said it was just a party."

"An arcade?"

"It's kind of a bar. How did you figure out this was happening tonight anyway?" I asked. "Are you on some kind of mailing list?"

"No," she snorted. "Believe it or not, they have a Facebook group."

"Geez. They do these all the time?"

"Yep."

"How'd your sister get pulled into it?"

"We were invited to the last one, heard about it through a friend. Her father was a real religious nut. He got put away awhile back, prison or something, I'm not really sure. Anyway, I guess he did time with—"

"Peter."

"How'd you know?"

"You mentioned it back there," I said, glancing at her as she walked up beside me. "Something about a madhouse."

"That's right. My friend Laura. Her dad mentored him or something like that. When Peter got out, he contacted Laura. Maybe her dad asked him to, I don't know. Anyway he invited her to one of his parties. Like she'd even be interested. She fucking hates her dad."

"But you went?"

"My sister and I did, yeah." She glanced at me and her eyes said: *sorry.* "It sounded cool."

"I can relate."

"We were curious. I mean, even if the guy running the thing was a creep, it seemed okay. Like a hippie thing, you know? And there were other people going too..."

"It seemed safe."

"Yeah. So, we went. At first it was fine. The campfire, cool people, all that. Just a chill little gathering."

"Super chill."

"Exactly. And everybody still had their clothes on. Peter played some songs on the guitar and then…well, you

know...they all started fucking. After that happened, we left.
Or at least, we tried to. Julie was really drunk. She wandered off
while I was looking for my purse and when I found her again,
she was in one of those tents with that fucking goon on her. He
had a lip back then. She was conscious and all, but she didn't
know what she was doing. That's why it would be tough to
prove rape."

"You know how that guy lost his lip?"

"No clue. He probably got it caught on the tail pipe,
sucking off his pickup truck."

"He seems like the big truck type for sure. What do you
bet he has one of those ball-sacks on the trailer hitch—"

"Hey," she said, stopping dead in her tracks.

"What's wrong?"

"Did you hear that?"

I stepped on a pinecone, turning, looking in back of us,
and the crunch was resounding. My senses turned to static,
probing the dark. We were surrounded. The trees were pressing
in on us, squeezing shut. It felt as though they'd made a
decision, a hostile one, and were now abruptly locking hands to
prevent our passage. I felt nervous, suffocated. I couldn't hear
anything, turning my eyes over the shadows, seeing nothing,
but I knew we were being watched.

Diane touched my arm apprehensively, moving closer.
We were shoulder-to-shoulder, listening to our own breath, and
breathing through our teeth.

I felt the urge to run, but where?

Forests are alive, we rarely consider that going in. Here
there are no walls to press against, no doors to hide behind.
Triggered by our own sudden awareness, we panic. And in one
swift motion, nature swallows us whole. Without our
cellphones and gunpowder we're dragged downward, kicking
and screaming, to a lower rung on the food chain.

"What's out there?"

"It's like something...not human."

We glanced at each other and locked eyes. Our hearts drummed against our chests. Then over her shoulder I saw it. It stepped from behind a tree, dragging a hoof through the weeds, and looked at us. A specter, dead-white and sallow, ribs protruding from shaggy ghost-like skin. Its horns were the shape of nerves in body charts, pronged and fingered and grey, spreading out above it against the black of night.

I grabbed Diane's arm. "Run," I said, pulling her after me into the trees.

We crashed through foliage, shielding our faces with our hands. Branches cracked beneath our feet. Limbs juddered and flexed, snapping off our shoulders as we ran, sinking to our ankles in the dirt and kicking up dust.

In the dark there are monsters, that's why we have candles and campfires. As kids we treasured nightlamps and glow-in-the-dark star sets. Nighttime reminds us of our vulnerability. Divorced from our light sources, the wilderness presses in. Up against nature, IQ doesn't even begin chart.

"What the fuck was that!" Diane shouted, slowing to a halt. She put her hands on her knees, catching her breath. Fear had driven us deeper into the woods than we had realized.

"Ghost deer," I gasped.

"A what?"

"A ghost deer or something, how the hell should I know?"

"It looked evil."

"Yeah exactly."

"Deer aren't evil."

"They're no supposed to be." I said, examining the endless tract of forest that surrounded us. "Well, this is just great. I think we're lost now."

"What do we do?" she asked.

"I don't know."

"Can't we go from here? We'll just walk in the same direction."

"What direction? We were running all over the place." I put my back against a tree and slid into a crouch. "We'll probably have to wait for the sun to come up."

She crossed her arms, idly kicking the piles of twigs that blanketed the ground. Crickets chirped, a breeze swayed loose needles and the branches creaked. The trees themselves were like cell bars, a boundless stretch of narrow grey trunks, thrust upward and blotting out the sky, receding row-upon-row into darkness. Here and there, their craggy bark was burst open, revealing trails of dripping yellow sap, and their roots lurched up from the soil in humps and elbows and ancient thirsting coils. Looking at the forest made me dizzy. I covered my face and pressed my palms against my eyes.

"Hey," Diane called. "Check it out, maybe we're not so lost after all."

"What do you mean?"

I pushed my back off the tree and stood. She was standing a few paces away, looking down at me from the crest of a small hill. "I think I can see the highway from here," she said as I joined her.

Through a breech in the forest we were faced by open sky. The ground below sloped into a short bed of angular scree then opened onto a clearing spotted with sagebrush and thistle. A narrow stream carved a tract down the center, feeding a thick copse of tall grass on either shore. The moon shone down, it struck the earth weightlessly and the tree-tops were dipped in silver. Taillights glided in the distance beyond the trees.

"Looks about a mile off," I said.

She put her hands on her hips. "Yeah, I think so too. We can probably make it in an hour if we go in a straight line."

I started down the slope, slipping through the scree on my heels and holding my arms out for balance. She followed behind me, scattering rocks. They leapt against the backs of my legs and bounded down, spinning into the thistles.

When we reached the base, she took a phone out of her coat pocket and ignited the display. "If we make in an hour, we can catch the people commuting into town and get a ride to my car if we have to. It's fucking five in the morning."

"You've had a phone this whole time?"

"Yeah, so? There's no service."

"A flashlight would have been nice."

"Nope. I'm on twelve percent. Once we're out of here I might need battery, especially if we can't find my car. I should have service by the highway."

"Tell that to the ghost deer."

"A flashlight would have changed things so much?"

"You never know," I shrugged, walking over to the stream. The grass and weeds were sluiced by silvery rapids where they overhung the banks. It was about two feet wide and three feet in the ground. The water itself wasn't deep, splashing over pebbles and gurgling pleasantly. Algae grew around the reeds and Jesus-bugs skipped beneath the banks in shadow. "You think it's safe to drink from here?"

"I wouldn't. You might catch giardia."

"You think?" I crouched down, dipping my hands in the water, and splashed my face. "It feels good on the skin anyways."

"Jump all the way in, I dare you."

I stand up, smiling, and my head explodes. *Crunch.* Old wood turning to powder against the back of my skull. Before I can recover, the branch comes down a second time, swung hard across my shoulders, and I'm sent sprawling into the water. I collide with the opposite bank, my shoulder strikes it and the soft ground turns to mud, giving way, while the rest of me is swept under and starts to drown. It's less than a foot deep but I'm dragging sand. I shove myself above the water, gasping, and a bootheel pushes me back under. Another rocket goes off against my head and my whole body turns to rubber.

Moments later the weight recedes. I roll onto my back, choking up water. Laying there in the slow current, against the rocks, and spinning. When I open my eyes, the sky drops down and hits me. *Wham.* A voice asks: *Does it hurt?*

I answer: Yes.

Any idea who hit you?

No.

I think they used a log.

I groan and stop responding. Annoyed, the voice recedes. And there goes consciousness leaving my addled brain. The darkness envelopes me and I sink into a noiseless oblivion. My body goes first. There's a tingle in my neck as my toes go numb. I'm laid out in cold water, but the current feels warm, splashing the back of my head. I'm about to go under, really pass out, then Diane brings me back. Her scream cuts through the fade and reaches me.

I come to.

Splashing, sitting up. Through a blur, I see her twisting on her ankles, grabbed by her hair. A big guy laughs and hauls her back. He's about thirty-percent beer gut in profile. She swings her arms at him and he knocks her down. His boot impacts her ribs and the flounce of her hair is a shimmering arch against the night sky. The subsequent grunt comes from deep in her guts as she struggles onto her hands and knees.

I crawl out of the stream and drag myself onto the grass. My clothes are water logged and my head feels like a beating drum. I make it onto my feet, scraping the dirt with my fingertips, and stumble forward. The assailant half turns and I'm able to see his face, a beaming network of scar tissue and teeth, the stitches catching moonlight and cutting across his jaw like railroads tracks.

"You want to know if I've got AIDS?" he asks, towering over her as she crawls through the brush. He snaps his belt loose and drags it free from his jeans. His teeth show through the old wound and his eyes are dark and sunken. He throws the belt over her neck, yanking her backward against his knees. "Nosey bitch. It's none of your damn business what I've got."

She chokes as he twists the leather, tightening the noose. "Come on, now." he says. "Speak up honey, I was hoping for an argument."

I slip trying to pick up a rock. Lifting it seems impossible. I have to roll it onto my stomach then heave, forcing it up over my head. He doesn't notice me. I'm insignificant, a worm on its back in the tall grass.

"Okay, fine," he says, letting the belt free. She drops forward, clutching her throat, and rolls onto her side, coughing. "Maybe that'll teach you to mind your own fucking business next time."

I come at him from behind, swinging the rock down against his neck. My aim is bad. I trip in the brush and it clips his ear and bounces off his shoulder. Instead of falling down he turns and shoves me backward.

"You little son-of-a-bitch," he growls, rubbing his shoulder. "You trying to kill me? I don't even know who the fuck you are. Lay down, go to sleep, whatever. This doesn't involve you."

"You'll kill her."

"Kill her? Shit. I just wanted to teach her a lesson is all. I'm done now anyway. They tossed me out back there because of her bullshit. She attacked my reputation. How do you expect me to feel?" He picked up the belt, ran it back through the loops, then tucked his shirt into his jeans. He cinched the buckle tight about his waist and smiled. "See? No worries. I'm done now."

Diane wasn't.

I watched her get to her feet. She reached for her necklace, swaying, then took the razorblade between her fingers and broke it away from the chain. He didn't hear her coming until it was too late. Something crunched underfoot. He turned in time to shield his face and she buried the razor lengthwise in his palm.

He reacted quickly. He might have broken her nose if she hadn't tripped. His fist glanced off her jaw, throwing her backward onto the ground.

"Jesus!" he howled, holding his hand up.

Blood streamed from the wound and ran down his wrist, soaking the sleeve of his shirt. He pinched the tiny blade, wincing, and drew it free of his palm. Moonlight struck the wetness, coloring it black. He dropped the razor and clenched his fist with an audible squelch. "You *fucking* whore."

He was on top of her before she could get away. He pushed her down and straddled her waist, pinning her arms beneath his knees. She kicked out, thrashing hopelessly as he used his good hand to squeeze her jaws apart. He forced her mouth open and shoved his palm against her lips.

"You really want to know if I've got something?" he shouted, smearing her face with it. "Now you can find out."

She gagged. Her head rolled from side-to-side and she tried to scream, choking on his blood.

I threw myself at him magnificently; you'd think I was well-slept and sober and with a firm cranium in lieu of one half-bashed to pulp. We tumbled through the brush then spilled into the water. The narrow banks sloughing into the stream, collapsing beneath out weight. Water sloshed the grass and I was on top of him, leveraging his face into the mud while his shoulders bucked. He tried to get ahold of me but his arms wouldn't reach. I ducked his hands. His fingers flexed, grabbing at empty air, and I continued to apply my weight.

Then I let off. He came up for air, gasping. I fell against the shore. Before he could recover, Diane wadded into the stream and stepped on the back of his head. She held her foot there, keeping him under, till the bubbles stopped.

"Diane." I said.

We looked at each other and she rolled her eyes. "Son-of-a-bitch." She grabbed him by the shirt and hauled him out of the water. He rolled onto his side, coughing as the water backed out of his lungs.

"Let's go," she said, walking toward the woods.

IV.

We made it to the highway just in time to see the sirens. There was smoke in the distance at our back, spiraling up from the forest in an ugly grey pillar. Fire engines came from the nearest town, barreling through. We sat on the roadside and watched them pass as the sun came up.

"You think it's them?" Diane asked. She was hugging her legs, resting her chin on her knees. There were still traces of blood on her face, a little in her nose and some at the corners of her mouth.

"It would make sense."

"I wonder how it happened."

"Who knows. It probably just got out of hand. One of tent might have caught."

"Could be."

"Pretty hard to tend a fire at orgy."

Several ambulances roared by following after the fire engines. We watched their flashing lights disappear down the road in a veil of dust. "If anyone got hurt," she said. "I'll probably find out."

"How's that?"

"I work at the hospital."

"Oh," and we were both thinking the same thing. About the outcome of the blood test she'd have to take. "We should have stopped one of the ambulances," I said.

"They're not supposed to stop."

"It's not like we're hitchhikers," I touched the back of my head where, beneath the matted hair and dried blood, it felt like a lump of wet cereal.

"They wouldn't know that."

"We could call, you've got your phone."

"It died."

We both looked down the road as a silver Mercedes came into view, speeding toward us. I hurried onto my feet and waved. The car slowed down as the driver peered through the windows at us. It pulled over fifty yards away and honked. I looked at Diane. "You okay?"

"Yeah," she said, stretching out her hand. I took it and helped her up. "Let's get out of here."

We walked to the car. I opened a door and eased myself into the back-seat while Diane took the front.

"Geez, what happened to you?" the driver asked as we buckled out seatbelts. She cringed visibly at the blood on our clothes coming into contact with the leather seats.

"We got lost," I said.

She asked if we knew anything about the fire. I told her we didn't, then we rode in silence. Eyeballing the blood on Diane's face, she offered her a business card. "I'm an attorney," she said, glancing at me in the rearview mirror.

I was fading. I'd pressed my face against the window and could hardly keep my eyes open. Through the glass I saw a carcass on the side of the road. Its legs were bent in every direction and its neck was broken. Its skin was a ghostly pallor. I put my hand on Diane's seat. "Did you see that?"

The driver overheard me.

"An albino deer," she said, glancing over her shoulder. "Really too bad. They're pretty rare. There's a lot a wildlife that gets killed out here. This stretch is infamous for it. I'll bet that gets picked up by the end of the day though. Someone will get it. Depending on the condition, you could make a pretty penny. Collectors go nuts for albinos."

"Collectors?"

"Yeah, taxidermy. You don't hear about it much these days, but it's still popular. From what hear, there's a huge audience for it up around Post Falls and Coeur d'Alene."

"It was a deer," I said, touching Diane's elbow. "Nothing but a white deer."

THE LEGS

This is an annoying consideration, but right now someone is out there putting in the work to surpass you. It might be at the office or at the gym. It might even be behind your back; with your husband or wife (casual text messaging is a dangerous game). You may know them or you may not. They might just as well be your neighbor as a complete stranger or your closest friend. Either way, they're getting ahead.

Zach had mild Hidradenitis Suppurativa and he wasn't happy about it. It's a relatively uncommon condition and it was nothing but dumb luck that he was possessed of it at all. It grew in his armpits primarily and sometimes against the backs of his ears, occurring in large tunneling boils like thick power cables swelling up from beneath his skin.

Funny, he thought on Friday night, driving his dinged, rusted, and yellow Datsun pickup truck through downtown Boise: there are gay celebrities, disabled celebrities, even dog celebrities. Celebrities of all race and gender. But there are no celebrities with skin conditions.

Name one.

Zach couldn't, and for that simple reason his dreams were shattered. He worked hard at the gym, lifting weights to alleviate his frustration or perhaps compensate for his condition. If somebody was going to be getting ahead, then, in this particular respect, Zach intended to be that somebody. His physique was exquisite for his efforts, although he never showed it off completely. He avoided going shirtless at whatever cost and didn't own a single tank-top in his wardrobe. A fear of exposure plagued him whenever he lifted his arms.

He imagined the Hidradenitis Suppurativa spilling from his armpits, thrust forth from his anatomy, swollen and purple and hanging there out in the open for all to see. Of course, Zach had no clue how fortunate he was. In more severe cases, Hidradenitis Suppurative can also occur in the groin area. This encourages even greater shame, halting all but the most vapid of sexual encounters. By comparison, Zach was oversensitive.

He, like most, was self-important in his suffering.

That night he wore a red tartan flannel, blue jeans, and his best pair of black Justin brand cowboy boots. His hair was freshly cut and his face was clean shaven. In theory, the glowing pride of a rural state. Dimples in his cheeks, good posture behind the wheel. The truck cab reeked of hot sun-rotted upholstery and dust, and his aftershave battled to mask the scent. He drove with the windows down, listening to country music.

It was the perfect summer night. Boise was alive with implants and locals alike. Thick legged farm girls dressed with belts and in boots with their windblown skirts pressed tight against their crotches, standing at the crosswalks while rangy tall boys prowled behind them in their tee-shirts as Zach rumbled by in his truck in search of parking.

It's the Californians, you know? They move here and take up all the parking. And then the city expands and puts parking meters way out where there were none before. Christ Almighty. Everything changes for the worst.

No, that's not true.

Change can be both forward and back, it's nonlinear. What we really mean when we say that things change is that they advance; like when cancer runs its course and winds up terminal. It's usually for the worst.

Yes. All roads lead to shit.

So after a while, frustrated, Zach pulled into an alleyway and left the truck outside an old grease spattered steel door and some trash bins. The police had better things to do on a Friday night than to pass out parking tickets. Besides that, what's to say that he, Zack, didn't work inside and that the truck wasn't parked there beside the door for a purpose? Like a pickup or a delivery.

Nothing.

It's fine, bucko.

Zach made his way back to the street with his hands in his pockets and then joined with civilization onto the sidewalk. He was meeting a friend outside the 10 Barrel at 9pm.

Yo, somebody said in passing. Nice boots.

Thanks, Zach replied, looking back over his shoulder at the guy. Then said, Prick, under his breath as he continued down the sidewalk. An implant form California, obviously. Frat boy cocksucker. Zach didn't need his approval to live.

Ahhh downtown Boise in the summer. So hot it burns your underarms. And your balls collect sweat for the licking in the confines of your jeans. Girls in summer dresses. And all the little sidewalk patios, crowded and caged off and cool with mistifiers and hanging plants and the delightful chime of wine glasses and laughter. Everybody is agreeable except for the homeless pantomime with the flowing beard and the bedroll, marching angrily down the sidewalk or sitting in Dawson Taylor waving his arms.

And Zach is glowing, positively radiant tonight. He rounds the corner and meets his friend and they shake hands and slap each other on the back and say things like: Geez, and Sonofabitch, and Hot Damn, and Hey Man. And then head down the street to a suitably rustic bar and order several beers and a platter of french fries before the kitchen closes.

I don't know man, Zach's friend said. You get what's coming to you. Girls deserve it.

Yeah yeah yeah, Zach agreed with his friend, sucking down another beer. They both drink their beer from bottle because it tastes better that way and because historically beer spills less that way if you need a cold one while driving the tractor, which they grew up doing and always did and so were predisposed toward having a preference for.

If you could have a little cunt now and then without all the baggage, boy wouldn't that be great. Zach's friend took a swig of cheap beer and belched. God damn it, how's the gym?

Been great, man. Really great.

Getting ripped?

Hell yeah bro.

Getting pumped?

Hell yes.

That's great, I'm really happy for you buddy, he slapped his gut through his bleach stained tee shirt and adjusted the bill of his hat. I'm a fat slob but all this extra gut turns to dick at night.

That's a good one, Zach chuckled. I like that one.

You get any pussy lately?

Nah, I've been focusing on the gym.

Why? he furrowed his brow. What's the point if don't get you laid?

Their table was set by the entry and at that exact moment the door swung open and crashed against the back of Zach's chair and in walked three young girls with wobbling breasts like jelly molds and their dresses clinging to their crotches. Zach stood up but didn't know what to say because Zach is a typical fuck-up hick and with a sickening skin condition that made him cripplingly insecure. He always felt it creeping out of his armpits like raw oysters. Big, runny, bulbous, tumescent, purple tunneling cysts on an otherwise perfect body. If not for that, Zach might have been the American Dream. Square jawed, red blooded, burgeoning born-again Christian boy with stars and stripes in his eyes. But Hidradenitis Suppurativa grew in place of hope for realized dreams. Instead of the America Ideal, Zach was a cunt.

Zach was tall.

Zach was stupid.

He excused himself and sat back down at the table while the girls giggled and bounced and waved their tits in the direction of the bar.

Jesus Fucking Christ! his friend howled, banging the table top and rattling the empty bottles together. You see the utters on that whore? The one in the center? Jesus! Why didn't you say nothing? What's the point of having all those muscles if you don't use them for snatch?

A man approached their table and slapped Zach on the back. He looked like a yuppie despite his unruly beard and mop of shaggy hair. Zach, my man, he said. Good to see you out and about bud.

Who are you? Zach's friend asked, abhorred by the intrusion.

Hello man. I'm his neighbor, I live behind him, he said then turned back to Zach. Hey, Zach buddy, you got a second? I was hoping to run something by you.

Uh yeah, sure.

Zach's neighbor waited for Zach to stand but Zach is a typical no-fucks-given oblivious moron and didn't budge. He takes hints like a latchkey kid with shit for parents takes discipline. Not at all. Stupid redneck.

When Zach's neighbor saw that Zach wouldn't be stepping out with him, he shrugged and resigned to shout into Zach's ear as privately as possible. He leaned close, conscious of Zach's friend glaring at him from beyond the cityscape of empty bottles and crumpled napkins on the table.

So, he said loudly, trying to penetrate the noise of the bar while whispering at the same time. You know since we've finished work on the addition to the house our master bedroom window faces yours directly across the alleyway.

Zach nodded.

It's really easy to see inside, his neighbor continued. And anyway, my wife is…well, she's really very okay with that. You understand? She likes it. She likes the way our bedroom windows face each other across the alleyway. And I was thinking, if you wanted to, you could look in and we'd leave the blinds open for you.

Yeah? Zach replied, puzzled. What do you mean?

I mean it wouldn't be free, that'd spoil the fun. But if you wanted to pass me like fifty bucks or something, we'd be totally down to put on a show for you. My wife is great, you know? Really wild. We would even be willing to take requests if you wanted. I mean, it turns her on you know? You have my phone number right, Zach?

Zach drained his beer, flushing the color of not-quite-ripe strawberries, and his neighbor stood up straight and smiled at him.

The bar was crowded.

People kept bumping Zach's chair.

You might not believe any of what I'm telling you about Zach and Zach's neighbor, but I can assure you, it's absolutely true. People are like this in real life. Perverted and sick. They're twisted even though they don't always seem that way. Even here in our blessed rural state of Idaho. Just a few days ago I was passing through Garden City when I was confronted by two grotesque prostitutes and—

"Alright, alright, get it moving. What happened next?"

Yes, sorry, I'm very passionate about morality and ethics and the way they both seem to be corroding and crumbling all around us, even in Boise. But back to Zach, yes. His neighbor standing there, breathing through his mouth like some asthmatic geek while Zach felt awkward and didn't know what to say. He didn't know how to respond to this sudden and perverse voyeuristic proposition so he drank his beer and his cheeks continued to burn red and his friend finally snapped the silence between them with a loud sigh and belch and then ordered more beer. Zach tried to avoid looking at his neighbor. He stared at the seams in the table where the joints had started to separate until the son-of-a-bitch finally took a hint and wandered off and his friend returned with several beers in amber bottles clenched by their necks between his fingers. He set them on the table with a crash and eased back into his chair watching the door as a stream of succulent young girls flowed through it and crowded around the bar with their tits on full display through their skimpy blouses.

Fucking good chicks here, he said.

I agree.

Who was that weirdo that was talking to you?

He lives in back on my place with his wife.

What did he want?

He wanted me to pay him fifty bucks to watch them fuck.

Perverts, he grunted. I'm sick to death of fucking perverts. Our morality and ethics are corroding these days. Even in Boise. But oh well, he said shaking his head. Jesus Christ, I'm horny as a fucking bull tonight.

Zach didn't respond because Zach was impudent and couldn't have sex despite his big muscles and the Hidradenitis Suppurativa was disgusting and the smell of his rotting armpits seeped from his shirt like windblown shit in putrid waves. Also because Zach is practically retarded. And most people don't

know that or even think it because Zach is tall. A great big
grinning all-American hick with dimples in his cheeks and a
preoccupation with the vilest pornography all involving saggy
breasted older women with stomach and thighs like cottage
cheese and a morbid willingness to deepthroat anything warm
and with a pulse.

The night wore on. Hours passed until the threads
stuck out and Zach and Zach's friend drank all of the beer.

They drank so much beer and pissed so many times
that the water company was notified of a volume increase for
the bar that night. For the whole block that night actually. And
subsequently all the restaurant owners were peeved because
their dues were increased.

So, very drunk they left at around 2am and said their
goodbyes outside the door on the sidewalk and shook hands at
first and eventually (drunkenly) embraced before parting, each
in the opposite direction. Zach scratched his groin and when he
reached the end of the street, standing at the crosswalk, he
realized he couldn't remember where he'd parked the truck.
Zach could feel the rage in his armpits. The Hidradenitis
Suppurativa was boiling over, irritated by the hot summer
night, and his armpits where chafed and the underarms of his
shirt were stained with medications and sweat.

I'm so very drunk, Zach said, wobbling, mentally
retarded and physically deformed despite how far ahead he was
at the gym. Do you go to the gym, detective?

"Just get on with the story."

Alright, alright. Where was I?

"We want to know what happened to the girl."

Oh, that's right. I'm sorry. You see my knowledge of
these things—events such as those presently being described, is
vast, and situations such as this are so very common that I tend
to lose track. The stories all bleed together, one into another.
And the perverts bleed together too, one into another and
spilling their seeds into each other, splashing semen and

spreading disease with their lips, mixing blood and lust and moral decay.

You understand, I'm sure.

As I was saying, Zach reached the crosswalk. Fortunately, he was quite sober. Being a born-again Christian and his mother's favorite child, Zach had chosen not to drink at all that night. Okay he had one beer. His friend drank all the rest. Zach watched him toss beer after beer after beer down his throat and it disgusted him to the core because it was a further evidence of morality decay and the desperate need to self-obliviate. Immorality sloshing against the backs of our teeth and chewing through the enamel then running down our necks and pooling in the warm chamber between soft breasts and bellies and the cunts of cheap whores in cheap redneck bars where Nickelback still gets played and the bartenders are all fulsome and tattooed.

Zach was at the crosswalk.

He was standing there.

Which way should I turn, thought Zach. Big stupid confused Zach. Big, tall, all-American Zach with a brain tumor and a skin condition and a seriously inflated ego because he was so much taller than most other men and worked out at the gym and was considered handsome and fit by some. When he rode in his pickup truck or worked on the farm or said grace before dinner or walked his dog it mirrored the country music he was always listening to on the radio. Except for the theme of heartbreak. Zach didn't know heartbreak. He was an impermeably selfish prick and only used women for their fat oily twats and to ejaculate in them and he never fell in love. That was where his life deviated from the lore of popular country music.

He left the bar and reached the sidewalk and was faced with the option of either waiting for the walk signal and crossing the street or simply turning left and continuing down the sidewalk until he reached a crossing without a traffic light.

Zach (*Zach Peterson*) was an idiot. A big dumb idiot. He looked out into the night and watched the traffic pass and the surrounding bars vacate and everything at 1am resembled a bowel movement as the city flushed its guts and everyone headed for home.

He was at the crosswalk, deciding what to do. But the nebulous fog that enveloped his head didn't help. It was the alcohol. He saw the world around him through an amber-glass tint. Too many beers. Rotten on the inside, all-American. And all the disgusting cunts out and about in their short little skirts clinging to their crotches and their tits hanging out like fuckable pendulums and makeup on their eyes and cheeks and foreheads and on their pouty red duck lips pushed out to imply good dick sucking like night itself is the grandest little whorehouse in the world on a hot summer night in Boise fucking Idaho.

Zach loved it. God damn he loved it! Nights spent in sweltering bars sucking on beer bottles and rah-rah-rah talking with stiff cocks and inflated egos. He loved it. Which was typical for guys like Zach with the dimples and curly hair. But Hidradenitis Suppurativa was alive and well and calling the shots with regards to his sex life and ballooning egocentricity, so he suffered from extreme anxiousness. Even the gym couldn't counterbalance his continual spiraling into diseased depression and beer drinking and pimple picking self-hate.

Zach despaired.

He left the bar and came to the crosswalk and forgot where he had parked his fucking yellow truck. When you're tall your brain doesn't get enough oxygen and heat rises and cooks the oily pink matter like bubbling egg and beef stew. And when you've got handsome Andy Griffith dimples the wind shrieks when it passes over the sides of your face and deafens your hearing to small signals in the same way humans can't hear dog whistles. And his brain tumor was raging, 9-months pregnant and stomping on his temple and screaming through his blood.

Where did he park the truck? That god forsaken rust spotted piece of shit yellow Datsun. It's because of the Californians moving in that there's no convenient parking in Boise anymore. I remember when parking was free and they used to drive into town and you didn't have to always wait at the crosswalks standing rotting like a dead houseplant in your tennis shoes or Justin brand cowboy boots and the women didn't used to sweat so much with their stinking crotches on display. Imagine being squeezed from one of those fatty vessels. No wonder we're all fucked and nothing is clean. We slough free from the gutter twat, putrefying in the decaying vaginal canal before being squeezed into existence with the sour scent of rot on our sweet baby faces and growing in our hearts already like God created shit-bag losers and ordered them to procreate for laughs.

The pursuit of happiness? Bah!

But Zach was good, clean, and all-American. His mother went to church and was a religious cunt, and she cooked and cleaned the house and vacuumed the carpets and made Zach's favorite (cornbread with molasses) every Tuesday night when the family gathered together and played cards or monopoly and sometimes Jenga. The Hidradenitis Suppurativa came as a shock of course and derailed Zach's plans for being famous and ruined his life, but fucking oh well.

Bucko.

He didn't tell his mom or his dad and he didn't tell the preacher. He imagined stabbing his dermatologist to death with a wrench. Good riddance, cunt. And beer quelled the urge, so he worked out in the bar lifting beer bottles and beer kegs and clenching his pelvic floor muscles whenever he pissed.

He worked out in the gym and lifted weights and did bench press and grunted while doing curls while staring into his own lopsided retarded brain-tumor eyes in the gym mirror like a man at war with himself. The Hidradenitis Suppurativa absorbed all the beer and muddled his memory. He couldn't remember where he'd parked the truck, so when he exited the bar and they shook hands and he walked left and his friend turned right, he came to the crosswalk and felt very confused.

Tall, dumb.

He was contemplating the crosswalk when he smelled their squeezed feet. Ankle buckles and hot cheese, swaying on bone and suede leather. Then the perfume and canned fish wafting from their armpits and legs, and their sour alcohol breath flowing between swallows and incessant giggling and silly girl-talk as they came to the crosswalk and stood behind him. Zach sensed their tits penetrating the pocket of air at the small of his back like missiles. Short, fat, and jiggling. Loudmouth girls jangling the buckles on their cheap purses with their chunky asses squeezed into jean-shorts and skirts and wearing black whore-boots of course with their thighs soft and thick at the knee. They get their nails done every other day and Zach was aware of so many points at his back, threatening his spine.

Blah-blah-blah, one of the bimbos said to the other two and they all tittered like hens and chickens and were probably drunk on vodka or high on something fashionable and colorful and cute as the signal blinked and they followed Zach across the street. One of them was Hispanic. Zach could tell without looking because he had eyes in the back of his head. She had a mean face and long two-tone fingernails with little plastic stones glued onto them at the base and lots of cheap metal bangles on her arms and wrists.

Zach was used to being around Hispanic girls. They didn't get pregnant as easily as the skinny white girls he knew that lived in trailers or in modular homes in Garden City and grew up fishing and wearing hunting jackets and baseball caps. Of course Zach wouldn't know because he had flowering purple cysts growing in the creases between his legs and swelling up from his skin like raw oysters, so.

But they reached the other side and.

Zach wasn't sure where he parked the truck.

Zach lashed out violently at a crumbled bag on the sidewalk and kicked it into the street and tripped at the same time and the girls that were riding his ass the whole way across the street crashed into him from behind and they all cackled and apologized and the Hispanic girl shoved her tits in his face as he tried to stand up and he staggered backward and blushed and hurried ahead of them so he wouldn't have to tell them about his skin condition.

Everyone has a skin condition, the Hispanic girl said. And Zach said, No. Screaming. And hurled himself against the door and climbed into his pickup truck and started the engine and slammed the pedal straight to the floor and the truck lurched backward because it was still in reverse and slammed against the concrete wall.

Oh shit.

Zach's yellow Datsun was a piece of junk and the tailgate was always down because the latch was busted. It had been that way for so long that he accepted that it was likely beyond repair and drove with it down. To hell with it. But tonight it actually bothered him because if not for the additional two-foot blade-like projection, he might have had the time to react before slamming into the wall.

Motherfucking shit cunt, he screamed and climbed out of the cab to take a look at the damage. The moon flooded the alleyway like semen and it was a long canal like the ones that burrowed beneath the skin in his armpits and were filled with pungent off-white green and yellow putrescence.

Shit fucking cunt!

He'd backed into one of the girls and crushed her between his tailgate and the alley wall, separating the lower disks in her spine. And the force of the blade-like edge against her soft midsection had ripped her organs apart and cut her in half. Zach pulled the truck forward after checking that nobody else was around and the body separated like a piece of warm cherry pie as the lower half dropped onto the ground and the upper half tumbled into the truck bed and rolled over and her fingers clenched and her eyes twitched a little.

Christ almighty, fuck me, oh shit!

Zach lifted her torso by her underarms, spilling blood on his jeans, and hefted her into the nearest trash bin amid the piles of greasy black bags and spoiled milk smelling chunks of ripped cardboard. The Hidradenitis Suppurativa told him to deal with the legs now and get the fuck out of there. And Zach did. He climbed into the cab of the truck and rolled down the windows and turned on the radio (country music). He pointed the wheels straight and drove from the alley, joining with the last push of traffic out in the street headed home from the bars.

He thought: the world has become a festering shithole everywhere and even in Boise and the women climb into their beds around this time at night like beached whales and spread their legs and touch the damp spot between their labia like sticking your finger into a rot spot on an apple after whoring all night and coming home lonely. But beer and clear vodka and loud music and so many manly men with their stiff cocks and hairy forearms and bugling muscles made it okay. And Zach's muscles were the biggest but it didn't matter.

Zach drove home.

The end.

"Well," the detective said, pinching his brow. "That's that. Book him boys. There never was a Zach Peterson. We've got him dead to rights even without the legs."

Wait please I haven't quite finished. I can tell you about the legs.

He paused. "Oh yeah? No more of this Zach Peterson bullshit? You'll give it to us straight?"

Perhaps with a cup of coffee.

"Get it," he told one of the lesser cops and the lesser cop nodded and vacated the room. "You're on a short lease, remember that. Now tell us about the legs."

The legs, yes. Well after Zach—

"No, I don't want to hear about him. Tell us about *you*."

As I was saying—after Zach chopped the girl in half with his tailgate, I ducked behind the dumpsters in the alleyway to shield myself from view.

"So you were there."

Naturally. I'd decided to cut through the alleyway that night as a shortcut instead walking around the circumference of the block. There I was walking through it, the alleyway, through the grease puddles and oil trails when I saw this giant redneck (Zach) backing his lowered and razor-sharp tailgate repeatedly into the wall.

And the girl was sliced in half, of course, by the pressure. And the blood, there was so much blood. You really can't imagine it. It came out in a thick sludge like strawberry jam with the chunks left in, and pulp, and it spurted from her stomach and onto the wall and seeped down her legs and pooled in the truck-bed. And then it ran through the opening in the gate and down onto the bumper, and I could see the hot-pink of her guts and the shit-brown glistening of her liver and the flashes of mulched bone and her ribs were crushed and pushing out through her skin beneath her tits in bent broken points and she was dead immediately of course, the poor girl. Women are subjected to so much unfair abuse because of their sexual impulses and vile urges and moral bankruptcy. And decay and because they're weak. They get what they're asking for when they behave like animals like that and corrode and get cut in half. And then there are guys like Zach who think they're getting ahead of everybody at the gym with their muscles and sculpted obliques when in reality they're harboring shame for the gross horror festering beneath their arms.

So I hid behind one of the grease splattered bins and held my breath against the waft of dumpster stink and watched while he hauled her torso into one of the receptacles atop a pile of shiny black garbage bags. And the blood dripped all over his pants and he drove off covered in blood, blasting country music. What Zach didn't know, what he didn't realize, was that her purse strap had caught in the mechanism of the tailgate and had ensnared her belt and as he drove away, he was dragging her legs, flopping, behind him.

Zach mopped the sweat from his brow and.

Oh, thank you. *I accept the steaming cup of coffee from the police officer and inhale its warmth, feeling the heat through the walls of the Styrofoam.*

Fortunately there wasn't a lot of traffic that night (Thursday) and no one seemed to notice it, the legs or the shit smear of blood on the road. And Zach himself didn't notice it at first, the legs and the flapping of denim and blood splatter, cartwheeling at his back, until one of her boots came loose and was slung forward by gravity, impacting his rear-windshield with a thud. Zach checked his mirrors and.

Fucking!

He pulled over immediately and untangled the strap from her belt and threw the legs into the back of the trunk. But then he thought better of it and carried them to the front seat and shoved them down on the floorboard where they wouldn't be seen or fall out while driving. He tried to free the purse from the tailgate but the strap ripped and so he threw the purse into the weeds and left the remaining material (faux leather) hanging off the broken latch.

It was 2am and the beer was still oceanic in his guts, sloshing around and making him anxious so he decided to eat first before determining what to do next. Country boy that he was he drove to the all-night McDonalds on Orchard Street and pulled into the drive through behind another Datsun pickup (this one a flatbed). He tried not to look at the legs and her pelvis bones while he waited for his turn at the ordering speaker.

"Where were you at this point?"

I was watching. Zach ordered—

"Where were you watching from?"

I was across the street. Zach pulled up to the drive-through speaker and ordered a large diet coke and four plain cheeseburgers. He hated pickles. When he pulled up to the next window, the person (a man) taking his money squinted his eyes and because he was so short. He was so fucking short he could only see their legs through the cab window and he mistakenly thought Zach was with a woman. A whole woman. So he chuckled and congratulated *them both* on their Friday night and handed them the bag of hamburgers and the diet coke and said, I gave you two straws! Like some fucking la-di-da, and like Zach and the lower half of some whore were lovers.

Son-of-a-bitch.

Zach piloted the Datsun toward home because in all honesty he had forgotten about the severed legs that were bleeding out on the floorboard beside him while he ate. The food distracted him. And the burgers worked well to soak up the beer in his stomach. He needed to piss now. Zach was still very drunk of course and driving in a manner indicative of booze cruising but nobody pulled him over because the cops are never around (sorry, officer). So he kept on driving, swerving between lanes in his rusty yellow Datsun with the bloodstained tailgate, running red lights and endangering dogs and little children and senior citizens.

Where were you that night, detective? When Zach needed pulling over lest he speed through crosswalks and ram into pedestrians and run them down in the streets. Sleeping, or were you out fighting crimes of a different nature like drugs? Where were your brothers in arms in their slick Boise patrol cars? Nowhere on a Friday night, I guess.

Oh well.

Zach pulled over. He was alone except for the legs in the backseat and the road stretched dark and empty in either direction. He'd finished the hamburgers and fries and drank his Root Beer and decided he'd never had anal sex so why not give it a shot? The night had gone bad enough already, he figured. Might as well sell your whole soul to Satan instead of doing it piecemeal.

Anal sex made sense since Zach was secretly gay and because toxic masculinity informed his conscious and he read all the men's magazines and was tall. Guys like Zach (country, born-again) all have a predisposition for anal sex. They're all obsessed with drilling the ass out of their girlfriends because they hate and don't respect women and because women put themselves on pedestals and condescend.

He pulled the truck over into one of those useless fields that skirt the airport side of the freeway and killed the engine. He finished his Coke and threw it out the open window. The night was calm and sweltering. Dirty hot, the kind that sticks to your back. And Zach's groin felt tight because of his throbbing erection and of course the Hidradenitis Suppurativa crowded beneath his balls, aching, as he slid across the seat and threw open the passenger side door. He took the legs by their ankles and, stepping out into the street, repositioned them bent at the waist over the floor then smoothed his hands over her hips and tenderly hiked her skirt up over her pelvis. She wasn't wearing any panties. Or if she was, they'd absorbed so much blood that they blended in with her skin. I didn't matter. He was drunk after fifty beers that night with his friend and the body froth didn't bother him.

Oh and she was dead and just a cunt and a pair of legs so there was really nothing to be ashamed of and nobody around to judge him for it.

Body froth is like steamed milk but it bubbles because of the pressure of bursting flesh between the tailgate and the wall and not because of any steam-wand or increase in heat; it's essentially bloody foam (or foamy blood) and it overflowed down her hips at the moment when her torso was severed. I saw it happen. I saw it from the second level of a nearby parking garage where I was standing, changing my shirt.

Zach loosened his belt.

He opened his fly and hoisted his cock out over the waistband of his shorts, then drew his scrotum forth also behind it, and fixed the shaft pointed at the base of her asshole.

It was like a warhead in his sweaty fist.

He idly wondered if the tip of his cock would be visible on the other side, through the wreckage of her stomach, that is, while he fucked her. If he'd be able to see it penetrating the gore on the top half of her waist, breaching the wound and entrails like an angry red whack-a-mole.

His cock was a zeppelin, a bright red blimp, and the Hidradenitis Suppurativa was there too, swelling up on either side like soft bombs from the folds of flesh. He gripped his cock and steadied the legs by pressing down on the left wing of the pelvis and then thrust hi—

"Okay okay that's enough. Jesus Christ, get him out of here. We know what happens next. Sick bastard. So maybe we don't find the legs. We've got your DNA all over her torso. Semen, saliva, the works. And we've got the hacksaw too. Her blood and your prints all over it. You're looking at twenty to life if the liberals don't put you into some state institution first."

I try my best not to smile, but I'm a very smiley person and on the way out I can't help myself. I tell him that my mother was a cunt. I explain how she used to screw me with a rolling pin as they take me back to my cell. But I don't have a mother and they don't know that and that's what's so fucking funny all of the sudden I'm laughing my fucking ass off. They don't restrain me because I'm nonviolent and because they're afraid I'll cut their daughters in half and steal the legs if they do. Which I'll probably do anyway once I'm out.

God made me this way, that's another excuse.

DESIRE

Restraining myself, I still want to gangbang you all by myself. What can I say? I want to fill you completely and simultaneously. I want you to collapse inward upon yourself like a burned-out star and implode. That's my desire. I want to split you apart by force. I want to flood your womb and hindquarters and throat. I want you to die over and over again in unceasing bliss, writhing, twisting in the sheets of the bed we'll share.

Life is a series of rebirths.

Pleasure and death comingle in the chamber of life. Orgasm is a tearing away, a peeling back; the one true emission of self as bodies collide and souls ignite.

I am the consuming star.

And this, your destruction, is my desire.

MAD STALKERZ

I.

I live in a death trap. A place where sex itself is a metaphor for the absence of love and we gun-tout, gripping pistols in place of diplomas. Misery, offset with drugs and swagger. It's called Hip-Hop. It's on the fringe, and you might get shot if you go there.

Because art is like that, right?

Like four walls and a chair, it's a state of mind. An embodiment. And if you stay there long enough—really pounding in the stakes, that is—it becomes you. You live there. You make it your home.

Really the world boils down to neighborhoods. Life can be as simple as a drive-by or a one-way ticket to the pen. Ziplock baggies store up the reprieve. Racism is a death sentence. You see, home isn't where the heart is, it's where the art lives. It's your mindset and the nitty projections you cast.

Me? I live in the music.

Literally I wear fucking headphones all the fucking time and I rarely take them off and I straight-up don't listen to anything white-skinned even if its related. G-Easy can suck my dick. I'm a black man at heart because I'm oppressed. Get it? Hip-Hop is a force of nature and it drives me. Headphones are the key in my pocket. Untangling the cord is like hotwiring a car. Understand? I smooth the cable out, plug in and roll. The sidewalk becomes a highway of hard beats and snare and I'm stepping on every damn crack like: *fuck you, mom.*

But it wasn't always that way.

I used to be an R&B guy actually. True love, consensual sex, marriage, monogamy, blah-blah-blah. You know the deal. I didn't strut in those days, I just sort of sidled. Then I outgrew all the love shit and gained a man's appetite. Tits and ass have more meat than a heart. Everybody outgrows their diapers eventually. Like: *hey, guess what?* Love doesn't exist, it's a fucking construct. Now I'm just angry. My heart is a target range with an open season on sentiment. I shoot to kill anything resembling an emotion and the little deaths make me stronger.

I'm mighty now.

Harder, tougher. My ex-bitch used to like country so I flushed her. Yeah. It's black music or bedlam with you and I choose Hip-Hop every time. It beats the hell out of simpering doldrum and insanity. That's what love is—crazy, schizoid. It's depraved.

Fuck it.

Mean streets with a gangster lean, that's my jam. And who's there to balk? In Boise the girls seem fundamentally opposed to smart insightful men. The glorious redneck reigns supreme, even in the suburbs. It's no big deal. I'm just passing through. What's love anyway, what's a lifetime? This bag of bones is a revolving door and everybody turns to dirt.

Like: *hey you?* Someday the love of your life will be reduced to fragrant grain in a cat-box; pellets kicked up in a cloud of dust, disclosing hard little finger-sized turds.

Yeah.

When I have an hour or two for a heart, I always wear a rubber and never call it love. Heck, a few extra bills on the bedside table make me a gentleman. You see, Hip-Hop is full of scholars.

"And in Boise, I'm number one."

"Cool..." she said, raising her eyebrows; a freckled blonde with green eyes and a latte, with her fingers poised on a rose-gold MacBook. "So do you rap?" she asked.

"No."

"Make beats?"

"No."

"Okay..."

"So, can I have your number?"

"Umm...no?"

My eyes flatten, aborting interest. Bitch. I ditch the smile and reroute my lips into a sneer. "Whatever," I tell her. "It's your loss."

I collect my americano from the bar and leave. I'm not that bummed out. It's like I always say, girls on their laptops in coffee shops are usually stuck up. And the ones dressed in sportswear are the worst. She wasn't my type anyway. She probably fills her head with songs off the Billboard Hot 100 and fingers her twat to Drake. Not my kind of music, not my kind of girl.

Not my jam, period.

I don't know why I even bother. Other human beings impede my course with their lack of comprehension and reactionary discord. I tend to ramble, sure. But she didn't have to be a bitch.

Her loss.

Someday I'll be a fucking king.

*

When I was a kid, I didn't have any heroes. Why would I? I was a child of the state. I had foster parents. The man I was expected to call Father, called me sweetheart. Yeah. Clark Kent by-day used to creep out on Lois and into my bedroom. Get it? After dark, he scrapped his disguise but instead of a cape he donned appetite. It happened more than once, but I'm no fag. He never touched me. He'd just sit there, stripped of his clothes, on the edge of my bed and masturbate.

I wasn't stupid. I knew what he was doing was wrong and I didn't like it. I didn't like the way it made me feel and I didn't like his straining face or the damp spots he left on my bedspread when he finished. One night I asked him, "Are you going to hurt me?" He said: "No." then wept for an hour.

That's how it was for nearly a year. The guy was a bitch, faggot, pedophile, and a coward all wrapped into one. And I wasn't his first, either. Nor was I his last, I'm sure. He and his wife were a celebrated couple and the adoption agency was a licensed buffet. Child Protective Services accommodated him. In interviews, they saw nothing shy of a saint.

So yeah, growing up I didn't have any heroes. I had hate the way other kids had cartoons. I used to sit in the grass and tear the heads off of dandelions. I gave the trees human names and abused them, lashing their stems with makeshift swords and whips. On hot summer days, the woman would drag me in from the yard and force me to eat.

It was on one such occasion that I discovered X-Men: The Animated Series. The television had been left on. The woman had dialed it to the children's station and the theme song reached me from the other room. I was skeptical at first. All of the characters seemed to have special powers and wore stupid blue-and-yellow uniforms.

When you're angry, these traits appear silly.

My skepticism was warranted. Afterall, they weren't really heroes. They were too busy fighting Magneto. Heroes rescue people, and what about me? Instead of saving little boys from their foster parents, they saved arbitrary things. They battled aliens and purple robots and the government.

Coming in from the yard made for a nice break from tormenting nature, though, and I had to satiate the woman anyway, so I started watching it daily. Most of the X-Men were fags, but I liked Wolverine. He was the only vaguely adult character in the show and I admired him because I wanted to be him, I coveted his strength. His was a street-level power, like a switchblade. Instead of laser beams and other bullshit, he had the claws. He didn't blast his adversaries at a distance with some intangible superpower, he dealt with them intimately. His skeleton was indestructible and his tissue regenerative. He had the attitude and the sideburns. Punching holes through steel doors and slashing the limbs off of cyborgs. Going berserk.

He was feral, blitzkrieg, barbarian.

An animal, and I liked that.

Then the first movie released. Claws protracted in live action. Hugh Jackman was cast as Wolverine, cage fighting and brawling it out in the snow with bikers. Gone were the spandex. He wore a leather jacket, jeans, and a tank-top, and smoked cigars. A few years later, the second movie showed him pushing a bullet out of his forehead and slaughtering a trove of mercenaries barefoot.

I was enthralled.

Whenever I got angry, I would pretend that there were claws secreted within my own fists; under pressure at ten-years-old, willing the flesh between my knuckles to sprout blades. The habit stuck. It lasted for years. What can I say? Popping blades out of my fists seemed like a solution to all my problems, all the pent-up rage and emotion.

Early adulthood inspired a change. My anger reached an apex, I guess, and the claws morphed into devil horns. I'd swapped symbols, but the sentiment was the same. Anything to radiate a threat. With devil horns and airs satanic, who'd dare to fuck with me? Nobody. That's right. *Pardon my horns, piss me off and I'll burn your fucking house down.* But I've grown-up since then.

I've got Hip-Hop now and I've traded the claws and horns for a handgun. Yeah. These days I just walk around with a gun in my pocket, squeezing the grip whenever I feel angry.

*

Morning blossoms like shit in a diaper. In this neighborhood, everyone walking or driving leaves a stain. Yuppie-greed trails from their pantlegs and tailpipes, or flips off their cycle tires, and onto the sidewalks. They jog up, grinning. Excitedly tethering their bikes and dogs outside the coffee shop. They parallel park their spotless SUVs and jangle their keys, crossing the street. It's another sweet Sunday in Hyde Park. Smiles as fingernail-deep as house paint.

I don't belong in this neighborhood, but I come anyways. You can tell that my presence here makes the yuppies nervous. They avert their eyes when they see me then turn their backs and whisper. I casually aim my gun at them through my coat pocket. I point it at their dogs and at the backs of their legs, imagining their shock if for once in my life I actually pulled the trigger. They pretend not to see me, of course. Even when I stare. Would they still pretend if I shot one of their dogs or put a bullet through their leg?

They're all a bunch of phonies.

But I'm a phony too. Who isn't? I hate coffee but I drink it daily. What's left of the americano has gone cold. I crush the paper cup and toss it into the trash. Then I cross the street and put my headphones in. *Time to get intense.* I scroll through the artists on my phone and open the one that suits my mood.

Dark, brooding.

But Danny Brown is too needling; his voice is like Christopher Lloyd, high. Sun warms the pavement, it's bright outside and almost noon. I opt instead for Doja Cat. She's not really Hip-Hop, she's sultry sex-pop with a dose of rap, but her music is smooth and I'm feeling nostalgic so the blend of genres works.

The album *Hot Pink*, the song *Juicy*.

I like it because it turns me on, it stirs the blood and gets me going. But I've got to be careful, bobbing my head like that. If someone were to find out I listen to *Doja Cat*, it'd be a bullet for my reputation. Street credibility is everything and it all starts with taste. In Hip-Hop, who and what you listen to means everything. But I don't need to worry. I'm safe. No one ever has to know about Doja Cat and Lizzo and Tory Lanez and Tinashe.

I'm safe from the world inside my headphones.

Fuck vulnerability.

Seated on the curb, smoking a cigarette. I stand out in this part of town; about as casually out-of-place as Johnny Ramone in the White House. I'm wearing sweat pants today and Nazi boots with the tongue open and folded down over the laces. The boots are beat to shit, same as my leather coat. Chest and sleeve buckles jangle when I shift my weight or walk. I took it from the Goodwill. There are bloodstains on the cuffs and some dirtbag wrote his name on the coat tag: Johnny. Like I fucking care. Beneath it, my t-shirt shows Britney Spears shaved, fresh out of rehab.

When people see me, they cross to the other side. I'm like a pile of dog shit nobody wants to step in, so they go around. It's like I exude thorns. I'm a degenerate because I still smoke cigarettes. And yeah, *I fucking know it isn't good for my health*. But I do it anyway. I like smoking and I enjoy the discomfort it instils in other people. In the North End especially. Here they frown on tobacco like its child porn. Like smoking is an afront on human decency. You'd think they all did yoga they're so stuck up and condescending, but they don't; it's a fugue state. Fuck them. *Just because you're on a diet doesn't mean the wolf won't still eat you when the time comes, bitch.*

With that in mind I consciously work to produce larger plumes, hoping they all get lung cancer. I'm like one of theirs now—the mega-rich—a factory spewing pollutants, letting the overflow of second-hand smoke pass back through my teeth and nostrils in oily grey trails.

Doja Cat is cream in my ears.

The song *Cyber Sex*. It's like getting a lap dance in a playground. An hour breezes by like it was never there and I'm down to my last cigarette by the time the blonde finally emerges from the coffee shop. She's wearing a *Fabletics* puffer vest and leggings, hugging her rose-gold MacBook against her chest. No bag for the computer, that could mean one of two things. Either she has a car parked close or she lives nearby— the latter option being the hope.

She stops just outside the door to pat someone's dog then continues down the sidewalk. I keep my distance, following on the opposite side of the street. I'm Jaws out of water, picking my teeth at the backs of her spindly legs. Cue the tubas.

Another thing about girls like this: they scare easily. That's the idea here. Follow her to her house, then break in later. Scare the freckles right off her face. And if she gets into a car, I'll just memorize the plates and trace them. It works out the same either way.

Maybe I'll even put a bullet through her MacBook.

That'd show her.

Piggy bitch.

Show her what? Nothing. I just want to scare the shit out of her. That's what she deserves. Horrorcore and paranoia for her eye-rolling bitchery.

Yeah.

Time to change the music. 21 Savage and Offset, their joint record *Without Warning*, the song *Mad Stalkers*. The beat fits the moment, her pony-tail flopping against her back like a pillow tassel in time to the bounce of my jacket buckles. I keep my hands in my pockets. The lyrics pour into my head, instilling confidence. I'm walking through fire now. I don't measure my steps. I'm extraordinary.

Fuck you.

The sun is out, casting shadows. I'm feeling the music in my bones. Yeah. And I'm not even high. I finger the gun in my coat pocket and the soles of my boots slap the pavement like thunder claps.

I'm goddamn Leviathan.

In a short while the neighborhood transforms. The houses swell and change and the cars parked along the curbs change with them. Everything grows in size and expense, giving way to newness, shiny slate and stucco, and the shrubs are tidied and even the gardens grow taller. These days going on a short walk through town is a lesson in alchemy—witness common real-estate morphing into gold overnight as the city swells, and houses are either torn down and replaced or they're old enough to justify restoration. It's like a march of progress for the people I hate.

Hip-Hop doesn't come here.

That's obvious. There's not a tag in sight; not a broken bottle, syringe, coke-spoon, or beggar with a bag from the liquor store. This isn't Compton, this isn't the Bronx. Street corners here go unclaimed. Kids don't play ball in the street and nobody deals drugs at the junction. The rims on all the cars are stock; newer model SUVs with no dents and not a single tinted windshield, parked outside freshly painted houses and doublewide garages. Window shades hang open on store-bought art and furniture that glows and the little wives that live inside haven't sucked cock for fun since high school. They think that having a career is enough; that DIY housekeeping skills engender cuteness and that everyman alive desires sportiness, sports bras, and vanilla sex.

Yeah. Hip-Hop doesn't live here, not in this neighborhood.

It's just a bunch of white people.

Men and women that work remotely but bicycle to the coffee shop wearing suits. They come here from California and Washington for cheap real estate, then invest, then drive up the prices. They push everyone out then expect empathy when the economy buckles backward.

Rich people, like it's a damn specie.

Welcome to Boise, fastest growing city in the nation. It's growing in on itself and soon it'll be fit to burst. Fuck it. Nothing a car-bombing couldn't cure. A few burglaries, break-ins, graffiti, whatever. Sound the alarm. I'm an anarchist. I'd deal drugs in a heartbeat for the hell of it. I'd pimp a bitch if she'd let me.

So what?

This is Hip-Hop. I'm in *your* neighborhood now.

I trip, catching my toe on the sidewalk—arms spiraling, jacket buckles jangling. I catch myself and when I look up again the bitch is gone. She must've turned a corner. I'm not surprised. Stuck-up girls have a gift, they evaporate just when you think you've got them.

WWIDIIWOD? I always ask myself that.

What Would I Do If I Was On Drugs? If I had a jumbo size styrofoam cup of codeine right now, what would I do? It's like *What Would Jesus Do*, but better. What would happen right now if I was high? Probably nothing. I'd probably pass out, showering the grass in promethazine, projectile vomited, with my lips stained purple and my shirt wrecked.

I don't do drugs, there's no money in it unless you rap.

I still ask myself the question though. It helps me think. Pretending to be drunk or stoned is a creative stimulant in its own right. I actually feel sharper.

Yeah. If I was to ever mess around with drugs, I'd just deal. Jay-Z did and he got Beyoncé. It's not like she mouthed his pole because of his skill set either. He kind of sucks. Those old school guys didn't know how to rap, they just rhymed.

I take a seat on the curb.

I'm all out of cigarettes. It's okay. She's gone for now but I never forget a face. Absence makes the heart grow fonder and revenge is a dish best served cold. I followed her here, this is her neighborhood. I'll see her again.

Yeah.

In the meantime, any one of these houses will do. I've got a can of spray-paint on me and an itch to scratch. Like Gandhi said: *be the change.*

Hip-Hop hurray, bitches.

The house is enormous. The walls are stone veneer and adobe, and the front windows are the size of minivans. It clearly doesn't belong here; it belongs in *Palm Desert* attached to a golf course. The backyard is fenced and huge, surrounded by trees.

The gate isn't locked.

I flip the catch and it swings open on an immaculate lawn. There's a firepit and a barbeque. Adirondacks and a swing-set. A sliding glass door reflects the sun and trees, and the deck is a beaming length of redwood. Breaking in is easy. The lock gives within seconds, pulling back on a strip of vertical shades that twist and flutter, casting shadows on the floormat.

Without Warning is looping tracks. I switch to SOB X RBE on shuffle, then step inside and pull the door shut. I'm in the living room. There's a stone fireplace decorated with pinecones and candles, and two giant leather couches. Wood floors stretch from front-to-back beneath gable-vaulted ceilings, and the hallways are strewn with Persian runners.

Paramedic fills my ears, storming the headphones and flooding my skull with a fresh dose of hype and endorphins as I breeze through the room and turn down a hall, spinning, twirling the spray-can against my palm like a pro; striking the polished floors with my bootheels and streaking the wood between the runners. It ruins the finish.

Yeah. Fuck shit up.

Family portraits hang on either wall.

Here, a smiling mom and smiling dad crouched on either side of a toddler. Then Mom and Dad married, taking their vows; Dad dressed for golf, lighting a cigar; happy baby sucking on a plastic spoon; and Mom laughing with her friends at a restaurant; baby slapping hands in a highchair, drooling on its bib.

They're plastic, stock middle-class money-mongers, and their child is too. Here he is again, a little older now, identifiably male, with sun bleached hair and rosy cheeks, arms tanned brown from kid's camp at the country club.

Cunts.

Maybe I'll spray-paint a combination of dicks and dollars-signs in their master bathroom. Swastikas in the shower-stall because it's there, naked in the water, that we're always the most exposed and vulnerable.

Another picture. Dear old Dad on a yacht, holding up a string of ocean fish. I pause and flip him the bird, smudging the glass with my middle finger. *Are you having fun? I am. And to think, if I ever bought a coffee maker for home, I'd probably never leave the house.*

Fuck you.

Their bedroom is at the end of the hall. Electric air fresheners keep it from smelling like sex but the deed is evident. The bed sheets are tangled, kicked down off the mattress, and there's a condom wrapper on the floor. Leggings, turned inside-out, overhang the rim of a laundry basket beside a pair of briefs, a t-shirt, and a lavender thong. It's like glimpsing the American dream. Despite their busy lives, careers, years of marriage, and having a child, Mom and Dad still indulge in impromptu sex on Sunday mornings.

I wonder if they both came.

And now they're out and about—at a park perhaps, raising their son—or maybe bowing their heads in church, blameless and rich.

Their closet door hangs open on a wardrobe large enough to clothe a militia. I flip the cap off the spray can, shake it, and grin. The music does cartwheels in my head, Slimmy B spitting furious non-sequiturs over a pulsing electric beat, then the song ends. Silence fills the pause between tracks. I'm about to spray gold paint across a row of their suits when I hear the blinds flutter, rattling in the rail, as the back-door slides open and shut. My heart stops. Then another song kicks off, deafening me. I'm disoriented, panicked. The volume toggle is out of reach.

I can't see or hear.

I'm tripping, panicked.

Instinct shows its teeth and I dart from the room. I run back into the hall and duck through a side door, ripping the headphones loose. It's the nursery. The floor is crowded with plastic dinosaurs and toy trucks, and I drop the spray can and kick it beneath the bed.

Floorboards creak as somebody slowly moves through the house. I put my back against the wall, peering through the door and down the hall. I take my gun in hand and wait. The steps are cautious. Creeping. Police maybe? I imagine the smooth pudgy face of a school-yard bully, sweeping the muzzle of his gun over doorways as he backs around corners, surveying the terrain.

He steps into sight.

A pasty white kid in a 2Pac tee with a septum piercing and *Beats by Dre* worn over a black beanie. His backpack clinks and clatters as he comes down the hall, swinging from door to door. He's checking the rooms, looking inside. Private security maybe? Families get what families can afford.

I back away from the opening.

There's a window above the bed but I'd never make it through in time. I flip the safety catch on the pistol. There's a closet in the room. Classic bifold doors with panel slats. I've no other choice. I step inside and pull the doors shut behind me. It's so cliché it makes me sick.

I raise the pistol into a quick firing position and hold my breath.

His steps sound nearer.

The bedroom door swings open.

My stomach clenches as he enters the room and walks to the center. Can he see the whites of my eyes, staring at him through the door slats? He unshoulders his backpack and props it against the wall. It looks heavy. He tugs the zipper open and reaches inside, bobbing his head. It sounds like he's singing, mumbling lyrics. The *Beats by Dre* headphones emit a steady thunder against his skull.

When he brings his hand out of the backpack there's a gun in it. Some kind of pistol, with a long blue-black barrel and extended clip. He turns it in his hand admiringly, watching the light play along the polished steel, then stands up, facing the closet, and flips the safety off.

My legs stiffen as he takes aim.

Coat hangers are pressing into my back. I tense up, anticipating the impact, the rain of bullets against my chest, ripping through me and into the closet wall, as the door explodes, shattering my concealment, in a burst of splinters and blood.

But he doesn't fire.

He smiles and lowers the gun. A wicked looking youth with evil eyes and acne pits on his jaw. Stubble grows in patches on his neck, on the verge of figure, but not yet a beard. He tucks the gun neatly beneath the pillows on the child's bed, then scoops the backpack onto his shoulder and leaves the room.

I'm paralyzed, stuck in place amid the hanging shirts like an ammonite, my hand frozen on the pistol grip, eyes open against the bands of light falling in on my face from the door shutters.

Relief touches me through the ice.

I thaw.

There's a commotion in the living room. The backdoor is jerked opened and slams shut, knocking the blinds together. I pull a blast of air into my lungs and push the slats, emerging from the closet.

I leave the gun where it is and vacate the property.

He wasn't hard to follow. I made a day of it, traipsing behind him, ducking behind cars and trees, as he traveled from house-to-house, planting guns.

His headphones formed a padded archway above his head and he moved robotically, like walking and kicking were the same interchangeable motion. Frankenstein's monster, stomping through people's yards, trying all their doors and windows and climbing their fences, with his backpack bulging and swaying against his shoulder blades.

He was brazen and unafraid, and for that very reason he seemed invisible. No one was ever home; it was either a stroke of luck or an evidence of careful planning.

He didn't carry a jimmy bar, key ring, or tool kit either; he obtained entry amateurishly, by trying all the doors and windows until he found one that opened.

The houses were always big and regularly inhabited, and he seemed to know which ones belonged to families because the ones he chose always did.

It wasn't coincidence.

Nothing about his selections exuded tactics on the fly.

He didn't steal or spray paint, he just left the guns. Always in the kid's rooms, well-within reach and with the safeties off.

I watched him from a careful distance, peering through the windows. His backpack contained an arsenal. Semi-automatics, sub-compacts, and machine pistols. He left them in toy chests, propped in closets, and on puzzle boxes; tucked beneath pillows in beds and baby cradles, or beneath the sheets.

The afternoon wore into evening.

When his supply was extinguished—the backpack smooshed in on itself, flapping, and empty—I followed him back into the city. It was near dark. He lived in a beige sedan parked in an alleyway off Lusk and Island.

He settled in for the night, laying the seat back. He rolled a blunt and cracked the window and the smoke crawled through the opening in a long murky trail. I watched him for a while, then got bored and walked home.

I could have called the cops, but why?

My phone was dead.

I hate police.

II.

Her name is Hannah I found out.

Hannah Blake. She sits at the counter and makes jokes with the baristas while they wrap pastries in cellophane and giggle; bonding over eye-rolls and trading sentiments with revolving declarations of *oh-my-gosh*. She's popular, yes. The type that preaches acceptance beneath glam-shots and boob-selfies on Instagram, and exudes smug self-importance.

She looks like a mid-tier Sharon Stone.

I've been watching her for a week. She sits at the counter behind her computer and does what? Nothing. Like she deserves a gold-star for sitting with good posture. Trying her best to look busy, pretty. Perky breasts. She narrows her eyes and types. The glowing Apple logo on the back of her rose-gold MacBook is pretentious as shit. She pauses, biting her lip, and fidgets. Then she looks around contemplatively— projecting diligence, but it's nothing more than a caffeine addiction. It's an act. Young people frequent coffee shops for the same reason they frequent clubs. It's to show themselves, and that's why they linger. *Look at me, I'm having so much fun. I'm free, white, and 21.*

I still don't know where she lives.

The last of the americano slides down my throat, dragging fire. I've spiked it with bourbon from the flask in my shirt pocket. Today I'm wearing jeans and the leather boots, an old army jacket and a red-checkered flannel. I'm feeling high. I scratch the pimples on my neck and fall headfirst in the whirlpool of an early buzz.

I'm dizzy, floating at one in the afternoon.

She closes her laptop and readies to leave.

While she's gathering her things, I slide off my stool and go through the door before her. She'll emerge and I'll follow. Today's the big day and I've got a whole playlist lined up for it. First up, Lil Uzi Vert, the song *Neon Guts.* I tap play and the music rolls free, unwinding as the synthesizers buzz and herald the beat, summoning track ringleader and lyricist, Uzi Vert, with his nasally voice and peculiar squawked cadence.

My headphones shiver in my ears, throbbing with enhanced bass.

I can feel the music in my toes and fingertips; it's electric and I'm 60% water. Hip-Hop fills me to the brim and overflows. I'm numb, following her now as she steps outside and starts to walk. I don't bother with subtlety. I couldn't give two fucks if I had two dicks and the Olsen twins lined up for a nude slumber party. The unlaced boots slap pavement and my jacket buckles jangle.

She doesn't even notice.

She's on her phone.

Her laptop is in a bag this time, hanging from her shoulder.

I follow her two blocks and then she climbs into a silver car and drives off. I'm left standing on the sidewalk, hyped on booze, hyped on coffee, and with my purpose snatched away and gliding down the street. It feels shitty. I watch the car turn and disappear, the signal winking, visible through the shrubs, and then gone.

Fuck.

I halt the playlist, feeling deflated. I shuffle the damn thing and land on *Black Balloons* by Denzel Currey. Fine. Whatever. I turn on my heel and collide. We crash into each other. Our shoulders smack and I'm thrown off balance, slightly drunk, and staggering backward. I slip off the curb and catch myself in the street. I'm in a parking space. A car slows to crawl beside me and honks, rolling forward then angling back as I regain the curb.

"Yo, what the fuck man!" I shout at the walker. "Watch where the fuck you're going."

"I was, asshole. Why don't you?"

My vision adjusts and I locate his face. It's black, mustached. *Wait, that's 2Pac. A face on a shirt.* I raise my eyes and find a living scowl as the kid wearing it rubs his eye. He's in the same clothes—the studded belt, jeans, and the shirt—and reeks of weed. His backpack drags at his shoulders, pulling the straps taut beneath his arms.

"Oh," I blink, straightening my posture. "Nice headphones."

"Thanks," he replied. "They're—"

"*Beats by Dre*. I know."

"They're the best."

"Have you heard Bang & Olufsen? They've got a line by DJ Khaled that's amazing for Hip-Hop. The highs and lows are—"

"His music sucks. Why would anybody buy his headphones?"

"He has a lot of good songs—"

"No he doesn't." His eyes are tiny black bullet holes, void of expression. They have a strangling affect and I can't make words.

He brushes past me and continues down the sidewalk.

It's like I was never there.

I turn dumbly, watching him go. His backpack is bulging; irregular shapes stress against the nylon in rigid lengths, battling gravity. "Fuck this guy," I mumble.

Young kid like that. Eighteen, nineteen years old. Early twenties maybe. Bag full of guns. Where does he get them? Who supplies 2Pac kids with heavy artillery in Boise, Idaho? And how does he afford it?

And who the fuck does he think he is?

I hustle forward.

Maybe to find out why, maybe just to follow.

He's no poser, I'll give him that. Living in his car. In the house that Hip-Hop built, like it was ever warm. Fucking beige sedan in an alleyway. Fucking kid.

What does he get out of it?

Instigating suburban dread with his guns; guns in the cradle or left amid the playthings in spotless upper echelon homes; secreted beneath bedspreads and quills. Bullets dumped in Lego-bins. A doll with a Glock-9 up her skirt. Why?

I see Elmo on a miniature bookshelf.

A box of hot wheels.

A plush Steve Jobs on a tiny bed.

Toys, shiny until they're considered dull and then discarded; totems of innocence, visible through the window. I'm standing on daisies and I don't really care, peering through the dirty glass, past a sill crowded by insects and dust, as he enters the room.

The song changes.

Lil Baby and Gunna now, *Drip Too Hard*, in my ears. I swallow twice as he takes the Elmo by the head and raises it. He scatters a few glossy books off the shelf and paces the floor.

He's looking for something.

In a fit of rage he swipes a Tonka Truck with his foot and hurls the Elmo across the room. He lowers a shoulder, dropping his pack. His septum ring catches a sparkle of sunlight as he crouches down and hauls the zipper back.

I duck my head.

Silly.

He reaches inside and his fist emerges with a MAC-10 in its grip. He pulls it from the bag and stands. He seems to be poising. Leveling the gun sights. Grinning. I bump the glass with my forehead and freeze, ready to bail, but he doesn't notice. He's too busy with his little gun dance.

It's Tuesday. I wonder what he's listening too.

I wonder if it's Hip-Hop.

He relaxes and lowers the gun. It's very sudden. Back to business like the end of a commercial. He throws open the purple door of a plastic play-kitchen and sets the heavy machine pistole inside. I feel my guts tighten up at the thought of a nine-year-old pacifying a tooth ache with the gun barrel; or excitedly bursting into the living room moments before blowing off a leg.

He closes the toy door, pauses—tilts his head, listening—then throws it open again and retrieves the weapon. He points it at the open bedroom door and *bra-a-a-ah!* He fires. Bullets rip into the plaster, tearing across the wall and splintering doorframe. They slam into the chest of a small Hispanic woman and drive her backward onto the floor.

It's a level of damage only Wolverine could sustain and survive; emerging from battle wearing stylized bullet holes in his flesh like pin-back buttons on a groupie's coat.

She's not Wolverine.

She goes limp right away.

A handgun slides from her grip as the wounds start to spout blood, welling up through her sweatshirt and collecting into a soupy pool beneath her in the carpet.

It happens fast.

The blood, the swamp.

There's an electric moment of pause. Sunlight catches in the blood. Silence blankets the room, pregnant with shock, as the gun barrel smokes, off-gassing it's bullet perfume, and the arm that supports it begins to quiver.

He lowers the weapon and stares at it, takes it in both hand and elevates it. It looks like a Scorpion without legs. He's not in awe of it; he's in awe of himself, the one that pulled the trigger, the one that traded life for death in an instance.

The wolf gets his teeth and smiles. Whatever he was before, he's something else now—*he's escalated.*

He wipes the gun down, running the barrel and the grip through the front of his shirt, then tosses it on the bed. He lifts his phone and changes songs. I can tell by the way his thumb maneuvers the screen, selecting artist, then album, then song.

My own music feels far away.

I've got a death grip on the gun in my coat.

WWIDIIWOD?

He takes his backpack, slings in onto his shoulder, and steps over the corpse. Her blood continues to spread, overtaking an acre of carpet; polypropylene stalks poke through the growing shallows and trails of pulpy splatter run down the walls.

He leaves the room without a backward glance.

I duck down and watch the back door. He comes through it, navigating the porch rail, then crosses the yard and calmly scales the fence. The urge to follow dissolves as he reaches the sidewalk and goes his merry way, whistling amicably.

I drop to my haunches and try to get my head straight.

WWIDIIWOD? I don't know. If I had a fat hypo and a rubber band; spoon and lighter; the strongest blunt in existence; hash sucked through an apple-core; a beer bong; ecstasy; horse pills; Percocets; glue-sticks; bath salts; NyQuil; rubbing alcohol.

Whatever.

When I was fourteen, I tried to kill my foster parents. I'd been collecting steak knives for a month, breaking the blades away from the handles and then sharpening them on the sidewalk. I kept them wrapped in a newspaper, stowed beneath my mattress, until I had six.

It was Easter morning.

They'd been drinking the night before.

I crept down the long dark hall toward their bedroom, still in my pajamas, with the knife blades held between my fingers, three in each hand, and projecting from my fists.

The door swung open on an empty bed.

Light spilled from their bathroom as the shower started. I glimpsed them, their naked bodies, as they climbed in together. I could hear their voices, the slop of washcloths and soap. Steam poured beneath the plastic curtain and the ceiling fan whirred overhead. The blast of water concealed my footsteps.

They were giggling, scrubbing each other's backs. Unnaturally happy after more than a decade of marriage. I watched them in silhouette. My foster father had a hardon; she was stroking it while he washed his hair.

I let the hate build to a maximum before I struck.

It happened in a blitz.

Roaring and punching, hurling my fists through the shower curtain with the blades held tight. I managed about four solid strikes before one of the blades slipped back through my fingers and into my wrist.

I almost bled to death.

Afterward I was sent to juvie, then reform school. I saw therapists for years, took meds, and slept in a dorm populated by psychopaths and rapists. Dear old dad lost a nut in the shower that morning and I punctured his gall bladder; the woman lost a finger.

They both lost body parts and I had won piece of myself back. Hip-Hop kept me alive after that. I found it when I stole a black kid's iPod. It gave me an excuse for losing, reasons to hate and keep on hating. Violence, drugs, parties. Sex without feeling.

Swimming pools.

Drank.

So what if it wasn't mine—my culture, my struggle—I stole it from a black kid but the feelings were the same. Life sucks, but if you slap it, it'll swallow. Hip-Hop understands that. It's deal, or be dealt. From gutters of abuse, oppression, and poverty, the sentiment is universal. Anger. Antipathy. Escape. It's that simple. And it's applicable daily.

You'll always be worse off than anybody else because you're the one living it. Yeah. That's why relatable art is eternally popular—people are selfish, it appeals to self-pity and dreams and projects emotion.

Holden Caulfield knew: write *fuck* and rebel.

I grip the gun in my coat pocket, squatted against the side of the house. I could pop off shots and nobody would hear. The yards are too big, the landscapes tall and deep, insulating the divide between neighbors.

The rich are the common foe.

See, I entered society at eighteen with a clean record. I made my way home on a bus, back to the house where the hate was born. I didn't have the gun then, I imagined myself with all-black eyes and devil horns. I carried a box of matches in my shirt pocket.

When I got there it was empty.

A *For Sale* sign was stuck in the grass.

I set it on fire anyways, then rented a room at the Motel 6 and fell asleep to the sound of police sirens, the rotten crackle of my childhood, burned at the altar in a blaze of glory.

Heroes don't exist.

I opened my eyes, walked to the porch, and slide the door back. The house smelled like Vanilla Bean, like sugared popcorn. A Yankee Candle sat atop a miniature piano, burned down to half in the scorched glass.

I flipped over a chair and smashed a few cabinet doors.

Fucking rich people

The music had changed. I hadn't noticed. How many tracks had passed on shuffle since *Drip Too Hard*? How many songs had I missed?

Immortal by 21 Savage kicks off appropriately as I stomp on a coffee table and overturn their couch. I like 21 Savage. If I was a rapper that's how I would sound.

I felt great.

I kicked over a coatrack in the front entry then walked down the hall toward the body. The sure smell of blood was immediately intercepted by a blast of flavor from a girl's room. The open door exuded floral scents. I looked inside, marveled at the spotlessness of it. Everything was white except for a rainbow painted over a vanity, tidy but for all the jars of make-up and face cream crowding the surface.

The kid's room was right beside this one, and the dead woman flooding the carpet with her blood. Big sister and baby brother would be sharing the stain even after they replaced the carpet, concealed between the doors in the floorboards.

I took a look at the dead woman.

Through the wreckage of her chest and spattered gore I could see that she was wearing an apron. Probably a house cleaner. Typical. The ones that work for the rich are always the first to give up their blood. Her tits looked like hamburger; ropes of fat strewn every which way like shredded balloons.

I stared at the fluid running from her mouth. It was very dark, almost brown. Must be coming up from her organs, I thought. Kidney blood, gut blood. Thick like syrup.

A bubble flared in her nostril.

Her eyes jerked open.

"Fuck!" I screamed, falling backward. I tripped over her legs and the headphones were ripped out of my ears. The music was gone and I landed in blood. The carpet felt like sponge cake beneath me. It made a sucking noise as I pushed off it and tried to stand.

I slipped, fell back again.

My face impacted, splashed, covered in blood. Blood everywhere. In my nose, ears, mouth. Sucked to the back of my throat. I scrambled for the island of a displaced laundry basket and latched on, dragging myself up. The woman was gasping, choking on the gush of blood that flooded her lungs.

I kicked her away from me.

My jacket buckles clanked, thrashing.

Her blood clung to my boot, sticking, dropping away like tentacles. She was AIDs, she was a vampire. Not that she was moving. It didn't matter. She was a disgusting gurgling thing, spouting fluids into the soggy carpet and still alive by some sickening miracle.

I grabbed the pistol she'd dropped and threw it at her face. It bounced off her forehead and skittered further down the hall. I shoved my back against the doorway then reached into my coat pocket and gripped the gun. I considered slamming it into her head repeatedly, firing off all the bullets until she was reduced to a splatter.

There was no gun of course.

Not in my pocket.

I never had one, I just pretend; it's something stupid I do to feel in control. I clawed the blood away from my eyes and started to shriek. It was futile effort, there was too much of it; wiping it off was the same as wiping it on. I could feel it drying in the corners of my eyes already, poisoning my vision. Her death was soaking through my skin.

I couldn't get up, I couldn't stand.

I saw my headphones where they'd landed, flung across the housemaid, sinking into her stomach via a ragged wet hole. My phone was in a blood puddle against the wall. I didn't hear the footsteps at my back. How could I? My eyes and ears were swallowed into the nigger's stomach. Keys in the front door, rattling the lock, then the scream.

Hannah Blake stood in the entryway

I'd finally found her.

THE BLOOD MAN

The blood is life. Therefore I share it freely, belching wet gobs and droplets into lattes. It stains the milk foam red like strawberry syrup. I share the blood and no one lifts the lid to notice. The blood is life.

You come in from the cold, into my parlor. With hands that are dry and shriveled. And your jacket is tightly wrapped around your shoulders with your face buried in the fleece-lined collar. Your nose is red.

I smile with my stained teeth and beckon you near, drawing you toward my station at the cash register. "Good Morning." I say. And then you say it also and tell me your order.

"Chilly outside." you say.

And you say it because you're cold and insecure and dead inside beneath all your clothes.

Fear not, loved one.

"The latte will warm you." I reply.

The blood will warm you when you drink it.

You hand me your credit card and I swipe it through the machine, then I hand you a pen and ask that you sign the receipt. After that you step away. You wander over to the tables and examine the newspapers while you wait.

I steam the milk and pour the espresso. Your back is turned when I impart my gift. I grip the paper cup and haunch my shoulders. My stomach heaves and the blood splashes my fingers and my wrists and the Formica countertop.

I wipe it clean before someone sees. The strong smell of bleach reaches my nostrils. It soaks into my skin and evaporates from the countertop. I place the lid on the cup.

And then I call you over.

You come running and collect your beverage and leave with the cup ensconced in your hands, leeching its warmth through the paper. "Have a nice day. Enjoy your latte."

The blood is life.

Everything you've ever heard about vampires is a lie. They don't burn in daylight and they don't feed by necessity. Immortality and pointed fangs are all a part of their fiction. The silly fantastic trappings of past centuries and superstition and popular entertainment.

The truth is straightforward.

There is no *us versus them*. Humankind is vampiric by design. We've just forgotten. The basic fact of our vampirism has been long erased by concepts of rightness and virtue.

But the instinct remains intact.

See it manifest in the uninhibited ones and their strange behavior. In common man, even: the day job, the car. His countless collections. Relations, materialism, and greed. We've supplemented blood-lust for money now, feeding off each other's wealth and wellbeing.

The modern vampire is purely economic. And such a pity, that. For the blood is life. Christ knew, hanging from that blood-soaked vehicle of martyrdom; he with the nails clenched in his fists and his blackened eyes turned in scorn toward all Creation. The lust for money is the root of every evil. We've supplemented our bloodletting with bank accounts.

This is the grossest perversion of all.

I feed in the early hours, in the dark place below. With the dirt and cinder blocks and sheaves of insulation hanging free, peeled back and away from the boards.

I hold my knees and ache, processing the gift. I am a factory, a refinery. Cramping between meals, churning fat, mulching meats to blood-wine. My stomach is an organic machine, fist-size and hard.

I am not selective.

I am carrion. Foraging for value amid the blind dead and garbage heaps. Those damned in their abject ignorance and mediocrity, discarding, faceless and void.

I am the lurker in the dark. The grandiose messiah. Incognito in the guise of common man, serving salvation under the guise of sweet strawberry; lattes and specialty drinks with fluffed dairy and the dark espresso.

In the black of morning the coffee house is very quiet. The customers are supremely isolated, rustling their newspapers and awaiting dawn. The time is ripe for the sharing of blood.

At eight o clock I am joined by Magda. She is a cold woman, dead on the inside. Her legs are crooked, causing her to bounce slightly when she walks. This deformity lends her the illusion of cheer.

Magda is the assistant manager. Her apron is purple. She is as an eggplant, misshapen and odd and dominatrix. Her breasts are heavy and her body is round and ripened.

I smile sweetly, knowing her.

"Hello Magda." I say. "Shall I make you a sweet thick latte?"

I pour the milk amid fingers of steam, the fluffy whiteness soon to be tainted by a dark shot of espresso and then further enriched.

She looks away.

I step behind the partition, working up a mouthful of hot blood as thick as chocolate sauce. I will feed her the sludge of life, smooth brown espresso and dark cherry milk.

It stings my throat, leaving my lips.

And the remnant clings to my jaw in ropes of bloody phlegm. I wipe my mouth and turn, and present her with the steamy blessed beverage, which she then greedily consumes.

You're back again the next morning with your red nose and shriveled hands. Today is the ninety-ninth consecutive day and I do as I have always done, betraying nothing. I pour your latte and smile, staining the milk foam with the usual beading of scarlet; little red rubies, like pomegranate seeds nestled in a blanket of down.

It's a rare achievement to find someone so consistent. You are the perfect addict. The ideal subject for this, my treatment. And tomorrow is the grand centennial of our affair.

You collect your beverage from the counter and I wave goodbye as you go. This time I pay closer attention than ever before. I see your vehicle, idling, emitting cold fog from the exhaust. And I lean against the counter, memorizing your license plate, the number that will bring me to you, as you pull away from the curb.

You are on the eve of transformation and entirely unaware. Tonight will be your awakening, your deliverance from the long night. Soon you will be saved from the pestilence.

And I will no longer be alone.

Your home is a well-situated manse, lodged amid brush, deep in the country. Acreage spreads in every direction, golden-grey. Your fields and farmland touched by dusk.

I can see your wife through the kitchen window with light poured down over her skin, shining on glistening dishes and soap bubbles that twinkle pink, clinging to her delicate wrists, as she turns the plates beneath the faucet, passing them through the water and then onto the dish rack.

She is pretty, full breasted. Her body is a soft fruit squeezed into a housedress. How many years has it been? Do you still find delight in her form? In the ripeness between her thighs? Do you yet suckle of those sweet juices in exchange for your own pleasure?

You live here while I live alone.

I live in town, amid the squalid mess of man, festering, in Room number eighteen on the third floor of a crumbling complex. Eighteen divided by three is three sixes. Satan. Here, you have fresh air and a loved one. Open spaces, fields of promise. But here you are also surrounded by lies.

I will save you.

Jesus Wept. I am here to enlighten.

I creep through the field, catching my socks on razor sharp weeds and sagebrush, and move to a different window. The moon watches me go, splashing through its pools and inching nearer the house and the warm glow of the interior.

The bedroom window reveals much about your habits. I sense your misery in the disarray of your closet, in the mess of clothing spilling from the opened door. Your television set and Guide Book with programs of interest highlighted, circled in red; the weary looking mattress, beat-down on both sides, and the unwashed sheets like wrinkled skin.

You don't have sex anymore.

Your desolation is reflected in the panties in the laundry

hamper. Her unsoiled effects, plain, white. Where is the little pink striped bag? She doesn't try anymore. There are no more secrets.

But tonight you will awaken and leave. Tonight you will be free from constraint and marriage and despair. Your priorities will simplify. Your attitude will shift. For the blood is life, and we will share in it together.

There is a fire and you are in your chair when she comes. She sits beside you on the large arm and touches your face. She kisses you and her hand is a serpent, slowly snaking below, working the evil between your legs. Her fingers massage you through your denim and she is telling you something, whispering in your ear.

Her face is flushed and her eyes are heavy. Her sex moistens; it is tangible and fragrant, pungent even through the window glass. You grip her arm and the both of you entwine, tongues entangling.

The firelight dances on your skin.

I sense that you are ready, but this creature, your wife, she has intercepted you now. You are distracted. The rebirthing has halted, clenched tight. Metamorphosis is upon you and she is ruining it, squeezing tight your ambition. She is a disruptive curse, a blight.

Evolutionary scourge.

She opens your zipper and takes you in hand, pumping her fist obscenely as you kiss and reach for her blouse. You pull the cloth, exposing her mammillae. And then you devour them, pleasuring the tender meat with lips and tongue while her arm continues to rise and fall, thumping against the chair.

And then you kiss her neck.

And when you draw back, her throat cords come away with you, caught between your teeth. Instinct wins you over. The blood comes all at once in a sudden steaming torrent as she screams and falls back, clutching the hole.

She collapses against the mantle.

She is on her back and trying to stand, flopping sporadically as she begins to die. And then she rolls over. Her sleeve catches fire from the edge of the grate and she lies still while she burns.

I am standing in the doorway when you see me. Deliverance, *en vogue*. You look up, aghast. "Who are you?" And I can see that you have been weakened by the events of the night.

"Loved one, I am Alpha and Omega," I say. "I am the one who stains the milk foam red..."

WOLVES

I.

I'm sorry, but there's a veritable bottomless pit of separation between what they're calling curvy these days and fat. This is most obvious on social media; dating apps like Tinder and Bumble, when thumbing through the deck and stumbling upon a pretty face with no body shots results in the dubious clause: Curvy Girl.

Christ, I go ballistic when that happens.

They should just say fat or overweight or say nothing at all. But no. Instead they make up their own rules, forgoing semantics, and call it a movement, dodging pretense under the guise of ideology like obesity and the hips on J-Lo are the same damn thing.

Well they're fucking not.

I'm afraid Body Positivity is trending perilously toward fraud.

Have you ever seen a sternum sag? Using the word curvy for the jowls on Droopy would be absurd. Tex Avery rolls over in his grave every time you fit your fluffy muff into a string bikini you fat fucking cunt.

The whole world has gone mad.

*

It's Thursday night and I'm in some rundown bar, *Cactus fucking piece-of-shit Pete's* or whatever, surrounded by vague shapes in the men's room and staring at my reflection on the surface of the urinal pipes with the gross unwelcomed smell of the puck rising up toward my septum. I look fucking retarded. The stainless-steel warps my face into a twisted arch surrounding the laser eye of the motion sensor. It blinks red; I zip my fly and wink back at the worst I'll ever look.

The urinal auto-flushes, splashing the porcelain, as I turn away. At the sink, the vague shapes bobble up on either side of me and snap into focus. They're human, though grey and formless; those desperate men in slim fit clothes with stocky builds, waiting for their shirts to reshape their genetics. They buy into a certain style and call it European, then dump their money into mall-brand clothing and wonder what happened.

These men—the men at the sink—I know what they're thinking as I smooth my hair back then walk toward the exit without washing my hands. But they're wrong, I don't need clean hands; the genital scent can be alluring and nothing like piss. The fragrance is an arsenal for seduction. They can keep their dive-bar liquid soap for themselves, reeking of chemical oranges and disinfectant. I exude attractiveness from every pore; a mellifluous diet keeps my body sweet, glands sumptuous as though dipped in honey.

I enter the arena weaponized, with pheromones on my fingertips like darts freshly tipped with poison, dancing momentarily, tracing the hussy jaw of a sultry tramp as I skirt the floor. She giggles, glitter on her cheekbones, a cute blond wearing concert bands and bracelets and holding a mojito.

I mark her for later and continue to the bar.

Getting a drink isn't difficult. The club is packed but I'm taller than the others and get noticed right away. Short guys are always the last to get served. The chain of order usually goes from best looking to worse: girls, then guys by height.

Social hierarchy, evidenced.

In Da Club, where the truth lies.

The bartender hands me my drink and I leave him with a twenty, waving no for change while the woman beside me screams *you never listen to what I want* into the face of her boyfriend. She's just one-half of a stereotype: the unhappy couple arguing and embarrassing each other in public.

I listen in, noting her face, the cluster of cherries tattooed in back of her ear, and log pieces of their argument in mind for future use. Pick-ups like that are always easy. The dissatisfied wench, unfulfilled, slightly drunk and untethered. Once the dissention starts there's no going back. Breaks in hard modern hearts no more heal than broken cliffs or busted teeth. All that's ever left is the jagged edge. Women like this—one show of appreciation and they're instantly DTF.

I'm an expert, I would know.

I turn my attention to the dance floor. It's like a bowl of earth, hard-packed and dark and full of worm-like limbs; damp flashing flesh, squirming in the strobe-lit darkness, all pink and blue and disco-ball beams; bare necks and shoulders, sweating beneath the lamps; beads of humidity like rhinestones on denim, glittering in the mosaic. It's pretty like glass pebbles in a firepit. Everyone glows.

I check my watch. 10pm and nobody over the age of thirty is drunk yet; just the young ones, already wild because they only have so many hours left to drink, fuck, and do homework.

Thursday's are the best for that. Midweek, the girls are easy. The ones that venture out are ones that couldn't wait till Friday or Saturday; mid-range hussies, lonely and insecure, frantic for attention and the kind of affirmation only sex can deliver. They're all whores and sluts, out for fun. And I'm a champion for girls like that. I love them and applaud them.

The Wolf passes no judgment.

I finish my drink and I've just locked eyes with a potential screw when Igor informs me of a Tinder match, pulsing twice against my thigh. Igor, that's what I call my phone. The "i" in iPhone stands for Igor because it's the perfect little henchman.

I open the app and peruse Courtney: slender and blonde. She's 5'6" and eighteen years old. A Snapchat filter magnifies her eyes in an angled selfie.

I grit my teeth and grin.

I send a message right away, breaking the ice with a wink-emoji. Then it's back to matters at hand. I return my phone to my pocket, order another drink, and cross the dance floor.

An hour later I'm in the house of a woman called Heather. She's middle aged with big lips and a smattering of freckles across her cleavage. The place is a cheap prefab with tapioca textured wall paint, light brown carpet, and caramel-colored couches. The furnishings are all department store stock and so is the wine she pours for us in highball glasses.

Cheers.

We clink drinks and swallow, watching each other closely; then we swallow again, desperate to keep the silence at bay because there's nothing between us—we're not here for conversation. Within minutes we get down to business and our clothes come off.

It happens in a rush.

We're on the floor and then we're halfway on the couch and I'm yanking her panties aside. I'm staring at the ceiling while she blows me in earnest; eating her out while she pulls on my hair and writhes. We move to the bedroom where the environment reeks of divorce, screaming out loud with scented candles and cast-off shoes. We cycle through a few positions then I put it in her ass.

She doesn't stop me.

I can see her face in the polished surface of the bedstead and it reminds me of what I'd seen in the pipes back at the bar. Her eyes are twisted shut in pained distortion and something tells me she isn't enjoying this. But she doesn't ask me to stop, she doesn't protest. Every time she sounds off it's just to grunt.

Even with that I'm getting bored so I turn my mind to the primo MILF in *Sperm Depository 3,* lapping up ropes of teenage spunk by the swimming pool. I feel myself getting close. Moments later it's all I can do to pull out. I wrench her backward and stumble forward, pushing my cock into her mouth like a fat felt-tipped dart, then watching as the cream flowed down her jaw.

On my out I paused at the door and looked back into the bedroom. Saying thanks is always an option, so I did; then I put my clothes on and left.

*

My Tinder Bio reads as follows:

Hey there ladies, new to Boise and looking for fun. 6'3" and a Pisces (voted most datable). I made more money last year than anybody else in my graduating class. If you have a dog that's great. Swipe right to get naked. I'm pro-equality so send me YOUR best pick-up line and we'll see what happens ;)

Here is Courtney's:

I like to work-out and my favorite color is purple. Interested in meeting someone with experience.

We agreed to meet the following night. The sooner the better I always thought, especially with Tinder girls; they're in and out of rotation like blueberry muffins at Starbucks. I suggested a bar but she opted for a restaurant, one of the trendier establishments on 8ᵗʰstreet. Upscale Mexican, a place called the Matador.

I figured the choice for a grab. She would be one of the smart ones then, the type that knew to always maximize her returns. She'd order the most expensive thing on the menu and a top-shelf drink, all of it on me of course. She was the trick after all; I was the John. This is the world's oldest industry, modernized for expediency. The rules are different but the game is the same and so is the reward.

Everyone plays.

Girls like that, they're the future; take note, here be the real entrepreneurs, available on every platform. Look no further than Instagram, Snapchat, or Tinder, each a racket with its own set of rules. Step aside escort services—sex has entered a new age and there's a new arena for it. Cellphone apps are the brothels of the future.

As I settled in for the night, I skimmed through her pictures again. Courtney, eighteen. She looked like a kid with her turned-up button nose and glossy pink lips; Snapchat refined complexion, cuddle creature cuteness overlaid with sparkles, filtering out the flaws.

*

I found parking and killed the motor. My face was reflected in the window glass atop a canvas of outer darkness. I looked good, refined but casual. Bruised moody eyes and hair effortlessly styled and tussled. It's the look every man aspires for; they reach and reach, but rarely grasp.

"Bro, bro!"

Passerby losers spoiling the mood.

Chuckling, high-fiving, headed no doubt for happy-hour and what would end in a lonely succession of rock bottom success stories and tall tales told amongst each other while drifting from one empty bar to the next. The type that spends their Friday nights looking for the party and never finding it; them with their bad breath and back acne, jeans and t-shirts and all matching haircuts.

They were probably on their way to Hannah's, the vile sort of college town club that passes out jello shots at the door; where the bouncers overlook the swarm of fake IDs and where happy hour lasts until midnight when the drugs arrive and the dancing starts and the stage volume goes way up. It's like slipping into a different skin, going there. Disappearing into the discord, everyone lost in stark ageless androgyny—the thrum of the millennials. An Idiot's guide to Generation Y.

With an ounce of charisma it's a sure bet for sex.

Places like that always are. Inequity needs a den and there's no app for it. Despite what most people think, success rates on Tinder are generally low—for me, higher, because I'm a) tall, b) have professional photographs, c) my alumni reeks of prestige. *Even with that,* most girls join up with no intention of responding to the messages they receive. It's not about sex for them. It's about the *illusion* of sex.

Pure flattery and narcissism.

But I'm not one to complain. Love, after all, isn't real; it's an urge, a reaching out and nothing more. I couldn't care less about other people's feelings.

I left the car and started walking in the direction of the restaurant. I figured I'd give her thirty-minutes to get sexual, flirty, or suggestive; if it didn't look good for a hook-up, I'd bounce and make Hannah's before ten.

She was there when I arrived. Recognizable even without the filters. The first thing she said was: *My name isn't Courtney.*

"Okay," I wasn't surprised. A lot of girls use aliases on Tinder. "So what is it?" I asked, sitting down.

"Cora," she replied, "Cora Schiller."

"Hugh Chambers,"

She extender her hand and we shook.

"Pleased to meet you," she said.

I glanced at the other tables and fixed her with a stare.

"Uh, Cora…" I said. "Isn't this all a bit formal?"

"What do you mean?"

"We just shook hands."

"Oh, sorry, I guess you're right."

"Let's start over." I suggested. "I'm Hugh and your Cora. Can I buy you a drink?"

"Sure," she smiled.

"Great. And you have a fake ID I presume?"

"No, why would I? I'm twenty-one," she dragged her purse into her lap and removed her wallet, "Here, look."

I raised an eyebrow at the ID she showed me.

"On Tinder you're eighteen." I said.

"Eighteen sounds better," she explained.

"Look," I leaned across the table and smiled. "You can stop being cute. Drop the act. You're not twenty-one and you're not eighteen either. What is it Cora, fifteen? Sixteen maybe?"

The smile dropped from her face and her mouth became a hard line. "But how did you—"

"Hello," our waitress beamed. "Can I get some drinks started?"

Cora shot me a glance, then lowered her eyes.

"Sure," I said. "I'll have a gin and tonic. *Hendrix* gin please. And whatever she wants."

"Can I see some ID?"

"Absolutely."

I reached for my wallet while the waitress fake-smiled and waited. She was possessed of all the characteristics of her trade: the prerequisite ponytail and bags under the eyes, heavily pierced ears and a few bad tattoos. I was sure she had a kid at home; the sag in her t-shirt said it all.

She took our identification and looked at it, returning mine with a nod of approval. I slipped it into my coat pocket and watched as she examined the fake. She squinted at the DOB. Looked up from the picture, to Cora and back. She ran her thumb along the edge and her mouth turned downward with apprehension.

She was about to speak when a diner party arrived. They took a large corner booth and started howling for drinks. I could see her weighing her options; the little gears inside her head going tick-tick-tick.

After a moment she gave the ID back and took Cora's drink order, her concern replaced by indifference.

Bystanders these days, nobody gives a shit.

"Thanks," Cora murmured after the waitress had gone.

"No problem," I shrugged. "So what is it, fifteen or sixteen?"

"Most people think I'm older anyway," she replied, avoiding the question. Her countenance was failing, sloughing off her and into the ether. Very little of the confident nymphet remained as she took to fidgeting with her water glass.

"Is vodka your favorite?" I asked.

"Drink, you mean?"

"Yeah. You ordered a vodka cranberry, right?"

"Uh-huh. I mean, I don't have like a lot of experience, but vodka is okay."

"That's good. Vodka is good."

The conversation drifted back into silence. A couple sat down at the table beside us and eagerly discussed the menu.

"You'll be wanting dinner I assume?"

"Nah, I already ate."

"Really?" I felt my eyebrows rise.

Surprise, surprise.

The waitress glided over with our drinks and set them on the table. Her eyes avoided us and her body language had changed. She asked if we were ready to order dinner.

"Turns out we won't be eating after all." I said, passing her the untouched menus. "The drinks will be all."

She said okay and left us, and I returned my attention to the girl. "So what do you want to do then?" I asked her.

"Umm," she raised the vodka cranberry to her lips and sipped tentatively. "Do you have a house?"

"An apartment."

"We could go there," she suggested, glancing up at me as tentatively as she'd sipped the cocktail.

"You don't have a curfew?"

"I usually study with my friend Michelle on Fridays. Dad hates it when I have homework over the weekend."

"And how do you get home...*usually*?"

"The bus. It runs late on weekends."

I nodded, holding the information in, sitting with it like I'd just inhaled a cloud of sativa. "Okay," I said after a pause. I drained my glass and pushed it to the center of the table. "Shall we?"

She liked my car of course, I drive an Audi R8.

Girls learn to spot quality at an early age. It's a survival mechanism as instinctual as the sex-impulse. She didn't have to know the make or the model to know that it was expensive.

She put her seatbelt on. The car roared to life and I pulled into traffic. Her hands were folded in her lap and her legs were clenched together tight enough to hold water. She was wearing a simple black blouse and jeans with sandals. It was the first time I'd noticed what she was wearing.

"What kind of music do you like?" I asked, switching on the radio.

"I like Rihanna," she answered. "You?"

"I like whatever's popular."

She nodded wordlessly and stared out the glass while lovelytheband performed their hit song *Broken*. I pointed the car south and thought about other things.

Like how off I'd been about her.

She appeared devoid of entrepreneurial intentions; had passed on a meal and even offered to buy her own drink. Could she be the proverbial virgin-minded slut—that veritable gem, like some sweet-sixteen plucked from a John Hughes movie and dropped into a street porno? She exuded naivety and inexperience like she'd gone to prom with her dad; she was shy like an amateur Juliette in a school play.

With the exception of a few minstrel pimples, the pictures I'd seen online had done her justice. Her teeth were straight and white, and her eyes were radiant baby blue. *An Instagram girl in the making.* She was strongly built and slender, pretty in a tomboy way; a princess with scraped knees and budding breasts.

I still wasn't convinced of her age. I made her for fourteen and not a day older. We pulled up in front of my apartment building and as she fumbled for the door handle and stepped out onto the curb I obliquely wondered if she'd done this sort of thing before.

"I'm on the third floor," I said, rattling my keys as I came around the front of the car. "The elevator's out so we'll have to take the stairs."

"That's okay." She hugged her arms across her breasts and followed me across the lawn, blades of grass glittering beneath the porch lights, wet from the sprinklers.

I slipped my key in the door lock and held it open for her. "Ladies first," I said. "The stairs are on the left."

We climbed to the third floor in silence. I kept waiting for her to hesitate, to panic and ask me to take her home, but it didn't happen. She entered my apartment without pause and stood in the living room, browsing the interior, while I prepared a bottle of wine.

"Do you like it?" I called from the kitchen.

Children are always comforted by small talk.

"It's nice," she said. "What are these for?"

She examined the fur-lined handcuffs I'd left on the floor beside the couch, evidence of a prior liaison.

"What do you think they're for?" I grinned.

"I like all the books."

"Good. That means I got my money's worth." I uncorked a bottle of *Louis Jadot Chambertin Clos de Beze Grand Cru 2016* and poured two glasses. "I've never read any of them, you know. It was my interior designer's idea. He's a real freak for that stuff."

"For books?"

"Yeah, should have been a goddamn librarian the way he goes on about it."

"So he just bought all these for you, you didn't even pick them out?"

"Nope." I came around the kitchen counter with the wine and handed her a glass. "I just wrote him a check and told him to pick out whatever got the best reviews. Oh, and no paperbacks of course. None of the cheap stuff."

She took a last lingering glance at the books that lined the shelves. "Can I see your bedroom now?" she asked, setting the wine on the coffee table.

"Of course," I smiled. I'd anticipated at least an hour of conversational foreplay, the usual nonsensical chitchat while the alcohol worked away at her inhibitions. For dates, wine is an invaluable component. It is to seduction what a coma is to authorship; that which separates the first kiss from the sex, the punctuation point before leaving the page delirious and uplifted. Tonight it appeared to be needless. She'd saved us both the time by cutting straight to the point.

"It's just over here." I said, turning down the hall. "But I must warn you, it can be a very dangerous place for girls like you."

"Girls like me?"

"Yes. Pretty girls are always at the highest risk."

"Why?" she whispered. She reached out and touched me and I felt her arms creeping around my waist. "Are you going tie me up and keep me there?" I felt her lips against my back as she pressed herself against me and pushed her hands down my waist. "Because you can if you want."

I spun, grabbing her wrists, and shoved her against the wall. A picture dropped off its nail and broke on the floor. We kissed and it was explosive. Her tongue entered my mouth like a flame.

"Hurry," she breathed, as I moved my lips down her jaw, tearing at her throat in the way that leaves marks. "Just do it, hurry up and fuck me now."

Her fingers were clumsy, undoing my belt. I pulled her blouse over her head and her bra came away with it, tugged up onto her neck. She was small breasted; they smiled up at me and I touched them. I covered them with my hands. Her nipples were bubblegum pink and thorny against my palms. I kissed them as she unhooked the bra and let it drop. She worked her jeans off her hips and down her thighs. I didn't even notice the color of her panties; they came off with everything else and were swiftly kicked aside.

"Take me to your room," she demanded. She was flushed and breathing hard. I pulled her down the hall and threw open the door. We staggered inside and collapsed on the bed. She took me in her hand in what felt like a bold move. I filled her fist completely. I pressed her face into the pillows. Rolling over, I pushed her hand away and shoved myself inside her.

It was like triggering a bomb.

She stiffened and her face contorted and she screamed, pummeling my chest with her hands and pushing at my shoulders. *"Don't!"*

I was confused. I tried to kiss her and she bit my lip, drawing blood. I slapped her for that. She slid out from beneath me and scrambled onto the floor. Then she curled between the wall and the bed, covered her face and started to cry. Her ribs stood out under her skin like the bones they were.

I felt angry and numb at the same time.

She only had one sock on and I couldn't help thinking how silly it looked, a single pink ankle sock on an otherwise naked girl. The moment passed and rage took over.

"What the fuck?" I shouted, touching my lip.

"I'm sorry, I'm sorry!"

"You fucking bit me you little bitch—I'm *bleeding.*"

Her body was racked by sobs.

I stood up from the bed and glared at her, taking hold of my cock. "And what am I supposed to do with this?" She didn't answer and I nudged her shoulder with my knee. "Huh?"

"I'm sorry, I just—"

"Just what?" I kicked at her. "How old are you?"

"I just—"

"How old are you!"

"I'm fourteen."

I fucking knew it. "Jesus Christ," I put my hands on my head and paced the bedroom. "What the fuck is wrong with

you? You thought we were just going to feel each other up?
What did—"

"No! It's not that, it's just...I...I *can't!*"

"Can't *what?* Don't tell me you've never done this
before."

"No!"

"Then what the fuck is wrong with you? Are you
retarded?"

"You're the only other...this, this is my first time
with...someone else."

"Someone *else?*"

She broke down; another seismic reaction accompanied
by enough tears to drown a whale. God I hate when women
cry. It makes me not even want to fuck them.

"Well?" I grunted. "Explain yourself so I can take you
the fuck home and try to salvage what's left of my night."

"It's not like...like it wasn't with a boyfriend before,'
she said, "I didn't want it to happen...he just, he made me."

"Oh. So you got drunk at a party, passed out, and then
someone decided to fuck you without permission? Yeah, great.
Get a therapist if you're so fucked up. Why bother even going
out. And why come here with me if you're so afraid of sex—"

"Because, I just..."

"Because *what?*"

"I want to feel normal...like other girls."

"Oh right, okay." I sneered. "Well then get on your
knees and open your mouth. That's what *normal girls* do when
they sign up for this sort of thing."

"It wasn't a boy," she whispered. "or anybody at a
party. I wasn't even at a party...when it happened...that
I...you know, when he raped me. It was...it was my dad. He
came into my room and..."

I rolled my eyes. "*Your dad?*" In truth I could barely
hear her; the blood was damned up in my groin and my ears
buzzed. "Is that what you said? Your fucking *dad* did you first?"

She turned her face against the wall, hugged her knees and nodded.

"Oh fuck. Jesus Christ." I groaned. "What next?"

I felt like breaking something, but something in *somebody else's* apartment; I'm only irrational when it doesn't have any lasting effect on myself.

"Look," I told her. "That's really fucked up. It's fucked up when parents have sex with their kids. But there's nothing I can do about it. So unless you want to get on with it, what we came here for—then you need to put on your clothes and leave. I can't do anything for you."

The room was stuffy all of the sudden. Stiflingly, overwhelmingly hot. She didn't move and she wouldn't look at me, and her whimpering, which had now diminished to sniffles, touched on my nerves like the incessant buzz of a fly. I started gathering my clothes and the act brought her to her feet in an instant.

She bounded over and threw her arms around my neck.

"Don't," she pleaded.

She tried to kiss me and I shoved her away. It was pitiful. She dropped her eyes, shame faced and more naked than ever, and I felt myself getting hard again.

"No more of this shit about your Dad." I said, whipping her spit from my mouth with the back of my hand. "If you want to stay then get on the bed. Lay on your back with your head over the edge and open your mouth. We'll go from there."

II.

I didn't see Cora again after that. Months went by and I never even thought of her. Why would I? She was too young for anything more than a one-off screw and even that had been forgettable. She was a dull lay.

All the praise for amateurs is a joke, the stuff of pipe dreams and pornos; twilit fantasies provided for menopausal men scared to death of having to face down their waning youth. Truth be told, inexperience is only appealing in theory. When they're that young they're starfish. They lay there inert. The act itself is about as exciting as ass fucking a subdued Patrick Star.

One might argue for the tightness of the orifice itself, but that can be had elsewhere. I'd risk a loose hole with a fuck-freak any day over a virgin.

But that's just me.

It was Tuesday morning when she made contact. Two months had passed. I was in a popular coffee shop in the trendy part of town—the neighborhood where everything is cute and all the women push around baby strollers and wear brand name tights. *Oh look, a yoga mom dressed in trending sports-wear spandex with breasts like eggs over-easy packed beneath one of those elastic bands that passes today for a bra.*

Her husband probably fucks her with latex gloves on. You know the type. Feminist politicos. They irritate me but I've screwed a few and they weren't the worst fucks on Earth. Strip back the veneer and they're just desperate. Desperate women will do anything to feel desirable, despite their banter and feminist politics. Cosmopolitan doesn't need to tell them the price of admission. Instinctually they know: their men want whatever scares them the most.

Facials, anal, deepthroat, whatever.

I was standing at the counter, waiting for my latte, when Igor quaked in my pocket. I had two Tinder notifications. One from a slut named Jessica and the other from Cora. Courtney, whatever. I opened the message and rolled my eyes at its length. Messages of any significant size are always a bad sign. They're usually soapy confessionals, crammed full of weak womanly attempts at seriousness and petty indignation.

The text read:

Hey so I have something to tell you. I hate to do this on here but I don't know your phone number and I thought it would be weird for me to come over. I'm pregnant. I don't know if it's yours or not but it might be. It doesn't matter and I don't want anything from you. I just thought you should know because I've decided to keep it. I'll tell my dad that it's his and I'm sure he'll take care of whatever other people think. Obviously he won't want any police involved. Also he's religious so I'm not afraid that he'll make me have an abortion. I'm just worried that he'll hurt the baby when he...you know. Sometimes he gets rough and he's not going to stop. Anyways, I just thought you should know...C

It affected me about as much as a patch of psoriasis might; annoying, but better than a melanoma. Certainly better than an AIDS rash. I would've been more concerned if the text had been emotionally motivated, or had concerned itself with legality, culminating in some rash childish blackmail scheme.

Actually, I was relieved to hear from her. The message showed me that she hadn't spent the past few months scheming. It was good.

I claimed my latte from the barista and thanked her with my best smile. She gushed, fluttering her eyelashes at me like kitty whips. The whole staff is like that; they all tend to gush when I come around.

Later that night I decided to stay in. I was in a rare mood, craving the kind of intimacy you can't find in the bars or clubs, so I poured myself a shot of Chivas Regal on ice and streamed a porno.

The storyline—atypically moot—involved the monstrous anal pregnancy of a stripper named Candy. The first scene took place outside a church where an impromptu rape quickly morphed into a gangbang and eventual orgy. Amid the various intercourses the lead actress is introduced and shortly thereafter penultimately impregnated by a soot-black Negro dressed in leopard skins. The rest of the film takes place during the course of her pregnancy as she spirals through a series of increasingly perverse and debasing liaisons, prompted by her unborn child—already a nymphomaniac, and gleefully encouraging these aberrant appetites from within the womb. Other than that it was a pretty straightforward sex-flick.

It didn't make me feel any better.

I lost interest about mid-way through and opened a book, a morose potboiler entitled *Andrea*, which served as a quick reminder of why I don't read. Books always take more time and effort than they're worth.

I poured a glass of wine and called my mother just to tell her that she is a cunt. *Greetings from Idaho you bitch*, I sneered, cutting the connection before she could respond. I finished the bottle of wine then went to bed.

I couldn't sleep.

I tossed and turned; something was nagging at me, something that Cora had mentioned in her message. She was worried that her dad might harm the baby, throttle the thing when he fucked her. *I didn't know that sex could damage a fetus.*

What also bothered me was the conception itself. I'm no amateur. I'd pulled out, I remember; she'd reached below and wanked me onto her stomach. I imagined my ejaculate flowing down between her raised legs and entering her womb with insidious prehensile dexterity. Improbable, but possible. I'd heard of drip-down pregnancies before; ass, mouth, and dry-hump pregnancies; pregnancies post-menopause and prepubescent and *divine fucking inception.*

Pregnancies happen all the time.

I saw my seed on her stomach, the downward journey, traversing the tender folds and entering nook. Anything was possible.

Anything, anything was possible.

I put on my clothes and hit the town. *Just to get out of the goddamned apartment. I must be losing my fucking mind, reading books. And what was that porno?* Like a fucking Borowczyk film. Hardcore porn with art-house aspirations. I only know about that from my designer who has a friend named Sean who had a sister I wanted to fuck—*that fucking guy*, he never stops. Always Borowczyk this, Borowczyk that. *Bora bora aurorabory fucking Borowczyk! Fuck, fuck, fuck!* It was all the freak ever fucking talked about, and he talked about it veraciously like a priest campaigning for church.

I'd had to endure his company on several occasions; worse of all when he'd accompanied my designer and I for a night out and kept on about Borowczyk in the fucking club, forcing it down my fucking throat like unwanted fucking medicinal syrup. My designer joined in too—evidently, he also likes Borowczyk—and it turned into a gangbang. They fed off each other's enthusiasm like ten-year-old boys hooked on crack and playing with goddamn wooden swords.

The wine, the wine, bad wine, creeping up my spine.

Borowczyk, faceless.

Borowczyk facelessly fucking Sean for an art film.

It was a hot night and the moon was a woozy, boozy, ragged hole, stopped up from bleeding iridescence by a wad of sopping clouds. I rolled up to a dive-bar with no name; no sign, just the words PARKING FOR BAR in white paint on a piece of plywood in the parking lot. Neon must be illegal in fucking Idaho because I never see it.

I vacated my car and stumbling through the dark toward the entry. I went inside and everyone at the bar was timeworn and wrinkled and diminished. Ancient Idahoans, prehistoric and geriatric and crippled up, with sex drives that had been buried long in advance, sitting at the bar, breathing mummy dust against their beer steins and dripping beer foam off their mustaches and onto their shirts.

Farmers: *fuck*.

The only young people in the place were a handful of scrappy cholos crowded around a pool table on the opposite side of the building. Their shirts and pants were too big for their bodies and they all had bad teeth. Beside them was a jukebox like something from West Side Story, with UFO-like lights and Frank Sinatra—subtly misogynistic—crooning oily standards through the speakers. The pool table had yellow felt.

Who does that?

Multicolored fairy lights were strung through the rafters for ambience, beaming through dust, and it felt like standing beneath a dirty rainbow. The smell of the place was rank with cigarette smoke, the old ghosts fossilized and entombed in the walls until reconstruction: *that day of judgment.*

The bartender was short—a pumpkin boy—shaped like a pear with bugling stomach muscles and fleshy little eyes that lived beneath the bank of his brow like frightened crabs.

Mollusks, whatever.

"Hello shorty-short," I said, flopping my arms onto the bar-top. "Get me a beer, house-choice, hold the earwigs—and a shot of warm tequila. I'm going to go piss right now but I'll be right back. Don't sperm in my latte."

The floor lurched upwards to meet my steps; and I walked, slightly spinning, like a pigeon on a record player. I wasn't feeling well and that was unusual. It wasn't *normal*. I eat salads and limit red-meat intake. I drink volumes of bottled water. Something was off tonight. My consciousness felt like a broken wheel, spinning, kicking up mud in the rusty harbor of my brainpan.

I found the door to the men's room and pushed it back on its hinge, then froze in the entry. *What on earth am I doing?*

The ladies' room was just down the hall, more compelling, more heterosexual.

It was obviously the better choice.

I went there and there wasn't a woman in sight. *How woefully disappointing.* I glanced into one of stalls, breathing deep because tonight the toilet seats were as close to a cunt as I was going to get. The current clientele had corrupted all the barstools by sitting on their balls on them and there were no women.

I entered the stall and pissed, splashing the seat, taking joy in the fact that women piss here also. And the polished green backsplash reflected my likeness like the tubes above the urinals in the men's rooms at other bars.

I looked fucking retarded here too. Because of the caulking, seams, cracks and graffiti. I looked like shorty-short bartender, but even then—even fucking retarded I was a hunk, pearlescent in the florescence, in the puke-stain aura of the ladies' room. *But no, no, not there anymore;* I was back at the bar and shorty-short wasn't anywhere to be seen. My drinks were on the bar top though and that was enough.

I took the shot of tequila and swallowed it. It burned when it hit the pit of my stomach. I looked up and around and there still weren't any women to fuck.

The ancient rednecks had grown quiet, listening to Mozart on the juke. The cholos, meanwhile, were sharing in the gangbang of a tailpipe—some asshole had backed his pickup truck through the exterior wall, engine chugging, pumping exhaust into the bar. It made the whole place foggy and mysterious, like London after midnight.

Maybe I'm Jack the Ripper?

Whatever.

I'm drinking piss-warm tequila from a beer stein, looking down into the liquid, eye-to-eye with myself, when my reflection leaps off the surface of the booze and onto the seat beside me. He's gained arms and legs, and he smiles because he's clearly stupid.

His eyes are vaguely lopsided and he drools.

"Hey Pal," the bartender says, now dressed differently and wearing a Carhartt vest with a heavy brass zipper. He reaches across the bar and puts his hand on my shoulder and his skin bursts open. His face falls back, hanging off his jaw in a long semi-transparent flap. Beneath the ruined skin, he is my interior designer. "Are the two of you related?" he asks, gesturing at my reflection. His prior visage is like bubble-gum, clinging to his lower lip. "You're practically identical."

"No, thank you very much, we're not *fucking identical.* Practically or impractically, surrealistically, twistedly, abstractedly or in any other fucking way you book-reading *cunt.*"

"Oh," was all he said. He was now slightly taller and bearing the likeness of my designer's friend's sister's brother Sean, the obnoxious cinephile who rattled on endlessly over drinks and dinner and at the club where there were actual women to fuck.

Borowczyk this, Borowczyk that.

I looked at my reflection. He was behaving strangely. He'd come from the beer stein, from the tequila, like a genie in a magic lamp. He was pale, squirming in his seat.

His eyes strayed toward the front entry as a crowd of women loudly burst through the door. They were whores, every one of them; loose women with loose labia that dangled down on either side of their short-shorts, pressed against their thighs in sour folds amid a turf of stiff black stubble and glistening wetness. They had wide painted mouths and lip cankers and none of them wore bras; their nipples prodded from their shirts like fingertips.

My reflection looked away, picking his nose.

I was repulsed.

The women surrounded the bar, cackling in cracked synchronicity. "You look the same," they told me, remarking on the similarities between myself and my reflection, entirely ignoring the old men and the cholos and Sean, who'd previous been the short bartender and then my designer. "Hey you," they said, poking my ribs. "You look—"

"Yeah," a blond giggled, going off on her own. "I think so too. He'd be attractive if he didn't look so much like that fucking kid of his."

"Yeah, yeah," the others crowed.

"His kid, the retarded one!"

"The down syndrome baby," one of them shouted.

"Like father like son!"

They were closing in on me. Their unity became dismantled as they each took turns degrading my appearance, hurling insults and unfavorable comparisons. My reflection became nervous. He got up and left, crawling inside one of the bottles behind the bar where I watched him scuttle from surface-to-surface in search of a harbor. "He should be beautiful!" one of the women screamed, smashing a beer stein across my face. "Oh, yuck! He'd be hot if I hadn't seen that disgusting kid of his!"

"Yeah! You can't un-see something like that! You just can't."

"Yeah! His DNA is written all over the child's face!

"Like a cum-shot!"

"Yeah! His gene pool must be a sewer!"

"So gross."

"It's disgusting!"

"Filthy!"

"He's done for good!"

"At first I thought…"

"But then I was like…"

"No way! They really do look the same!"

"The same! The same!" they cooed, their voices coming together again, merging like oil in a lava lamp. "The same! The same! The same!"

Their gibbering was eclipsed by the sound of bursting bottles; they were smashing them on the bar and then taking them in their teeth, holding them in their jaws, broken off at the neck and jagged, like translucent beaks. They crowded in on me. My stool tipped, the legs shattered and broke and I was thrown over. I fell onto the floor beneath them and raised my hands, screaming as the broken bottles plunged into my arms and sliced my face.

They plucked at my eyes, picking at the meat around the sockets; they were birds, thrusting and stabbing, hooking their glass beaks beneath my skin and rending it from the muscle. I was blind. I was choking on gore; it came from my mouth in a fountain as one dragged at my neck and hauled a rope of tendon out from beneath my jaw.

I woke up and puked.

It was 5:00 am. I was on my hands and knees staring at the wine stained carpet beneath me. A scale of mucus coated my lips and my throat felt raw.

We need to talk.

It was the first thing I did that morning; send her a message, dragging myself up off the floor and over to poor discarded Igor buried beneath the bedspread.

Here's my number.
(509) 520-4080
Call me.

Igor was low on power, as raw and unrested as I was. I plugged him in beside the bed and massaged my eyes. I was shaken, no point in trying to sleep. A bird chirped outside my window, oblivious to pain. Sunlight touched the glass, grey-blue on the blinds. I brushed my teeth and took a shower, scrubbing the nightmare from my pores with an organic loofah and a bar of artesian coffee-and-cranberry soap.

Afterward I felt better.

I styled my hair and put on some clothes, selecting a pair of loafers from the closet to go with the khaki slacks and blue summer-weight button-up. I didn't feel like wearing a watch, so I didn't. I didn't feel like shaving either.

I left the apartment and drove downtown, avoiding all of my usual haunts. I went elsewhere, to an anonymous spot in the rising sun where I bought a coffee and waited for her response. It came an hour later.

She said: *Sure. Why?*

I swallowed my annoyance and replied: *Because we should talk. I think you should reconsider having the child.*

No, I want to have it.

Cora. You're being immature. I have a say in this too.

No you don't. It's not even for sure that it's yours. And even if it was...wouldn't that be problematic for you? If people knew.

You're being unreasonable.

It's my body.

And I don't deny that. I just want to discuss it properly and make sure that you make the right decision.

Why do you care?

Don't be dumb.

So you want to meet? Again.

Or you can just call me.

I'll be at your apartment tomorrow night. I don't know what time. I'm deleting my Tinder account so you won't be able to contact me here anymore. Bye.

My apartment won't work. I'll meet you outside the Safari hotel, but you'll need to give me a time.

I don't know when.

Text me when you do.

She went offline and that was that. An hour later I checked Tinder and her account had disappeared from my messages.

In anticipation of our meeting I did some research. If I couldn't provide her with absolute proof—proof of even the slightest chance of our child being born retarded—she'd never submit to the abortion. I would need to be convincing. Persuade her with facts.

I googled *sex with pregnant women* and most of the results were pornographic. I rephrased my query and tried again. It didn't help much. There isn't a lot of information out there substantiating the concern; generally intercourse during pregnancy doesn't result in harm. Of course *it could*—but there weren't any credible sources to reference and I certainly couldn't tell her about the dream I'd had.

I called my interior designer and offered to pay him whatever he wanted for a faux article on the subject. Expectedly, he said he would. He entertains writerly aspirations and the idea of getting paid for something was enough to prevent him asking questions.

"It's got to appear legit," I explained over the phone. "None of the arty crap. Write it with professional airs. Dry, surgical precision, you understand? And use whatever doctor's name you want on the thing as long as it's pulled from a credible source—I want the author to be searchable and discoverable, without being particularly noteworthy or having any significant online presence. Okay?"

"Sure, and what—"

"I don't care what you say, as long as it's believable. Do your homework. Find a way. Maybe the cock-friction gives the kid a rash, some obscure nuptial condition that promotes Down Syndrome—I don't care. Just make middle school pregnancies look bad. Quote statistics, whatever. *There's a seventy-two percent chance your baby will be born retarded or dead,* or at least *look retarded*, etcetera. You know, like that."

"Gottcha."

"And maybe attach some pictures too, medical stuff, pictures of retarded infants and their small malformed heads and droopy eyes and what not. And have it ready for me by tomorrow morning."

"Can do."

"I'm counting on you Bowen," I said, easing a threat between the lines. "Don't let me down."

"I won't."

"Good."

I hung up and poured myself a double shot of Glenlivet XXV. Once the child was disposed of, I could get on with my life. *What does a fourteen-year-old girl want with a baby anyway? Shouldn't she be at the police station, reporting her father for incest?*

No. Instead she swells contentedly, stealing my joy, as the shadow-self grows inside of her.

The thought made my skin crawl; that he'd be out there, ornamented with my likeness, beholding life through those dreary lopsided eyes, and that our two separate paths would inevitably cross. A chance encounter in a bar perhaps, bumping unexpectedly into each other amid a sea of witnesses, our resemblance rendered clear in the flashing lights. That moment of terror, frozen in time. Showdown between a man and a funhouse mirror; a man confronted by his own warped reflection and the crooked eyes of fate.

I'd have to leave town.

I could do that, run away.

But no amount of distance put between us could obliviate my knowing; the infernal nagging awareness of an imposter. Not a man—a shadow, a sucking black hole, drifting through life on the spectrum; spawn of deficit, culled direct from the Uncanny Valley of his mother's underdeveloped underage hole.

Look there! stood upon the ledge—my features dismantled, pulled apart and reassembled. Twisted together to bring out the worst. *Tick, tick, jaw wet with drool, shirt stained. Hey look it's me. Hey Dad. Are YOU two related?* My mannerisms imitated brokenly to a fault, put through a spin cycle and destroyed.

Charlatan!

They'll say that I have bad genetics, DNA that sprung the additional chromosome. He'll be Humpty Dumpty, held together by tape. A nasty, drooling, driveling, warped reflection, forever marring the way people process my appearance.

I knew a girl growing up. She was very pretty with distinct feminine features and eyes the size of crown jewels cushion-cut to piercing polished perfection, green like emeralds on a copper tray. I wanted to fuck her—until I met her brother, that is, and saw that they were identical. They looked the same in almost every way. They shared their eyes and eyebrows, had the same ears, nose and mouth, jawline and shape of face.

After that I couldn't even look at her without seeing her brother. It irreparably destroyed her appearance for me and I never spoke to her again. I cut her off completely. She became someone I chose to forget, an accident; reduced to what I will always think of as a brief unintentional foray into same-sex attraction.

I wouldn't see myself resigned to similar fate.

Night came and again I couldn't sleep again.

I was parked outside the hotel, watching for Cora, when the passenger door opened and she climbed inside.

"Drive," she said.

"I guess you're feeling bossy today," I started the car and pulled off the curb, merging with the flow of evening traffic. "Where am I driving to, exactly?"

"Nowhere. Just driving."

"Okay."

I stayed on Grove till 16th Street then hung a left toward the greenbelt. It was hot for June and several of the homeless population went shirtless, exposing their tattoos and beer-guts over emaciated ribs and sunken chests. They gravitated here, in the underpass by the skate park, where they could hackle traffic with their signs and woe-is-me God Bless America hobo bullshit. I drive by on purpose sometimes just to flip them the bird and make remarks.

"So," I told Cora, "I wanted to discuss—"

"Things have changed," she said, cutting me off. "It's different now."

I waited for her to continue. If she wanted a reaction, she wasn't going to get one. I turned off into Ann Morrison park and drove toward the back, looking for a privacy. The blast of the air conditioning filled the silence as I pulled to a stop and killed the motor.

"Okay, what?" I groaned. "What now Cora? What could possibly have changed?"

She undid her buckle and turned, sitting with her back against the door. "He wants to have it tested."

"Tested? So you told him then."

"Yes. Last night."

I felt exhausted all of the sudden. I rubbed my eyes and wished I could delete my involvement with her as easily as she'd deleted her Tinder account.

"*Why?* Why would he want to have it tested—surly he knows that *he's* the one fucking you right? Or have you started sleeping around since we—?"

"No, it's not that," she balled her fists in her lap. "I told him it couldn't be from anyone else but he doesn't believe me."

"Well, he'll have to. There's a higher possibility that it belongs to him anyway."

"Maybe," she shrugged. "He's taking me for the test next week."

"And how long for the results?"

"I don't know. A few days, I guess. He'll probably want to have it expedited."

I nodded my head—*fuck, fuck, fuck, fuck*—I could always murder the girl but with the messages between us preserved in some digital archive I'd never get away with it. The police would access the Tinder database within days of her disappearance.

"Do you have a cigarette?" she asked.

"I don't smoke."

"Too bad."

"So why are you telling me this Cora? What do you propose I do for you exactly?"

"Nothing really. I just figured you'd want to know. So that you could still leave the country if you wanted to."

"*Leave the country?*" I hissed, draining the blood from my knuckles as I tightened my grip on the steering wheel. "Why *on Earth* would I need to do that?"

"Because the baby is yours. I'm sure of it. And if my Dad doesn't kill you, you'll be arrested and go to jail."

"Don't be so sure you little bitch, you don't *know* that it's mine." It was mine. I was sure. "And besides, wouldn't he be endangering himself if he reported anything—wouldn't he be concerned that the police might discover his *own* incestuous transgressions if they started digging around?"

"Not necessarily. They'd be looking for you, the man that got me pregnant."

"You wouldn't tell the police you mean? About your father?"

She shrugged. "If they took my Dad away, I'd just get put in some fucked up orphanage. I probably wouldn't even have my own room. Besides, I'm used to it by now. It's not so bad. Just so long as the baby's okay."

Who was this maniacal, hard-bitten child? This version of Cora was steel-eyed and sneering; a far cry from the squeamish

little girl I'd taken back to my apartment in April. Where were
the shy sidelong glances? The fidgeting and blushing. She'd
become a ball of un-emotion and apathy, indifferent even to
her own abuse and certainly indifferent to whatever outcome
might be in store for me.

I could see it now.

Hugh Chambers: pedophile and rapist, imprisoned for
an indefinite term while supposed victim bratty little Cora
Schilling gives birth to his mongoloid facsimile. That would be
the end for me; twice over, my reputation decimated; lose-lose,
fucked at either end.

"Cora, I…"

"I just wanted to let you know," she said, opening the
door and swinging her legs outside. "Too bad you don't smoke.
It might make you feel better."

"Where are you going—"

"Don't worry," she smiled. "I can walk back on my
own. Goodbye."

She climbed out, shutting the door, then walked off
toward the path that bordered the river. Her turquoise
backpack bounced on her shoulders and the wind kicked her
ponytail up into a golden streamer.

*

I closed my eyes and went over it again. I was on my
back on the apartment floor. I'd been there for an hour like
that, thinking. I didn't know what time it was. The phony
article my designer had provided for me was spread all around
my ankles, torn to pieces. I was waiting for my phone to ring.

It had been three days since the meet with Cora.

My mind was spinning like something wet, like sludge
on a turnsole. I was searching for a plan, a way out; gradually
exorcising a shape from the fear-clay; something I could use to
evade suffering and penance.

By the time the phone rang I'd exhausted all the fear. The panic had died back and there was nothing left, no more governing emotion. I felt in control again. Igor unlocked with a swipe of my thumb.

"You told me an hour," I said into the phone. "I don't like it when people waste my time. Remember that."

"Sorry, it took longer than I thought."

"Did you get what I asked for?"

"Yeah it wasn't a problem. You want it now, over the phone? I could always just text you the address—"

"No, no texts." I hissed. "When I requested that our business remain anonymous, what did you think that meant? Tell it to me, I'm ready with a pencil, and when you're done— *we're* done. You'll receive your check in the mail this week. Now start talking, you've wasted enough of my time already."

"The address is..." and he rattled off her address like the seventh trumpet of the apocalypse.

Cora lived in a nice neighborhood in the East Boise hills, where row-upon-row of upper middle-class prefabs mimicked suburbia proper with sparse landscapes and porch Jacuzzis and double-car garages. Boise doesn't have suburbs yet. Not really. Not like San Francisco does or L.A. does or New York or Chicago. It's too young and too underdeveloped and the wealth is still too evenly distributed.

I give it two, three years at best.

All life succumbs to growth.

Her house was a two-story affair with a tiny front yard. Hedges bordered the porch and a clean cement driveway lead to a modest garage, decorated on either side by matching rock gardens and old wagon wheels. Various boulders decorated the lawn. It was painted sky blue with white doors and trim. I imaged that her room would be upstairs, at the front of the house, where I could make out the frill of a pink curtain in the window from the street.

I imaged myself walking into their yard. No one would be watching. No one would care. Once upon a time the nosy neighbor existed, the little old lady, or the neighborhood watch. But not anymore. People are busy these days.

No one gives a shit.

I drove by twice more, then checked my watch; still early, plenty of time to kill before dark. I headed back into town and bought dinner. I ended up going to the Matador, where Cora and I had first met. I don't know what drove me there. The decision was impulsive. A coincidence? No, nothing is by mistake. I was driven to it by subconscious engineering, the subliminal voice inside my head.

I ordered enchiladas and drank Patron Platinum until the sun died down in back of the buildings, smearing its blood on the horizon. It took twenty minutes to pay my check because the waitress was inept. I didn't tip. Fuck her. I hate it when people waste my time.

It was ten by the time I left.

I drove back to Cora's drunk on Patron Platinum and weaving from lane to lane uncaringly, blasting the radio and singing along with song lyrics I wasn't aware of ever knowing. I felt good. I didn't worry much about the risks involved in my endeavor. I never do. It's my greatest strength, actually.

Supreme fucking certainty.

The night filled me with courage as it always does. My confidence blossomed and I felt invincible and beyond reproach. I refused to be this child's Goliath. She would put down her sling and submit to my will; she would bend or be broken. It was too late for apologies. She'd tied her shoes and had knotted them together, tangling the laces, and now the little bitch was going to trip.

I'd prepared the perfect stairwell for her ruin.

I pulled up to the curb and my vision bounced slightly like the tracking on an old TV. I killed the engine. The light was on in her window, visible through the drawn shade, a dull pink hue. I put my foot out on the moonlit asphalt and left the car.

I felt like howling.

Rows of teeth in the night, *just like a wolf.*

III.

My feet were stuck. I'd dropped over their fence and into darkness, and I was slowly sinking in it—twisting, like through a small intestine, amid strange flashes of light. I saw pain; it was beautiful, blossoming in soft electric showers; and I was dipped in black syrup, reaching for a heartbeat. My fingers stretched toward light in slow motion. A jet of air left my mouth, ripping through the darkness in a fray. Had I screamed?

I saw below, down into the zero.

Some of us never come back.

The darkness dispersed in yawning plumbs and spirals and I was kicked.

"Wake the eff up already you sobbing SOB," he said, prodding me with the toe of his boot. I opened my eyes and saw my feet. They were far away and my shoes were scuffed and dirty. The man was sitting across from me in a chair. I seemed to be on the floor, propped up against something. My legs were splayed out in front of me like two separate objects.

I felt nauseous.

My vision was blurry and brown.

A light bulb hung from the ceiling by a cord; outside of its glow, the surroundings were lost in a bank of darkness. The air was damp. It could be a basement. It could be anywhere without windows and a concrete floor. The light from the bulb was so dull and orange it was like glimpsing hell through honey.

My captor wore a wrinkled grey shirt and black jeans. He had bloodshot eyes and a delicately veined nose and his hair was slicked away from his forehead in an oily sheen. He'd been leaning forward but now sat back, confident that I'd come to.

"Hello Hugh," he grinned.

I couldn't speak, I was gagged and breathing hard through my nose.

"Now don't be bothered by me knowing your name," he said. "I took a look in your wallet while you were out is all. No big deal, right? After all, you and me, we've got a commonality between us."

I tried to move my hands, but couldn't. Presumably they were bound. I couldn't see or feel them. My entire body was an unknown, I felt detached from it, and my mind was splashing, gasping for air at the surface of an icy cataract. How did I get here? I couldn't remember what had happened. I remembered going over the fence. The rest was a fog. I remember seeing the moon, looking up at it and then back at my car and at the boulders in their front yard, feeling powerful.

"Oh, I'm sorry. I haven't introduced myself. My name is Tom Schiller. You know my little girl, Cora. Met her on Tinder awhile back, that right?"

My eyes widened: *Her Father.*

"Look, Hugh," he frowned, pushing his tongue into his cheek. "If you can't speak because of that sock I put in your mouth—and I presume that you can't—then at least show me the respect of nodding your head when I talk to you in a manner that requires your participation. Or when I ask you questions in a non-rhetorical sense. It's the least you can do after you did what you did. After you tried to seduce and do-in my little bride and then come out here after dark to do who knows what else."

I tried not to panic. My eyes were adjusting and I could make out that his initials were embroidered on his shirt collar.

"Now I'll explain what brought us to this moment. And how you ended up down here, handcuffed to a post in my basement. Alright?" He gestured: nod. Holding a finger beneath his jaw and commanding an exemplary back-and-forth movement of his head.

"Darn it to heck!" he shouted. "Why don't you just nod, Hugh? It's not that difficult. Just nod your blasted head. Do you want to hear the story or not?"

I pressed my tongue against the sock and felt a stream of spit running down my chin. It was hopeless. I still couldn't feel my arms, just pinpricks here and there, and my legs were dead and worthless. I glared at him, pushing bullets into his head with my eyes.

"Geez Hugh, if looks could kill..."

They can't, cocksucker. I just tried.

"How about we do something a little different?" he offered. His smile was corn syrup. "You just sit there and listen, and I'll talk. We'll pretend you're inanimate, a mannequin—like a dummy in a department store, how about that? You can just sit and listen while I do the talking."

He gripped the chair and shifted, scooting to the left.

Beside him stood a porcelain Jesus Christ and an upside-down cross. He struck a match against the statue's face. Its eyes had been painted over with black and *cunt* had been written on its forehead. Match-tracks marred its cheeks and chest. Cupping the flame, he leaned oved and lit a large black candle on a wrought-iron stand. The wick took fire, casting the shadow of the porcelain Christ flickering against the cross.

He shook the match and tossed it, crossing his arms.

"So, Hugh," he said, carrying on. "You met Cora on Tinder and the two of you went out on a little date, is that correct? Heck, I already know. I set the whole darn thing up," he smiled. "You and Cora went out and then she did what she does for Daddy to get you here. You see Hugh, we knew you'd be coming. Once a wolf catches the scent there's no turning back. So we waited. And last night, sure as Satan, you showed up, all drunk off your you-know-what and trying to get over the fence into our backyard. That's when I got you. Came up right behind you and put you out with a little chloroform on an old dishtowel. Just like in the movies.

"Did you know Chloroform could be bought online? Comes in two days, right to your door, if you've got the Amazon Prime. Free two-day shipping at no extra charge, just like that," he snapped his fingers, shaking his head in wonderment.

I tried to move my arms again. I closed my eyes and focused on following the blood up through my veins and into my hands. I squeezed my fingers against my palms and felt the handcuffs biting into my wrists, the wooden post pressed against my back.

"Carrying on, the whole reason she's out there—Cora I mean, on Tinder and whatnot—is for me. The sweet girl does it because I ask her to. She's to find suitors and get them *here*. So that I can, well...adhere to the rules of my religion. You see Hugh, I'm not originally from Idaho. I spent most of my grown years in North Carolina as a member of the LDS. That's the Latter-Day Saints. Mormons you know? Then I got some real bad news. I lost my job and some of the properties I'd invested in—this happened back in 2008, of course. And as if that wasn't enough, for no apparent reason, God decided to smite me down further. Lash upon lash, Hugh.

"I found out I was sterile, shooting blanks. My hormones were all effed up and my back became a regular *moonscape* of cysts and boils, all up and down my back and over my shoulders, creeping up my neck even and on into my hairline. I lost four molars to bad dentistry and the rot they left in my jaw gave me a blood infection that nearly killed me. And on and on," he wiped his brow with his shirtsleeve and sighed. "You get the picture, Hugh, I'm sure.

"To make a long story short, I abandoned my beliefs and absconded from the church. I decided if God was going to do me dirty—I mean if he was going to be a regular a-hole, then I'd do the sanctimonious crapper one a whole lot worse. And do you know what I did? I got on the internet and I joined a forum. Big online thing, whole mess of people—and I mean lots of people, Hugh—going on about and in support of his dark majesty, Satan.

"Oh sure, at first I was just pissed off. I didn't mean nothing by it. I got angry and then I got even. So what? But I stuck around and after a while things started to get real for me, you understand? I converted, like. Came to Satan like a pup to the wolf-shepherd himself. And then you know what happened? Everything got better, Hugh. It really did. My whole darn life was turned around. Everything I'd ever wanted was added unto me.

"I got a new job—better one than before, even. Full benefits, more pay. And my complexion, all that junk on my back, it cleared up lickety-split. And if all that ain't a good cause for faith, I don't know what is.

"Anywho, that was all a little over a year ago now. The new job brought me here and I bought this house—a nice safe place for me and my little bride. You see what I'm driving at, don't you Hugh? Life has been good. Real good. And there's only one little thing I got to do to keep it that way.

"You see, as a disciple of the Mourning Star—that's what we call ourselves—I'm required to tithe. You know what tithing is, Hugh? Most religions do it, churches and whatnot. It means to contribute, to donate funds or whatever to the organization. What we do is. Well, it's not monetary. Each of us in the community, we've got to get us a live one every so often. Bout twice a year, I guess. And that's where you come in, Hugh. And where my darling little bride comes in as the illustrious lure, the proverbial bait. The catfish, what-have-you.

She brought you here. She delivered you unto me and now all
I've got to do is—"

A swath of light cut into the cold hell of the basement
as a door was opened; heaven's conduit, glowing at the top of a
stairwell. The steps were ignited and the banisters glowed in
golden tandem, dropping down into the black, as a figure
stepped onto the landing. Tom turned in his chair. He raised
his hand above his eyes and waited.

"Tom…?"

She was backlit, her child-body visible through her
nightie as she glided down the steps in her bare feet and leaned
on the balustrade.

"Hello sweetie," Tom smiled. "I was just explaining our
little system to Hugh here, and the origins from whence it
came. How did you sleep?"

She rubbed her eyes and yawned. "Good."

Tom looked at me.

"Beautiful, isn't she?" he beamed. "I bet you wish you'd
been able to get her in bed with you. But that was never going
to happen, Hugh. My little girl only has eyes for me. See, I took
her away from her Daddy back in Raleigh. The SOB was
abusing her. I offered him four-hundred dollars to sign the
marriage license and he took it.

"She'd just turned fourteen," he smiled. "And in case
you're wondering, Hugh. In the state of North Carolina, that's
perfectly legal with the consent of a parent and court approval.
Once I got the new job, it weren't nothing. Her daddy signed
her over and we moved out here as far away from the SOB as
we could get. I had to tell her everything, of course.
Fortunately, Cora took to the new religion like chicken and rice.
And she's been my little partner in the whole thing ever since,
haven't you sweetie?"

"Why do you always have to do that?" she sulked,
coming closer but not quite into the light. "You're always
telling people the story."

"Because, little girl." Tom chuckled. "It's a testament. Every darn time I tell that story it's a witness to the nonbeliever. I'm sharing our gospel here, darling—offering them a final stab at eternal life in the hell that is heaven. We've got our ministry too, just like the Christians. And besides," he scowled. "I want this degenerate to know that he never stood a chance. That despite my shortcomings you love me, love me good and only. I was the second man to know the sweet fire of your loins and I'll be the last. I want this *wolf* to know that—"

The letter opener plunged into his neck, then pulled back in a bleeding arc. She held it high, clutching it to her breast and showing her teeth. Tom was slow to register the damage. He lifted his hand and touched the wound, still smiling, as Cora stabbed him again.

The little blade pierced his fingers. Blood splashed the floor and his eyes rolled back. He gurgled, slumping forward. The hole in his neck blasted small steady streams in every direction as he rolled from the chair and collapsed onto my legs.

It was a quiet death.

The smell of his blood was like copper. I felt it seeping through my pants, touching my skin, and entering my pours.

I felt numb.

Cora stepped into the light. She brushed a lock of hair from her face and smiled. Blood splatter was smeared on her cheeks and teeth. She nudged her husband's legs and exhaled, relieved that it was over. The stain on his shirt had grown into a Rorschach blotch the size of a dinner plate. I pulled at my restraints, rattling the cuffs against the post.

Get the key you stupid bitch! Get these handcuffs off of me!

She carefully stepped around him and took his place in the chair, crossing her ankles and smoothing the hem of her nightie against her thighs. Her bare-feet were pale in the honeyed glow of the lightbulb, hovering just above the floor.

She scooted forward and pulled the gag from my mouth.

"Cora," I gasped.

"Don't call me that," she said, kneading her feet against the dead man's back. "I mean don't say my name. Don't call me anything."

"But—"

"But you're wrong."

"Cora, I..."

"I told you not to call me that. You thought I was going to save you, right? That I killed old Tom for you and that in my infernal fucking naivety I actually thought you came here to save me. Yeah right. Is anybody that stupid?"

"He's not your father," I said, wincing at pain that was blossoming at my wrists. "You lied to me."

"You're right on both counts. I did lie to you. He wasn't my father at all was he? He was my husband."

"Why would you—"

"Because I wanted a baby, and I want money, and I want to be alone. And now I have all that and it's entirely legal too. I turn fifteen in two weeks. In the state of Idaho that means I'm adult now. I can be independent. I'll get the insurance money from Tom's claim, plus whatever benefits a single mom—"

"You're not even fucking pregnant, you fucking bitch."

"Oh," she grinned. "That's where you're wrong, that part wasn't a lie. I really am pregnant. And it's definitely yours too because Tom couldn't have kids. See, he didn't think I *actually* fucked you. But I did, obviously. I had this whole thing planned out from the beginning. At first, when you didn't cum inside me, I thought I'd messed up. But then while you were in the shower, I tried putting it inside with my fingers and I guess it worked out," she shrugged. "Geez. You must have so many questions. I'll admit, it's pretty confusing.

"So, the money I mentioned? Tom took out a big old life insurance policy—they all do that, the Satanists, just in case of what might be required of them. Tom called it an act of discipleship. It's all so stupid. I mean I hated all that. All this crap," she kicked the candle and the inverted cross, and the cross fell over and broke, echoing sharply in the confines of the basement.

"Actually," she continued. "In case it wasn't obvious, I hated Tom. He thought he was this great person to me, like my knight in shining armor. But he wasn't. All that stuff I told you about him, when you thought he was my dad? I mean we were married but still, he's like fifty, so."

It felt like a bad movie. I was far from relaxed, but the threat was gone. This disturbed child wasn't going to hurt me. At worse she'd leave me down here with her husband's corpse and run away. Somebody would find me. I'm an important enough person that they would come looking. The neighbors would see the car parked across the street and call it in. Whatever.

"Did you know that's legal?" she asked. "To get married that young?"

"Cora, look. This is all fine, you can have the baby and the money and whatever else you want. I can give you more money if you think you need it. But you have to let me go. I won't tell anybody about this, I just want—"

"Well, you can't always *get* what you want, Hugh," she sneered. "That's not how this works. Besides, I need you. You're part of my plan."

"You need me?"

"Yeah. You're very important. See, this is how it went: I met you on Tinder back in April, right? And I went out with you and then you raped me and got me pregnant, and when I refused to see you again you got violent and started threatening me. Then when you found out about the baby you went ballistic, so I blocked you on social media. I deleted my Tinder and all that. But somehow you found out where I live and then came here to my house last night. You were crazy with jealousy when you found out about my husband and so you killed him. And then you tried to kill me and…well, it didn't work out. I'm a lot stronger than I look. And you gave me no other choice, really. I had to kill you in self-defense."

The fear welled up inside me again like blood in a punctured lung. "You'll never pull that off you fucking bitch, you stupid fucking cunt. I'll make sure that you get—"

"Also," she said. "This is your letter opener." She held up the narrow blade, shining wet with blood.

"No it's not."

"Oh," she shrugged. "Well, your initials are on it."

She dropped the letter opener onto the body and it rolled into my lap. It was a delicate little tool with a fine point and mahogany handle. It looked like something I would have— an expensive souvenir, a gift from some past lover stowed away in a desk drawer and forgotten. Sure enough, my initials were stamped on the handle just like she had said, engraved in the wood.

I felt the blood drain from my face.

"What about all of this Satan stuff?" I croaked. "The police…"

"I'll just move it up to my room," she smiled. "Teenage girls go through phases. Maybe I'm a really big Sabrina fan."

"The handcuffs," I stammered. "They'll see these marks—on my wrists! How will you explain that? It will be clear to them that I was held against my—"

"No, not really," she said. "I mean, sure, they'll *see* the marks. But in your apartment, they'll find your own pair of cuffs and a penchant for rough sex."

I thrashed against the post some more and felt my inner-engine rev, prepping for a fast trip down memory lane as scenes of my life started to flash, hauntingly, before my eyes. *This evil little bitch is really going to kill me.*

"Oh, Hugh! I forgot to mention, one more thing. You really were good in bed. I mean, good at fucking. Like, way better than Tom. But I guess that isn't saying much..." she frowned. "Never mind. Anyways, you probably want to know the rest of my plan. I hate to say it, but you're a pretty selfish guy Hugh. But also that's what's going make this part of the story so exciting. Are you ready to find out how you die?"

I looked at her: at an ageless face frozen in time on the spindly bones of a child, captivated by torment and evil. I could see her excitedly tearing off the heads of her Barbie dolls, and now she'd graduated to flesh and blood.

"How are you going to kill me?" The words left my mouth ghost-like; they were the dead echo of my soul's departure. I'd already been evicted, alienated. The voice wasn't mine anymore, it was a memory.

"That was tough actually, finding something that appeared organic. I mean it gets difficult when you're just an innocent fourteen-almost-fifteen-year-old. So I went through all the options that a girl like that would have at her disposal and would think of to use and have convenient and so on...stuff like nail files, hairbrushes, razor blades, and all that stuff. But nothing stood out. Fortunately for me—me being an Ex-Mormons wife and all—my available options practically *quadruple*. I get access to the whole kitchen and all sorts of other housewife stuff.

"So," she said, reaching behind her. "I chose *this!*"

She pulled it into the light and beamed. I didn't know how to react. It was so absurd that I felt a flicker of hope kindle momentarily in my chest.

"It's a turkey baster!" she exclaimed.

"How..."

"How am I going to kill you with a turkey baster?" she asked. "It's easy. I'm going to suck your eyeballs out of your head with it."

The silence between us held; it felt tender, like the words had left a bruise, and the hopeful fire within me continued to blossom. *She was just a little girl.*

I tried to smile.

Play along. Kids like it when you play along with them.

She bit her lip to keep from giggling but couldn't hold back. "Just kidding!" she burst out laughing. She slid off the chair and into the dark, gliding toward the faint impression of the stairs. I heard her rummaging, jostling through boxes, and then the slap of her feet on the concrete as she returned.

"I chose *this* instead!" she shouted, stepping into the pool of light with her arms held behind her back.

"Have you ever seen one of these before, Hugh?" she asked, bringing it around from behind. The rubber phallus quivered in her fist and the leather harnesses jangled, dragged against her knees. "It's a strap-on dildo. Tom couldn't…well, sometimes he wasn't able to," she explained. "But don't worry I'm not going to fuck you to death with it! I'm just going to kind of hit you with it."

Her left eye twitched and she looked very pale, ghost-like. I noticed a power-cord trailing between her feet.

"And then," she said, squatting and feeling around in the dark. She stood abruptly, revealing a second object with a broad theatrical swoop: a fiery glowing shaft. *"AND THEN I'M GOING TO FUCK YOU TO DEATH WITH THIS!"*

It was a curling iron.

CRATERFACE

I don't take fucking drugs; I stay healthy. She did and she was clear as a bell. Free of rust. Like a clean skinned sun. How generous of me, thinking that. After all, gutter suns all get shit stained eventually. Lucky her for now. A porcelain doll on the verge of collapse. And what am I left with? CRATERFACE.

Tonight, again.

I am the moon.

I can feel it coming on. The divots swell, the old scars start to pound. Pockmarks, stains. Mankind grasps space but can't comprehend flesh. Science has taken us to the moon, we've sat in the craters, we've built microwaves, but we haven't resolved the soup pockets that form in the skin.

Acne is God, cystic.

Sort of.

Pustules are His fingertips working their way out, boring up from the flesh cavern, sickly lit. When you have God, everything is awash in hard florescence, highlighting the disease. We sweat, forcing our oils out through the clogged pore, the malformed gland.

I had a dream that I died once. I fell. Or maybe I jumped. Now I dream of farmlands, of fields, of lying in the furrows, corn stalks and crops growing up out of the holes. Ragged wet holes. The stems piercing, lancing, rearing up toward the wicked sun.

Out of my face.

My wormy wretched face.

Skin squirming, nascent.

I lay on my back, watching the clouds. My expression is lost in bubbling soup, upturned, boiling over from some ineffable internal source.

Hormones, they say.

They say, they said.

Take these ANTIBIOTICS.

I don't take drugs, fucking cunt.

She shrugged, "I didn't offer you any," and then snorted a line of coke off the bedside table.

There's a Bible in the drawer just below.

Take dick, trick; that's what I pay you for. To kiss the bumps, the boils, run your fat fucking tongue over the hills, the cities. Miniature landscapes, mountains; colonies of ants building out their mounds from within. *Your mouth*, meet the Rockies running up the sides of my neck, the small spires, Mount Rushmore on bone, the mountain ranges on my jaw that I think of as Swiss, famous for milk-maidens and cleft-riddled cheese.

Head cheese.

Scar tissue.

BITCH.

You haven't lived. You haven't hurt. Dresden, Germany is rubble on my left shoulder; ruinous clumps dig into your soft underarms when we embrace. And my hairline creeps back away from you, away from the mask and the spotted brow below, receding to escape the reach of encroaching cysts that swell from my forehead. Inflammation is there.

Hellfire blistering the surface.

That's the worst.

She crawls between my legs and attaches her mouth. She fits the hitch, chasing the root with her tongue. It's an evasion tactic. Avoidance. This way she doesn't have to feign indifference; she can skip facing the boils, the ejaculate blossoming from my neck. Infection spurting, off white. Dabs of blood. Running down her jaw, her lips. Sliding down her throat in an oily trail.

Yuck.

Purulence, swallowed.

Moments later it happens like she wants it too: I cum from my balls. Her shoulders jerk as she takes it down her throat. It sounds like sucking tapioca through a straw. Her lips tighten against the blast and she breathes through her nose, not wanting to break the seal.

It's something a harpy would do.

I slowly whine.

Cumming is like a slow death.

It's true: sexually active men ejaculate when they die. That's how the soul leaves the body. The substance is sticky and opaque, of swirling marbled off-whiteness; no flecks of gold like party Vodka, but she takes it down, chokingly like champagne loaded with glitter.

I pay the bitch and leave.

Stepping outside.

The motel has the ambiance of an oil stain. The front door shuts, closing on the image of her in the bathroom, cleaning her mouth with a rag. I look at my feet. The sidewalk is illuminated by an ice machine. The doormat is dirty; you wipe your shoes off when you say goodbye.

I head to Jerry's house. My name is Tom. Rats chew through my fucking face.

I ring the doorbell and wait. He's home of course. He answers door in stained green sweatpants, scratching his balls. In one hand he's holding a game-controller. His expression is as impassive as stone. Wordlessly he turns, returning to the bowel of his apartment.

I enter, shutting the door behind me. He resumes his video game; I hear the gunshots, then head for the bathroom to wash off the spit. I use a rag from beside the sink. Warm water. Her lipstick is like cherry red nail-polish, hard to remove.

I drop the rag in the sink, finished.

Close my pants.

When I look in the mirror—dirty, toothpaste-spattered, finger-printed, smudged, and pus-dotted from examined and pinch-popped pimples—I see red. Bright red because it's on my face. Because acne, because rage.

I am the moon.

I get angry in an instant, self-inflate. I see myself reflected there and then I howl. I'm a werewolf: when I look in the mirror I CHANGE.

Sup CRATERFACE.

Sup fuck face.

Jerry's toilet doesn't flush.

I scream and punch the wall. Pain gets me hot and I can feel the fur bristling beneath my skin. It never breaches though, just curls in on itself, bunches up, and welts. The hair becomes ingrown, the follicles inflamed.

Swelling into horns sometimes.

I could swallow pills like silver bullets. Sure, but I don't do drugs, so.

"JERRY!" I scream.

"What?" he asks without pausing his game.

"Your toilet again."

"Oh," he says. "Leave it. I'll take care of it later."

Jerry doesn't work out. He's a nerd and he's not

healthy. I leave the house without saying goodbye. He wouldn't understand the werewolf thing.

He drinks too much.

Back to the streets; this time, the wolf. I don't walk. I prowl. Carhartt coat, cargo shorts, Merrell boots with long socks. FUCK YOU.

It's hot outside.

Boise is a monster.

I don't relate to anyone anymore. I lick the CarMax off my mouth, walking on paws veiled by human feet. Longer nails will sprout from my hands eventually like railroad spikes pushed through glove-fingers. Volcanoes on my face, geysers on my neck. When will I be born?

There's a crack in the sidewalk that rips through to the base of a black storefront. A display window just above where the weeds have started to grow. I put my foot on the crack, leave it there: *Hurting Mom.*

I peer through the security bars and the occupant therein stares back. She wears a black silk nightie and thong, and plum pointed brassiere. Her complexion is unblemished milk.

Erotic Shop, meaning what?

I lose track of time.

The ants come hard against the skin, furiously banging their heads and pinchers against the hive. It feels itchy. Like gripping nettle; masturbating rose thorns and barb wire. I go numb as they breed and beat their wings inside me, a farm for the parasite.

The moon.

Incubating.

As a planet, I cast shadows; they cross the blank face of the mannequin but she doesn't blink. Inside me the tendrils spread and my heart flexes with growth. New arteries form, accommodating the ire. Something chews my ribs and I want to howl.

But all of the sudden...

I'm not alone.

You've joined me on the sidewalk. We stand there, breathing. It's faint but a train. You look in the window because you've just turned fourteen. I look because the moon. And because rage and hate.

You're young.

I'm the face of lasagna; the aftermath of a potluck, my jawbone is the glass edge of an oven dish and the skin there is the last of the scalloped potatoes and cheese.

Scrape me clean in the dishwater.

Harvest Moon.

Very orange soap and steel wool.

You recognize that I'm watching you in the window and you suddenly turn. That's fine. God didn't fuck you. You've only just learned how to bleed.

You walk away on Bambi legs. UGG boots keep you from being a woman. Those and the glitter in your lip-gloss. And you don't like it when the sun goes down and the dark comes stumbling in like a drunk and shambling corpse and drops dead on the city. But I do. That's night. When the streets became wet with pain and the sky bleeds dreary luminescence through star shaped holes.

Run little girl, the sun has abandoned you. The shadows have been unlocked and the wolves run free.

A bad moon rises, echoing.

CRATERFACE, CRATERFACE.

Sparkling blue ocean and bamboo umbrellas; the mountains in Thailand, rising a stone's throw from the shore. Beautiful polluted beaches. Child trafficking. I see acne like seamounts, jutting up from the water; like icebergs summoned from the flesh-depth by the shifting of great tectonic plates.

I see it all in the poster plastered outside the door. Hordes of beach-goers, smiling and bright, with their manicured toes in the golden sand.

I rip it from the bricks and hurl it into the dark. Propaganda makes me sick. The pelt beneath raises in ire, hackles pressing back against their root at the base of my neck. I restrain a growl and ring the bell.

The door pulls back on a chain and a man grins through the opening. He extends his hand and asks for a credit card. I give him what he wants. He moves aside, arms straining as he rolls backward, gripping the thin grey tires of his wheelchair.

He leads me to a low table and shows me pictures in a binder. I select the whore with the biggest breasts, a hard-looking redhead named Rose.

"Old Rose, she's a pro," he tells me. "Has a hole you could drive a pickup through, wouldn't even scratch the paint. But how about them tits?"

He removes a key from a drawer and drops it on the table for me. "Room 18," he says. "Up the stairs and down the hall. Go get comfortable. I'll let Rose know you're here, horny as a jackrabbit."

Inside the carpet is a deep mustard shag, the walls are white, and the ceilings are beige with tatty plumbs of water damage. The bedspread is red paisley and so are the pillow cases; the sheets below, burnt orange, showing at the edges. I sit down and wait, facing the door.

Time passes.

I let myself go, drifting.

My eyes lose focus. My member swells. My thoughts wander un-shepherded. There is a cliff, an ocean raging; blank contemplations fall prey to the wolf, halted by the angry sea.

Guileless sheep, swallowed whole as the jaws of lust close on darkness.

I tap my foot and contemplate the swarm. My hand snakes into my coat pocket, clutching the straight razor. Soon enough, I tell myself, fingering the grooves of the bone-handle, the hinge, and the anatomy of the closed blade.

Soon enough, I think, cajoling the bristling wolfskin, adrenaline, and bloodlust. Soon enough, I tell myself, calming down.

The images come in flashes: split, parting tissue as the razor draws down, slicing. Opening wounds. Clean cutting and smooth. It makes me shiver. That satisfying ejaculate, shot from the blood-groove and into the soft white cloud of becoming.

Sperm on mink, phlegmy and opaque; the soul drips down the wolf hide like raw egg.

I let go of the razor as the door swings open and the whore steps inside. She's taller than expected; a fuchsia negligee worn over plain white panties; burst little blood vessels bleeding into the milk of her skin at the back of her thighs as she turns and closes the door.

She puts her hands on my shoulders and I'm faced with her breasts, freckled, straining the gossamer cloth of her negligee. Her nipples are the size of wine-corks. Maybe she expects me to lick them.

"You do drugs, of course?" I ask.

She draws back, looking down, and sees me for the first time, mouth flexing involuntarily as her mind registers disgust. "Who doesn't?" she shrugs, dropping her arms and turning away.

"I don't."

"Good for you. So why don't you undress, I've got a long night ahead of me."

"I need you to do something for me first."

She paces to the other side of the room, as far away

from me as she can get. Turning, studying the air above my head. She rests her hands on her hips, "Oh yeah, like what?"

I reach into my pants, remove my wallet, and then take the money from inside. "There's six hundred dollars here," I say, holding it out for her. "I want you to go to your man and buy drugs, whatever kind you like, okay? Then bring them back here."

She took the money without hesitation. Then, pausing at the door, "Hey this isn't some kind of..."

"No," I reassured her.

Twenty minutes later she returned to the room with a bag of junk the size of enough flour to bake a cake with. We avoid eye contact.

It's not easy for her.

Being with me.

I have one thousand eyes; eyes in my face, rolling in their sockets; the eyes that surround them; landmines in the topsoil, ripe to burst; itchy on my forehead, my neck and shoulders, and creeping down my chest beneath my shirt. I undress while she turns her back and lays the powder out for us in lines.

It doesn't take long; we run it up our noses like model trains, like prayers for rain, and finish the bag together.

Line-after-line-after-line.

It's very informal.

Time doesn't pass, it stops.

We're both high and glazed over on the floor at the foot of the bed and the carpet is so yellow it hurts. Blood pushes between my legs, running a fist through an empty sock. The stimulant chips away at gravity. I get hard. And I can smell myself, sitting there on the yellow floor, as release blossoms from me like a shaft of asparagus, straining free from the root.

I slap her hand away from my cock.

She blinks her eyes several times and starts to OD while I fondle her private parts and withdraw the straight razor. *This is the part where you look away.*

You stop reading.

You know I'm sick and I've gone too far.

Let me ask you. Have you ever used a straight razor, little-girl-on-the-sidewalk, wherever you are? Surly hating night. Have you ever spread your Bambi legs and shaved?

Look away now.

I dare you.

You're thumbing open the razor. You unfold the blade from its frame and expose the wanton edge. I press the weapon into the whore's open palm and ask her to amputate.

Dissect.

Run your razor across my skin. It's easy when you're high, slobber staining the corners of your mouth while you jerk and spasm.

When I was fifteen, I was afraid to shave; when I turned twenty, I couldn't use a blade without accruing scars. The acne was too widespread, the craters too deep. I cut my face and bled but never had the courage to go all the way. To scrape clean, cut to the bone and extract.

This is a plague.

I beg the whore now: do it for me. Set me free. We're both high. We don't feel pain or empathy. The drugs have worked their miracle, breeding indifference. We laugh, we howl. We paint spirals on her breasts and beat our wings. The hackles raise, the boils rage. I pray to God, make me GQ. *Give me darkness, I am the moon. Allow me please to accommodate your divine disgust and transform.*

God is a monster; and tonight, so am I.

AFTERGLOW

Whenever we finish, rolling onto our backs beside each other on the sweat soaked sheet, she tells me how she feels; how she is falling more in love with me, and I close my eyes, bathed in something like euphoria, and agree.

I want to sleep.

I feel anxious. Sentiment has disappeared, swept away with the passage of climax, and I crave solidarity. Time has slowed for the duration, but it's picking up again and my youth flashes before me in a series of stills. They're like windows on a passing train. Thunder in motion. And when the whistle blows, I know in my guts that every sequence has its end.

How long will we last?

Tonight I suggest putting her in handcuffs. Tie me up, she says. We both know she'll deny me nothing. I remove the hot blue silicone cuffs from the dresser drawer and fit them over her wrists against the small of her back. Fuck my face, she says. First, I want you to fuck my face.

I take hold and give it to her mouth. She gags. Looking at her, you wouldn't think she enjoyed it. After a while she backs her head away and coughs; we lock eyes, tendrils of spit and semen connect us via her lips. Tonight, she says. Tonight we're going to cut me in half. There's a saw under the bed, the blade has no teeth. Draw it across my skin while you take me from behind.

I do this, twisting her body.

Without the support of her arms, she's helpless. The side of her face is pressed against the carpet and slowly abraded red. She breathes through her mouth. Her flank quivers and she bits her lips. Her legs give out and her body goes flat, and I finish inside her, feeling nothing.

Afterward she wears my cum in her panties so as to feel loved.

We don't shower.

Pulling on her stilettos, she tells me that she enjoys the silicone cuffs and that her cervix is bruised from the depth of my penetration. You were very rough, she says, adjusting her bra straps evenly onto her shoulders.

She smiles at me, piercing my heart.

It wasn't always like this.

She likes talking about when we met. It's her favorite subject. She's obsessed with it to the point of neurosis and brings it up in bed, whispering *remember when* like a personal mantra. She speaks of it in passing and drags it into conversations without context; our friends have all heard it a hundred times and sometimes I'll even catch her telling it to strangers.

We met in a bar, of course. And like most adult relations, it started with a few drinks. I was interested in her sister at first. But her sister was interested in somebody else, so I settled for Abigale. I fed her alcohol and she let me kiss her. It was great. We went for a walk and later on I finger-banged her in the washroom. Mid-way through she started to bleed. Her menstruation had run the length of my arm before we noticed, and a drunk had started to kick the door.

And she loves this story?

Then again, it's very different when she tells it. For her it was romantic, our instant magnetism and desire. One of the first things she noticed was my well-kept beard and fingernails. In her version of the story she picks me up, not the other way around; I was shy but attractive, she says, and everybody listening laughs. Then she smiles at me and reaches for my hand while inwardly I cringe. This is a common occurrence.

After we left the bar that night, I brought her to my hotel. We took a shower together and she washed the blood off her thighs while kissing me. We fell on the bed, wet, drying our bodies against the quilt.

Anxiety deprived me of my erection and she squirmed between my legs in an effort to bring it back. Moments later, she crawled up onto my chest and told me that it was okay. We held each other in the cool darkness of the room murmuring sweet nothings until the sun came up.

It's not a story I'm proud of, but maybe that's the point; romance is the absence of pride. Men aren't usually open about such things because it shames them.

The next morning saw me on a train. She ran along beside the tracks, waving at me through the windows. I remember walking to the station with her, hand-in-hand, dragging my suitcase through the snow on its tiny plastic wheels. I kissed her on the platform and promised that we'd meet again.

And we did. Again and again, bridging distance without a thought. Two years passed. We moved in together. I loved her quietly and we never spoke of marriage. Years later, the exhilaration died but the feelings remained.

I wound up in bed with a teenage girl one summer because it brought me joy. Anything to escape the doldrum. Madness comes in many forms. Hearts are not exempt. Sometimes love turns rotten in the afterglow.

It's amazing how a relationship can be summed up in a few paragraphs like that. Or in a few images, snapshots like touchstones. Today I'm going through my phone, cleaning up space. I'm deleting all the pictures. They're all backed up in the cloud and I never look at them. More room for apps I'll probably never use.

Here is a picture of us in San Diego.

We're at the beach and we're both smiling. I've got my arm around her waist. Despite appearances, I remember it being a lousy day. It was overcast and windy and it took about an hour to find parking. The whole time we were there she felt self-conscious about her weight. She felt that I'd bullied her into buying a sexy two-piece swimsuit instead of the one she'd wanted. Which might have been true. I don't know. It doesn't matter anymore.

Here is another picture of us.

This time we're outside of our apartment, flexing our arms beside an empty U-Haul truck. It was the day we moved in together. We'd just unloaded the last of her things off the truck and she'd set her phone atop a stack of boxes for the picture. We look happy here because we are. Working together is a growth hormone for the heart; for couples especially, look no further than good sex and the combined effort it takes. Salsa classes, ceramics, whatever. Shared satisfaction is un-tempted selfishness.

Here's a recent one.

It's Abigale outside my favorite bar. She's wearing a skirt and little red cowboy boots and she's smiling, poised against the curtained window. She made me take it. I don't know why.

I skim through the rest of the photos and then delete them all. As they disappear from my phone, sucked into the ether, I watch our past evaporate one little square at a time.

Afterward I go online and order nipple-clamps and a ball-gag. Tonight I think I'll cum on her face.

Abigale hates Chinese food. That's why I come here. I don't need an excuse, only appetite. I get to be alone. It's not the best environment, sure, but for a buffet it's not bad at all. Silk screen landscapes run the length of the walls, backlit for ambiance, and all the waitresses wear flower-petal patterned kimonos and powdered white complexions, fluttering down the aisles beneath paper lanterns and dragons.

Several banks of food make up the buffet. Everything from noodles to rice to vegetables and meat cooked apart or together in a dozen different sauces. I fill two small plates with a little bit of everything and take them to my booth. I ask for a Sprite from a stone-faced waitress who bows and evaporates, then returns moments later with the drink in hand and sets it on the table with a straw. It's the only thing not included in the buffet price. Chinese are very cheap when it comes to beverages, I've noticed.

I work through the first plate, then the second. When it comes time for dessert, I load a third plate with jello squares and fruit. On my way to the dining area, I see a few men from the kitchen loading a tray with pale golden meat. I've never seen it before.

"Excuse me. What is that?"

Special is all they can tell me about it; one of them leans closers and says, *"Seasonal. Very good, very uncommon. Very special ocean meat."*

"It's fish?" I ask.

"No, not fish. Very special."

They pushed their trolley back to the kitchen and I took a closer look. The meat glowed with the odd suggestion of color, like something chemical. Vague little prisms sparkling beneath the food lamps, off-gassing rainbows. It looked like chunks of Unicorn, something mythical and fantastic.

Why not, I figured.

I took the ladle and helped myself to a portion of the strange meat, loading it onto the plate beside the orange jello and fruit. When I looked up, a line had formed behind me.

I returned to my table, slid into the booth, and primed my taste buds with a ribbon of ginger and a lemon slice. I washed it down with a mouthful of Sprite and took up my fork. With Chinese food you can never be sure what to expect. The flavor palette is incredibly diverse. Sweet, sour, spicy, savory. The possibilities are endless. You never know what you're going to get.

I skewered a chunk with my fork and brought it to my nose. It looked and smelled like fish, but held together like pork. I opened my mouth and set the piece inside, drawing it free from the fork with my teeth. Chewing. The texture is firm, the taste is like salmon wrapped in bacon. Special indeed.

It's delicious.

When I was finished, I shoved the plate aside, leaving the fruit and jello untouched. I went to the buffet for more but the tray was empty, the meat was gone. Grease swirled in the stainless-steel bottom, reflecting the lights. I flicked the ladle in a flash of anger and rolled my eyes.

There's nobody around of course.

The waitresses are like cable-cars, they flit down the aisles on a stringent grid, bussing plates and delivering drinks. I smile and wave and they pretend not to notice; their faces are like powdered white steel.

I gave up trying and resorted to the front desk where an old woman stood at the register, monitoring the door. Dark red lips punctuated a perpetual frown and her skull was sinking in on itself. She watched my approach and raised a single, sharp, immaculately plucked eyebrow.

I asked about the meat.

"No more today," she yaps, turning her attention elsewhere. *"You come back tomorrow."*

"You'll have more?"

"Maybe. Very special dish. You come tomorrow. OK?"

Abigale crawled into bed beside me, freshly showered and smelling of soap. She kissed my cheek. "Lunch tomorrow? I can meet you at the office."

"Actually, I'll be going to the buffet."

"Chinese food," she groaned. "Again?"

"I'm in a mood. Why not?"

Before she could respond I clasped a hand over her mouth and rolled on top of her. Her tongue instantly pressed against my palm, licking and kissing as she closed her eyes and surrendered and I pushed myself inside her.

I was shown to the same booth as before and, without sitting, tossed my keys onto the table and headed straight for the buffet. I could make out the little rainbows from a distance, leaping off the golden skin and sparkling beneath the heat lamps.

My guts clenched when I saw the line.

There must have been a dozen people waiting their turn. They were all as desperate for it as I was, you could see it on their faces, weighing their odds against the remainder each time a portion left the tray. I plucked a sesame-ball from one of the neighboring trays and popped it into my mouth, stepping in line.

The wait felt very long.

When my turn came about, I looked down and the tray was empty. The man before me walked away holding two plates. I stood there, seething, then went after him. I found him in a corner booth. He was already eating, sucking his fingernails after each bite.

"Excuse me."

"Yeah what do you want?"

I asked him for some of the meat; it didn't go over well. I returned to my table and dejectedly ate a variety of lesser offerings. I ordered a Sprite and sulked. When I paid the check the old woman told me to come back the next day. *"You come again,"* she said, waving me along. *"Come earlier."*

I left work very early the next day and made it to the restaurant just as they were opening. A man outside was tethering a string of red and gold balloons to a stone dragon beside the entry. We exchanged hellos as I hoisted the door back and went inside.

"Not ready yet!" I was told, pleadingly, by a Chinese girl in oven mitts. She was loading trays of hot food into the buffet from a trolley.

I ignored her and took the nearest table. I had a direct line of sight on the kitchen door. This time I would eat more than my share. This time I would be the one to gorge. Others, the late commers, would look upon me with envy and regret. I would be almighty in their eyes, in the face of their cold quite acquiescence.

Ten minutes passed.

Ten long unblinking minutes. Then it happened, two men in uniforms slammed through the kitchen door pushing a trolley between them with rainbows glittering against their stained white jackets, springing out from one of the trays.

I swept a plate into hand and met them at the buffet. We exchanged smiles and nods while they loaded the hot tray in place beneath the lights. They were nervous. They could sense the impatience lifting from my skin in a hostile vapor.

By the time they'd finished, there were others there too, standing behind me, wearing their dourer and hollow expressions as I reached for the ladle and helped myself to several heaping portions. I took more than I could eat. My greed was insatiable. The next person in line hurried forward immediately as I stepped away.

"Cheers," I said, glancing smugly at the diminished stock.

I walked to my booth and collapsed into the seat with a sigh. The only gold at the end of the rainbow is the rainbow itself, low-hanging but impossible to grasp. The unattainable. It's supposed to represent an ideal, not literal wealth.

I loaded my fork with a share of bliss and that ideal was realized in a bite. For once I wasn't thinking about Abigale. My joy was complete and impartial. A pleasureful reckoning between the living and the very dead. The salted, the cooked. The sautéed in butter perhaps.

Pleasure is one-sided; mutuality is a farce.

I cleaned my plate over the course of an hour. It was the best sex I'd had in an age. Simple, clean. Some would say vanilla. But I had chewed and swallowed rainbows, wasn't that enough? What need had I for roughness?

Satiated, I ordered a drink.

Saki for once.

It was Friday, I wouldn't be returning to the office so why the hell not? I drank several small stoneware cups of the pungent wine then teetered to my feet. I wasn't drunk, the meal had filtered the booze; I was woozy with contentment.

I wandered down the aisle and cast a glance at the now empty tray as a woman turned away in disgust. Her plate was empty and held at her side. Her eyes were drained of hope. Too late, sweetheart. Try again tomorrow. I felt bloated and very glad. Cheerful even.

I needed a toilet.

They were in the back of the building down a hall lined with plastic booster seats and wooden high chairs. A few tired signs marked the way on dirty white walls.

The men's room smelled like bleach. There were two empty stalls and a pisser, all stained and splattered the same golden brown.

I stepped into place and undid my fly, rolling my head against my shoulders as the toilet water splashed in the shallow bowl. The feeling comes close to orgasm, bordering on agony.

Sweet fucking relief.

I finish and wash my hands. They're out of paper towels. The mirror is streaked and I look like death; a beautiful boy but with dark patches beneath his eyes and hollows in his cheeks. It had always been part of my charm, that peculiar gauntness. But we all get older, don't we? Charm wears off and the tarnish settles in.

Recently I'd been looking grim.

Abigale wanted to have children.

I stepped from the bathroom and came to a halt. There was a door I hadn't noticed before, hanging open on the opposite wall. The bleak living quarters for scores of illegal immigrants, working off their transport debts? I imagined their dirty faces illuminated in the beam of a flashlight, starving and hungry, crowded together and sleeping on the floor on bamboo mats.

Stairs channeled down into a chasm of darkness.

Curiosity is a bitch.

"Hello?" I called, stepping toward the opening.

Why do we always say that? We cry out to darkness like we expect a reply. We cast the runes, hoping for a welcome reception.

Nobody answered, of course.

I glanced down the hall toward the restaurant, the active clatter of dinnerware, plates, and glasses, then stepped into the open door. I raised my cellphone, casting a watery beam into the darkness. A trail of colorful grease was dripped and splattered on the steps. I looked down, shifting my weight, and saw a swarm of rainbows.

And then I slipped.

Love is a lot of things, not all of them good.

Falling in love is a tricky one. It is perhaps more defined by the falling than the feelings it beckons. It's all sentimentality. Butterflies in our stomachs as gravity sweeps us off our feet. But how can long can anything remain airborne?

Without puking.

Falling from great heights is not in our nature. We don't have wings. Love is the Dramamine for the tumble, it quiets the chaos but poisons the butterflies. When the magic is gone, our guts get twisted. We don't fall in love, it seems. We feel it, then fall through it. Fuck.

Love is a cloud.

Love is burning. Love is saying I am incomplete. I am horny. I am alone and I am in need. Love is the match that burns the witch. I am in love—the fist that shatters the glass, the knuckles that bleed. Love dissipates. Love is anger, love is on fire, blackening into the ashes of hate. Gradually, the support beams snap and the roof caves in. Things fall apart. Love is selfish. Love is beautiful, love is ugly.

Love corrupts.

It drips off her face as I push her backward: how's that for falling in love? I raise my pants and go for a piss. Afterward I collapse against the closed door and silently weep.

I wasn't sure if I'd opened my eyes or not. It was that dark. Dust tickled my cornea and I blinked. I couldn't see shit. I was on my back at the bottom of the stairs. My head was bloody and it ached. I sat up and my left shoulder felt like a disaster. My ribcage burned.

I found my cellphone on the floor beneath the stairs. The interface was shot, gone all-white beneath a cobweb of cracks. Turning it toward the room, the glow penetrated the darkness all of an inch. It was useless.

I stood up feeling sore.

What time was it?

I grabbed the rail for support, and started the blind trek toward the top of the stairs. My body ached. I could feel the imprint of the steps swelling into purple bruises across my ribs.

I reached the door and it was locked. I banged my fist against it, shouting hoarsely, then slumped against the railing and gave up. How long had I been here?

I searched the wall for a light switch and found one. The basement burst into luminance, lighted by a single green bulb at the base of the stairs. It was dim and muffled by dust, set into a dirty porcelain ceiling fixture and surrounded by mold. For the first time I noticed the dampness of the place, the peculiar suffocating humidity that filled the air. It smelled like the sea: a miasma of fish scales and stale tobacco.

I descended the stairs. My eyes adjusted and I swept my eyes across the damp interior in search of an exit. With a pipe I could probably force the door.

With a role of ducktape I could hang myself.

There was a shelf within range of the light, opposite the landing, crowed with jars and glass buoys netted with hemp and boxes gone grey beneath furry coats of dust. The walls were unfinished sheets of drywall, spotted with mildew and rot, and the far reaches of the basement were lost to shadow.

I stood at the bottom of the stairs feeling uneasy, hesitating, resisting panic and the urge to cry out as I was gripped suddenly by an overwhelming fear of the dark. I could wait for help, sit on the steps in the murky glow of the lightbulb and stare at the backs of my hands, turned swampy

green. Someone would come. The restaurant would open.
Tomorrow I would try the door and they would hear me.

Then it happened: the darkness spoke.

A single drop of water struck the concrete, resounding
in the tomblike silence of the buried room. Something glittered.
Beyond the reach of the light, I heard what sounded like a
chain being drawn and then a sucking noise.

Something writhing.

A shape stirred in the darkness.

I narrowed my eyes, straining my sight. Listening. My
heart beat faster and my skin prickled as I sensed shallow
breathing; something alive, something wet and glittering, and
attempting to conceal its presence.

"Hello?" I whispered. "Is somebody there?"

As my eyes continued to adjust, I was able to make out
a form slumped against the wall. Dark prisms winked in the
shadow; the flicker of scales. I moved closer, raising the broken
phone against the blackness to an applause of colorful flares,
pink and green, winking in the yawning void, as the shape
gained dimension.

It almost looked like a woman.

Pale trembling flesh.

She was holding her mouth against a drainage pipe that
protruded from the sheetrock. Water slowly leaked down her
jaw, catching in the delicate pink netting of her gills as she took
the liquid down her throat in slow inhalations. She was naked,
nipples stiff at the end of heavy breasts spattered with blood,
streaked with long muddy tracks, and a chain swung from her
neck, attached to an iron rung in the floor.

She watched from beneath the wet curtain of her hair.
Her ribs glittered where the flesh had been peeled back and
scraped clean, the fatty layer sliced away from the bone; and
what was left of her tail was coiled beneath her, a butchered,
bloody, reflective mess, webbed with scummy secretions.

She pulled her mouth away from the drain pipe and her lips twisted into a perverse mockery of a grin. She gestured: come.

Numbly I went, moving closer. The smell became overwhelming, a sickening coalescence of ejaculate and rot. She took my hand and pulled me to her. Coarse fingers slid beneath my shirt as she lifted her face and kissed me.

She tasted of ocean.

Her tongue was filmy and slick, entering my mouth as she undid my belt and stroked me through my undershorts. I couldn't move. I'd lost touch with reality. She pivoted her hips and guided me into place, standing in back of her.

I couldn't see, so I felt for the opening, thinking back to the trout my father used to gut in the kitchen sink, the small teardrop shaped hole. There was only one, a puckered orifice surrounded by folds of ruffled flesh, sucking eagerly at my fingertip.

I lowered my shorts, took my cock and thrust inside her. She pitched forward with a grunt and I held her shoulders, working it in; straining, penetrating her at an angle that forced her back into an arch. I could feel her muscles contracting as I pushed myself deeper. It was a new sensation, like working a finger down through the center of an apple core; the resistance was incredible.

I imagined her mouthing the drainpipe while I was inside her. I imagined that I was the drainpipe, cramming myself down her throat simultaneously while I fucked her from behind.

I hadn't made a backward motion when the pain shot through me, needles in my groin, followed by intense pleasure and urgency as my hips started to buck, slamming into her. I could hear the bloodied flaps of skin slapping against her stomach and the harsh rattle of the chain, swaying from the iron collar as her breasts impacted her ribs.

She gasped, a sharp intake of breath that echoed throughout the total darkness. I tore a chunk out of her shoulder, scattering rainbows with my teeth.

"That's right baby, fuck me good," she huffed as I drove myself at her core. "Fill my cunt with your shame."

THE NIGHTMARE

I was in Thailand—or maybe it was Laos, I'm not really sure. But I was traveling with Harry at the time, I remember that. And I'd fallen in love with a few different girls and I wasn't sure how to feel about myself.

It was a hot night. I was in a derelict pub, built into a catacomb. A dugout or a bunker maybe, left over from the war. Low ceilings, dirt walls. *Primitive real estate.* Light bulbs made the air glow orange. I remember it was thick down there, humid. It felt like breathing beneath a blanket—like inhaling at the pills of a cheap duvet, strands of polyester holding together a matted quilt.

There were other people there as well but I couldn't see their faces. They sat around tables like it was after work in any old bar. Laughing, drinking, brooding. And maybe it was.

For them, but not for me.

I proceeded to the next room, drawing aside a curtain in an arched passageway. The space on the other side resembled an ancient grave with shelve-like cubicles cut into the walls and privatized, cordoned off by curtains. There were candles lining the floor, guttering in piles of wax. A single light fixture dangled from an orange extension cord with a 40 watt bulb attached.

The visitors here weren't preoccupied with booze. They'd come for a greater form of release. Local men, dirtying their shoes on the earthen floors, dirtying their hearts, ensnared by harpies—the lithe painted oriental women who earned their living on their backs; faces bleary in the lowlight, features obscured by acts of seduction, giggling as they lured their patrons toward the cubicles.

I seemed to know what I was doing. I felt comfortable there. It was as if I knew the place, but not like I'd been there before. I knew it in the same way some people know their dreams—obsessively, intimately. Almost in Déjà Vu.

Nobody acknowledged me. Nobody cared. I stepped inside and walked to the back where the light was nearly void, a single candle holding its own. Holding the dark. Back where the humidity seemed to absorb sound, deadening the noise of the harpies at work.

I came to the end and reached for one of the curtains on the top half of the wall. There was movement, a shadow beneath. Light fluttered at the edges. I ran my fingertips below the covering and found the ledge, grunting as I hoisted myself up and crawled inside.

The chamber was tiny, a single berth with a flimsy mattress. Bare walls lit by another candle, an ugly trail of green wax slowly dribbling down from an enclave. I shifted onto my elbows and pulled my legs in under the curtain, stretching them out behind me.

A girl lay motionless in the bed, tucked beneath the sheets, her shoulders and neck glittering with perspiration. She looked European, light skinned with tendrils of dark hair spread out on the pillow like the coils of a soft black snake. Her face was dirty and her septum was pierced through with a silver hoop.

She looked at me, and her eyes absently wandered my face before settling on a spot in the corner of the ceiling. And then she glazed over, the candle wax crawling down the wall above her head. I could see where it had stained the pillowcase and where little beads of wax had hardened in the strands of her hair. I shifted my elbows and kissed her.

She shrunk away but her mouth opened beneath me nevertheless, like a delicate flower, submitting itself to nature. Her tongue found mine and they danced. I fell into the rhythm of it, losing myself; tracing her jaw with my fingers, sinking them into her hair as the fire built inside me. She bit my lip. I kissed her shoulders and neck and our eyes came together, locked—she was alive now, eyes smoldering beneath cake patches of old mascara, driving the blood between my legs.

I pushed my tongue into her mouth and she tasted metallic, like blood and lipstick, moaning as I lifted the sheet from her shoulders and drew it back. I needed her then. I needed to *unspool.*

I tore the sheet from her in a tangle, exposing her nakedness, and looked down at what was left of her body. I saw that she had no arms and no legs, and that her flesh was riddled with piercings, red welts raised against the bite of the steel. Her breasts were flattened, battered blue, and perforated. And I remember seeing the moist cleft of her sex, nestled between her mutilated appendages, glistening.

I woke up in a cold sweat. The dorm was quite. Harry was in his bunk with an arm draped across his backpack, and a German girl snored soundly asleep in the bed above him.

I lay there wondering what kind of a man I was that I could love multiple women at once; wondering if there wasn't a rot spot somewhere deep in my heart.

DARK

God save me from this emptiness, all-consuming
Save me from this dread
Lift me into light, the darkness is deafening

I no longer feel the sun upon my heart
Save me from this defeat
Hold me in Your arms; support me with Your Love

I cannot rise—encourage me to breath
Fill me, complete me as you complete the sky
Bring me stars, Lord
Save my eyes

Ignite my night—bring me life
Make what is wrong, right
And save me

Noah Abner Bowen is an Idaho native.
When not writing, he does whatever it takes to pay his rent.
He has been an interior designer, drywall taper, bag-boy,
barista, manger, rapper, furniture mover, and Christmas tree
salesman among other things. He has traveled extensively and
currently resides in Boise, ID.